CHURCH OF WIRE

CHURCH OF WIRE

Andrew Hook

First published in 2015 by Telos Publishing Ltd
5A Church Road, Shortlands, Bromley, Kent, BR2 0HP

Telos Publishing values feedback. Please email any comments
about this book to feedback@telos.co.uk

ISBN: 978-1-84583-912-3

Cover Art: 2014 © Iain Robertson
Cover Design: David J Howe

About church: the trouble with a mask is it never changes.
Charles Bukowski

Prologue
Tailing In A Tailback

Mordent was out tailing a Buick in heavy traffic.

Reflective Tony was in the Buick's passenger seat. The Frame was driving. Mordent had picked them up at the bottom of Tony's road just as he had been turning into it. Fortuitous, maybe, although it had necessitated a surreptitious U-turn, and after five miles he couldn't be sure that they were unaware he was following.

Why he was following, of that he also couldn't be sure. After his meeting with Kovacs at police headquarters, he had picked up a voicemail from Isabelle Silk enquiring after progress on her case. He needed something to give her, but he had nothing that was concrete. And he had more pressing things on his mind than a small-time crook with an unstated association to an organisation that he didn't know he was working for.

Mordent had searched for Isabelle Silk on the internet, but nothing had been forthcoming. If she was high up in some company, then she didn't advertise it. He could take that two ways: either she didn't want people to know who she worked for, or the company was so insignificant that there was no reason for it to have anything other than a perfunctory web presence. Either way, it rankled Mordent that information was held back. That he was asked to do a job without reason. Albeit, with payment.

Maybe he was just getting curmudgeonly in his old age.

The traffic had slowed to a crawl. They were in the business part of town. Pavements were crisp and clear, guys in freshly-pressed suits strode confidently without worrying if they were going to step on bubblegum or dog crap. The women were also suited here, power dressing as though it was still the '80s, in garments so sharp they would have your eye out if you looked at them too long. Which was a shame, because most of them you did want to look at too long; with their perfect lipstick and shoulder-length hair, and their legs that rose underneath their skirts.

Mordent crawled forwards. The car immediately in front moved into another lane, and he found himself right behind Reflective Tony. That wasn't the best situation. Distance led subtlety to a tail. Although when the traffic was bumper to bumper he could hardly be faulted for following too close.

At this distance, though, he could see the Frame's eyes reflected in the rear-view mirror. A deliberate attempt to view Mordent or a run-of-the-mill traffic check? It was impossible to tell. There was nothing for Mordent to do but sit it out.

His gaze wandered across to the buildings that flanked the street like giant glass waterfalls, umpteen storeys high. It felt as though he was driving through a lane created by the parting of the Red Sea. The sun was – unseasonably – out again, and all the windows reflected blue. Would this be the city of the future as imagined by H G Wells or our other forward-thinking ancestors? Only here perhaps, away from the dealers and the pimps and the rubbish and the smells. Away from the vendors and the poor and the graffiti and the dirt. Yet no-one lived here. At weekends, this quarter was deserted. It was all façade and no substance, a bit like the banks and businesses that these glass houses represented.

Recession was a great leveller, but it hadn't happened here yet, Mordent thought, as he watched another blue sock stride in another shiny shoe.

The traffic started to thin. Reflective Tony's vehicle began to pull away, the distance between them gradually increasing until Mordent was able to allow another car to come between them.

He felt comfortable with that buffer, idly turned on the car radio and listened to some jazz before spotting his tail turn right at an intersection. The traffic lights turned red, just allowing the car immediately in front to slip through, but not Mordent. He cursed under his breath, and then more loudly. Considered banging the steering column. Didn't.

He turned off the radio. Drummed his fingers on the dashboard. The music hadn't soothed his savage breast. He felt the tail slipping away from him as inexorably as our ancestors' tails fell from our bodies during evolution. There was almost a pull within his body as it happened, a protracted sense of loss. Then the lights changed in his favour and he continued the chase. Reflective Tony's vehicle was nowhere to be seen.

At the back of the financial sector the roads criss-crossed like a potato waffle. He didn't know that area well, was unsure which tinier businesses – dodgy or otherwise – were hidden in the maze. Feeling like a rat in a controlled experiment, he turned alternately left and right at each junction, not actually expecting to see the prize: the car, the cheese. Yet luck was in his favour. As he cruised by what seemed to be a disused office block, a metal gateway on his right opened out into a small car park. There was a Buick there, empty, and the plates were Reflective Tony's.

Mordent considered his options. He could wait until they came out, make a note of where they had been, continue tailing and then check on the building once he had returned home. Or he could be foolish and park inside. Risk being seen. He wondered: what would Kovacs do? And then he chose the latter option and reversed up, turned into the compound and parked a good way away from his mark.

He switched off his engine, heard it idle. Took a look around.

Considering the glass towers that punctured the air not more than a couple of hundred metres away, this part of the quarter was run-down and forgotten. The car park tarmac had ruptured, greenery pushed its way through like cress in a baguette, nature forcing itself on the manmade environment as though approaching from underneath in a bear hug. Glass bottles lay incomplete, smashed, against a back wall that bore the tags of graffiti artists with more aerosol than talent. Rubble littered the floor, making it resemble the landing site of a meteor shower. Mordent soon noticed that the four cars parked in addition to Reflective Tony's were burnt, slashed, smashed, dismantled: wrecked. In short, it wasn't a salubrious neighbourhood. While his vehicle wasn't in the best of condition, it still stuck out like a sore thumb.

As did Tony's. But Tony had a reason for being there. Mordent's only reason *was* Tony, and that would be as clear as second-hand daylight should either Tony or the Frame return to the car park.

Mordent was hiding in plain sight.

He glanced quickly at the surrounding buildings. While there were several entrances, and a couple of the doorways were not boarded up or broken, none of the offices bore an indication as to the nature of its business. It would be easier to back out, watch from a distance and then make enquiries about the area rather than wait. But before he had the chance to gun his engine, a door opened on the far side of the compound and a figure turned sideways to pass through: the Frame.

If you dressed a block of concrete in an ill-fitting suit you would have the Frame.

If you made furniture flesh and put a wardrobe through boot camp you would have the Frame.

If you took a haulage truck and compacted it in a car crusher you would have the Frame.

If you took a mattress, righted it, then sprayed it with adhesive you would have the Frame.

What Mordent had, advancing toward him, was the Frame.

Surprisingly the man wasn't as ugly as his descriptions attested. But then he wasn't a pretty boy either. His face was fairly nondescript, his expression casual. But it was still a face that you wouldn't forget.

The Frame had to come some way before Mordent could see Reflective Tony stood in the open doorway behind him.

If Mordent had been wearing red, he might have imagined the Frame as a bull. He certainly imagined steam coming from the Frame's nostrils; but on closer inspection there was a cigarette clamped between his teeth. The Frame held his hands as fists. His feet were encased in black boots that could only have steel toecaps. Mordent imagined those fists and boots inflicting a variety of injuries on his body. But he remained in the vehicle and didn't back away.

Instead, he wound down his window.

'This is a private car park,' murmured the Frame, as he drew close.

'I took a wrong turn,' said Mordent. 'Ducked in here to get my bearings.'

The Frame stuck his head in the car window, looked around as if checking for a map. Smoke hit Mordent's eyes and he blinked: once, twice. Then he realised the cigarette in the Frame's mouth was one of those electronic ones. Those to help you stop smoking. The 'smoke' dissipated quickly, even in the confines of Mordent's car. For some reason, any danger disappeared with the smoke.

But just as the presence of the false cigarette concealed the addiction of an actual cigarette, so the negation of danger was a thin veil concealing the real violence just behind it.

'I guess,' said the Frame, choosing his words carefully, 'that tailing us for twenty minutes was also a way for you to avoid getting lost in this city.'

Mordent shrugged. The Frame reached an arm through the window and pulled the car keys from the ignition. Then he stepped away from the vehicle and threw them across the compound, where they bounced, kicked up debris and finally came to rest beyond Mordent's vision, making a tiny metallic sound as they did so.

'Shame,' said the Frame. 'I guess you better go and retrieve them.'

Mordent watched Reflective Tony, still leaning against the doorway. He was smiling.

The Frame leant back through the window once more. 'I'm

waiting for you to get those keys.'

'No rush, is there?'

The Frame opened the car door, extended an arm as though he were a chauffeur. 'After you,' he said.

Mordent ran through the options. They weren't great. He decided getting out was the only solution.

'Look,' he said, 'I'm not quite sure what you're thinking ...'

Before he could finish his sentence, the Frame had yanked him out of the vehicle. His arm pulled taut, his body trailing on the floor. Stones scoured his jacket. There was a kick, only one, to his stomach from one of those boots. They were toe-capped, as he had guessed. Somewhere inside him a kidney moved position. He gasped. Then his arm tightened again and he was pulled to his feet. Eye-level with the Frame, who wasn't as tall close up as he appeared from a distance. Not that height was much to do with anything.

The Frame's other hand grabbed Mordent's collar, pulled his face so close that the electronic cigarette was an inch from Mordent's eye. 'What's your business, chum?' he said.

Mordent kicked out at the Frame's left shin. The manoeuvre was ineffective. The angle was wrong, and he achieved no more than the removal of a couple of dead skin cells. Probably from his own toe.

The Frame tightened the grip on the collar. But then he got clever and began to lift Mordent off his feet. Mordent swung his legs either side of the Frame's body, and leant backwards fast, causing the Frame to overbalance and fall forward on top of him. Mordent locked his legs and rolled sideways, pinned the Frame down. Shook his arm free and connected – once, twice – with the Frame's face. The blows landed soft, as though he was hitting putty. Mordent wasn't sure if it was his own strength at fault or the texture of the Frame's face. Either way, he had a fight on his hands.

It was a fight he needed to finish to get out of there. He had to debilitate the Frame to such an extent that he could look for his keys. He was thinking it was a fight he wasn't going to win.

If this were the movies or a tenth-rate pulp novel, then a

nose would have been broken by now. As it was, Mordent had a few scuffs on his knuckles and his jacket was dirty, the Frame had a swelling no bigger than a dime under one eye. Real fights were hard and haphazard, luck more than judgment. They almost always ended in tears.

The Frame jerked but couldn't shift his weight off the ground. His strength worked counter to his agility. Meanwhile Mordent was thankful for a diet of microwave meals and alcohol. He punched again, three times, his knuckles connecting with the Frame's teeth, drawing blood on his own hands. He pushed himself backwards to a standing position, kicked the Frame between the legs, hard. Then pulled out his gun and trained it on the hulk of a man reduced to a temporary wreck: eyes clenched, hands clutching his genitals.

'You'll excuse me if I go and get my keys now,' Mordent said. There was more bravado in his voice than he felt. He glanced toward Reflective Tony, who was stood still in the same position, regarding them impassively.

Mordent backed away from the Frame, aware that the distance he needed to cover was more than ideal. From that distance, firing a shot would be ineffective. Again, the accuracy of guns in the movies and in books belied their use in real life. Not that he intended to shoot anyone. Unless he had to do so to stay alive.

After he'd reversed a good dozen steps, he turned his head and saw his keys glinting in the sun, half-hidden by a patch of yellowing weed. He stooped and retrieved them. The Frame had got to his feet and Reflective Tony had beckoned him back to the doorway. His progress was slow, but no doubt it was his pride that had been hurt more than his physicality. One thing for sure: Mordent had made an enemy who wouldn't hesitate to exact revenge, if he got the chance.

1
The A-Z

It had started with a missing body. Everything starts with a missing body. Except for the alphabet. Which starts with A.

Then come the other letters, but they're never in the order you need them. Mordent's task was to rearrange those letters so that they spelt something. Something that was usually someone's name. Either the victim or the perpetrator. Sometimes, if he was lucky, both.

Occasionally, the name came up twice. If it was the perpetrator's name that wasn't unusual; if it was the victim's name it was. He had this before him now. A puzzle. Against the window, with the night a backdrop for the reflection of his face, rain speckled the darkness and distorted his features, scrambled his thoughts.

Across the way, lights were on in some of the facing apartments. But unlike in Hitchcock's *Rear Window*, nothing played easy on the eye. Murder, theft, all the petty crimes, these didn't roll out on some big screen, some TV-plotted panorama. The city spread out in all directions simultaneously: desperate people lived disparate lives. Loose threads were like frayed carpets, or intertwined like a cat playing with a ball of wool. Even when it was obvious, it was rarely *obvious*. Establishing motive, opportunity, fierce desire, tracking down a perp even once they had been identified, these were all tricks of the trade.

And Mordent was a jack of all trades: a master of none.

It was after midnight. On the windowsill bourbon dregs hardened at the bottom of a dirty glass. Around the edge of the glass ran Mordent's fingerprints. He had been drinking alone. Behind him, the bedcovers sprawled misshapenly – if there was a body underneath it was bent and broken. In a corner of the room, a fan purred and whined alternately, pushed hot air into the crevices. Mordent stood in his shorts, off-white, once-white. Sweat gathered on his forehead, water tension holding it back like police officers talking a suicide off a bridge. When he sighed, the sound was old and low, filled with life's disappointments and an aching need for sleep.

Two months earlier, Bernard Maloney had entered his PI office, looking as dishevelled and confused as Mordent felt. They exchanged glances. Mordent knew in an instant it was a missing person case. Either daughter or wife. Probably wife, because underneath the loss was a hint of release. It was always that way. No matter the love: a closed door on one relationship opened possibilities of another. Eventually. Children were different. The loss of a child was a fundamental loss. The death of self.

'Mr Mordent?'

The voice wavered, whether holding back despair or uncertainty Mordent couldn't tell.

'Just Mordent is fine.'

He beckoned for the guy to sit. His office was sparsely furnished. A filing cabinet rarely used, a computer on the desk. Mordent liked the basics. Life was complicated without adding clutter.

Maloney gave his name. Didn't sit comfortably. Not that Mordent's office chairs *were* that comfortable, but Maloney sat as though he was waiting to be folded in two.

'What can I do for you, Mr Maloney?'

Maloney cleared his throat, words fighting a reluctance to leave his mouth. 'My wife. Tessa Maloney. She's been missing over a month now. She took nothing with her. Her accounts haven't been used. The police have been informed. It looks like abduction. Plain and simple. I want you to find her.'

'You think she's dead?'

Maloney jerked his body straight, relaxed it. 'That's direct.'

'Direct is the best way to find her. Take me or leave me. That's how I work.'

Maloney gave a tired shrug. 'Well, there's no trace of anything. The police can't make up their minds as to whether she's run off or if it's homicide.'

Mordent had been leaning back against the window, but now he sat down. He fiddled with a pen on his desk. One that he rarely used and was probably out of ink. 'What do you think?'

'I want to think that she's alive.'

'Even if she's with some other guy?'

'She wouldn't be.'

'So you think she's dead.'

Mordent wasn't comfortable when guys cried. Maloney fell into himself like soaked origami. He sat and watched. Nothing else to do. On the wall behind Maloney a fly made a staggered vertical journey, and through the frosted glass door panel there briefly appeared the shapely silhouette of one of the agency girls walking down the hall.

Everyone was taking a journey. But Mordent would have bet both the life of the fly and the life of the girl that the journey of Tessa Maloney was at an end.

Maloney pulled out of his pocket a handkerchief that looked like he'd used it to clean windows. He blew his nose, wiped his eyes, mumbled an apology that was neither necessary nor unnecessary. Then he cleared his throat again.

'This isn't the first time,' he said.

'What isn't?'

'She was abducted before. Over twenty years ago. But she escaped. This was before I knew her. She was convinced she might have been a victim of Richard Cottingham, the Torso Killer.'

Mordent knew about that case. His interest in Tessa Maloney quadrupled.

17

'I'll take it on,' he said. 'Give me all you got.'

Two months later – after Maloney had given him all he'd got – the body of Tessa Maloney had been discovered by police in a disused warehouse downtown. Disused warehouses accepted this city role just as dog walkers accepted the role of finding bodies in rural areas. Mordent never knew why the police didn't check them out first. Maybe they didn't like life too easy.

Life. The big A-Z.

Mordent turned his back on the night. It glowered behind him like an angry wolf. He could feel its breath on his neck. Sometimes he imagined the corpses of those he had been unable to save returned as ghosts, pointing toward him with accusing fingers. But Tessa couldn't do that, because they had only her torso. And she'd been dead before Maloney had turned up in his office; probably dead before he'd had the chance to call the police, to realise she was missing.

It was all in the timing. Maybe she had been dead when she had escaped from the Torso Killer back in the '70s. But it wasn't Cottingham who'd done this, regardless of the spec. The alphabet had been shuffled and Tessa's name had turned up twice. Quite rightly, it wouldn't a third time.

Mordent got into bed. The covers were damp. He stilled his thoughts, then his body. Sweat crawled over him like fleas, but within minutes he was asleep.

Sleep: just a conscious candle flicker from the unconscious state of death.

2
Confessions of a Psycho Cat

Morning broke like eggs thrown against Mordent's window. A yellow glow permeated dissipating fog, soon replaced by smog that hung over the city like a fire blanket. Mordent woke, scratched, drew a hand across his stubbled chin and decided against shaving. Some days were better than others, but this was destined to be a bad day. It might as well have been signposted, the feeling was so strong.

Opening his refrigerator he sniffed the milk, drank it anyway. His head stung. The liquid washed over his tongue, lined his stomach, curdled. Breakfast would be fresher outside; a snatched bagel or an early-morning hotdog. Not only armies but cities marched on their stomachs. Every worker, bum, housewife, lowlife – all of them would be foraging this morning. Searching for sustenance, both physical and spiritual. In the city there was always a place to do so.

He rode the elevator down to his vehicle, exited the underground car park like a mole forcing through soil, turned up radio jazz that assaulted his ears as much as the sunlight assaulted his eyes. Immersed within the city in seconds, he navigated the traffic, kept an eye on pedestrians exhibiting death wishes, ignored cyclists who were too foolish to get out of his way. Downtown he passed Morgan's Bar, his usual haunt, still open at this time of day, not that it advertised. The awning looked shabby. The whole area looked shabby. Still, it was always an attractive proposition come night.

He pulled up outside Bukowski's and picked up a bagel for now and a baguette for later, then re-entered the traffic like a caught fish thrown back into the stream. At this hour, all traffic headed one place, like spawning salmon, leaping against the flow to cut a living in dead-end jobs lined with false promises. Or for those whose earnings were way above the average, to sit around playing with executive toys in large, air-conditioned offices, just as much slaves to the wage as those on the lower rungs, only with a better standard of living.

The drive for commercial success puzzled Mordent. It was a crime – both figuratively and literally. Lives wasted working for the Yankee dollar, scraping together a living because society dictated no alternative. And then the actual crimes that resulted from subsequent feelings of entrapment without escape: murder, theft, embezzlement. Or those that went missing, obliterated their previous lives in a desperate urge to be something other. Mordent had traced many superficially contented fathers and husbands who had abandoned their families to live not dissimilar lives with not dissimilar wives in not dissimilar suburban houses. The grass was always greener, even when it was sun-baked and brittle. And of course the suicides, the bungee jumpers without the bungee, the deep-river swimmers without the aqualungs, the marksmen with the guns pointed in the wrong direction, the boy scouts who knew only the hangman's knot.

All failures of the state. A failure to supply health and happiness without a nose to the grindstone. And as Mordent was sucked deeper into the city, like detritus into the open maw of a vacuum cleaner, he knew he was one of them. They all knew it. And yet they *all* did it, all the same.

Above them, there was a blueness to the sky beyond the smog. If only they could see it. If only they would just look up.

He parked. Entered the building that held his office. Recently some of the other residents had gone under; the corridors were bare, echoed. The saving grace was the temp agency on the same floor, which disgorged a bevy of beauties day and night for secretarial jobs across the city. Mordent dreamed of the day when he would earn enough to employ a secretary. But then window-shopping was always more fulfilling than making a purchase.

Sometime that day he would have to make a call to Bernard Maloney. Apologise for not finding his wife. It wouldn't be news to Maloney as such – the tabloids had seen to that. But as a matter of courtesy Mordent wanted the case closed. And then, hopefully, reopened. If Maloney would re-employ him as part of a murder enquiry then it would keep him in bourbon and bagels for some time to come.

If Mordent was a hard man, devoid of emotion, then it was just repetition of experience that had carved that granite heart. On seeing his first dead body he had almost fainted, his eyes reduced to colourful kaleidoscopic images, his forehead creamed with cold sweat. Curiosity kicked in the second and third times. Anything subsequent was nondescript. Familiarisation bred contempt. The body itself became reduced to crime-solving details. The flesh transmuted into flagships of mortality, a distasteful reminder of our corporeal state, which – through religion, alcohol or the pursuit of earthy dreams – each of us tries to avoid.

To do his job properly, to be as good a PI as he needed to be, he had to divorce his mind and emotions from the reality of death. Empathy could only be false. Sympathy in moderation. Without that exterior shell he would be dragged down like the rest of them. That shell hadn't been fully formed when he left the force – it was one of the reasons he was a PI – but now he was a fully-formed cockroach and almost indestructible. If he had a weakness it would be a woman.

And there she sat. On the wooden chair in the corridor outside his door. Her heels were in his eye-line as he ascended the stairs, and each step led to a gradual reveal. From the polished black tips through to the curve of the calf, bare legs, lightly tanned, straight black skirt, one edge stiff over a crossed knee like a visor, white blouse – office wear – freshly ironed and formal, average-sized breasts contouring the fabric, shoulder-length brunette hair with a twist at the ends. Then on the final few steps her face came into view.

Hard, mannish, possibly cruel.

Tentatively intriguing.

Mordent swapped his brown bagel carrier into his left hand then shook hers. Their grip was equal.

'Mordent?'

He nodded. No requisite *Mr*, here.

'My name's Silk. Isabelle Silk. May I talk to you for a moment?'

'Certainly. I imagine that's why you're here.'

Mordent unlocked the door of his office, placed his breakfast-cum-lunch on the desk. Proffered Isabelle a seat.

Meticulously-applied red lipstick cut a gash across her thin mouth. Other make-up was sparingly applied. Her fringe concealed a high forehead. Her jaw was square. Mordent would have put her age around mid-thirties. Not severe enough a personage to invoke fantasies of school matrons or BDSM mistresses, just how a distant aunt might appear to a boy on the cusp of puberty. A suggestion of something other than one of life's usual channels. Despite her essence of unattractiveness, Mordent found it difficult to keep his eyes from her.

'How can I help, Ms Silk?'

Was that a suggestion of a smile at his use of a title? If it was, then it vanished as quickly as a chameleon on a Cheshire cat.

'Can I count on your discretion, Mordent? You have come highly recommended.'

Mordent hung back on the question as to who had recommended him. It was surely a trap to test that discretion.

'Whatever you say stays within these walls,' he answered, tapping his forehead.

'Well, then I imagine it's best to be honest with you, Mordent.' She leant back, crossed her legs, her brown eyes catching the light from the window, which enlivened them briefly, before a passing cloud turned them dull again. 'It's like this. I'm the head of an organisation the details of which you don't need to know. We have some concerns over one of our clients, and seek some information about his activities. Nothing serious I'm sure.' Here she gave a little laugh that left Mordent in no doubt as to the actual seriousness. 'But it would be of great interest to us to determine some background on this gentleman so that our organisation can be best placed – *best placed*, Mordent – to make a decision as to whether or not we need to interact with him at all.'

If Ms Silk considered that honesty, Mordent would have hated to be her husband. Not that she had one; her ring finger was bare with no trace of an indentation.

'You're not giving me a hell of a lot to go on.'

Silk reached into a plain brown handbag that Mordent hadn't previously noticed. Sleight of hand. She passed over a piece of paper containing a name and an address. The address was downtown. The name was Tony Runcorn. Mordent kept his opinions to himself.

'Straightforward surveillance?'

Silk nodded. 'That's right.'

Mordent told her his daily rate and she reached again into the handbag and pulled out a bunch of notes, well used.

'I do prefer cash to cheques,' she said; again, a smile toyed on her lips.

'However it comes,' said Mordent.

He opened his desk drawer and carelessly chucked the money inside without counting it. 'I'll report back within the week; sooner if necessary.'

Silk stood and extended her hand. She was taller than Mordent. Five-eleven, at a push. This time her grip was a little softer, and Mordent wondered about a release of tension.

'Goodbye Mordent. I look forward to hearing from you.' The door closed with a click.

Mordent took a few steps around the side of his desk and pressed his ear against the glass panel. Locked the door. Then he sat back down, opened the desk drawer and counted the money. There was plenty to be getting along with. He rose and stood at the window. According to one of the city clocks it was close to 10.15. The streets had disgorged their commuters, and their places were being taken by tourists – either singularly or in groups. Mordent often wondered how people in one place always wanted to visit another, instead of being content with where they were. Another case of greener grass.

He watched as, on the street below, Isabelle Silk hailed a cab and entered the fray. He needed an angle on her, couldn't pin one. For a moment he was reminded of Eileen Lord in the '60s B-movie *Confessions of a Psycho Cat*. The plot involved a wealthy deranged woman who offered large sums of money to three men so long as they could stay alive in Manhattan for 24 hours. Then she went and hunted them down. Mordent had an inclination that Ms Isabelle Silk wasn't beyond hunting. He couldn't remember how the movie finished, but was sure it wasn't a happy ending.

Meantime, there was Tony Runcorn. Mordent looked at the address on the piece of paper, wondered at the connection between Tony and Isabelle and her undisclosed organisation. It was a puzzle, that was for sure. And a puzzle to which he already had one piece. Tony Runcorn was a name that was known to him.

He stepped away from the window. Tony needed to wait. Before Mordent could engage himself there was another matter to settle. He sat at the desk and dialled the morgue.

3
Calling In Favours

Mordent had contacts in the force from his previous involvement in policing. Some of these were readily forthcoming; others were tight and needed to be prised like oysters. Oysters that didn't guarantee pearls. Kovacs was an oyster, to be approached only in extreme circumstances. But in the morgue, Martens was in Mordent's pocket, due to the memory of an indiscretion. It was Martens he dialled now. Not that he needed too much information. Again his mind was drawn to the tabloids and their splash on Tessa Maloney's death. But despite phone-hacking, the tabloids didn't know it all. And there were details that required clarification before Mordent made another call.

Martens would hopefully be finishing his night shift. Mordent needed to catch him before Clements took over, because otherwise his fishing would be for nothing.

The phone rang twice before Martens picked up. Evidently he hadn't been buried to the hilt in a cadaver.

'Morgue.'

'Martens, it's Mordent.'

The sigh at the other end of the line was expectant. 'What do you want? I'm at the end of my shift, need to get home, get some sleep.'

'You'll get that soon enough. I need some information.'

'Hasn't my debt been called in yet?'

'What do you think?'

The pause was pregnant. 'I think you ain't never gonna let me forget it.'

'The thing is, Martens, you're your own worst enemy. For you, working in a morgue is like being a kid in a candy store.'

'It was just the once.'

'Sure it was. But you got caught with your fingers in the jar. Careless.'

Another sigh. Resignation in the voice. 'What is it that you want?'

'Information on Tessa Maloney.'

'The papers got all that.'

'I want the info that the papers didn't get.'

'Jeez Mordent, I don't know. It's not like you work here anymore.'

'That could be both of us, Martens. It's your decision. Always has been.'

Again, a pause. 'There was just a torso; no head, no limbs. Body identified by an engraved St Christopher. The chain of which had been pulled tight into the flesh around her neck so it wouldn't fall off; without the head to hold it, if you know what I mean. Subsequently confirmed by DNA. Husband's been spoken to and he's due to make a formal identification this morning, although the papers appear to have beaten him to it.'

'So, that's the stuff I already know. I need the rest.'

'Seems to be a copycat killing. Method imitated that of Richard Cottingham, the so-called Torso Killer, who was incarcerated in the early '80s. Husband reckoned his wife claimed to have had a lucky escape from that guy, although I don't know the details. Obviously it isn't the same guy. Straightforward copycat, as I said.'

'What's Kovacs doing about it?'

Mordent could almost hear Martens smile. 'He's out looking for the rest of her.'

'Anything else?'

'Not a great deal. The papers have left out the references to Cottingham, although I don't know how long that will last.

Knowing their predilections, they'll be hoping this is the first of many. Cottingham was convicted for six murders, but he reckoned it was nearer one hundred. Serial killers like to brag when they're caught, of course. Improves their ratings, so to speak.'

Mordent glanced out of the window. Wondered how many of the populace would take on the mantle of a serial killer if given the chance. The media had romanticised the public's fascination, yet everyone looked at a car crash.

'Okay Martens. Give me a head's up if another torso comes in.'

'Very funny. Maybe I should give you the finger.'

'Your fingers are safer in your pockets, Martens.'

Mordent hung up.

He removed the bagel from the brown paper bag and took a bite. The chewy, doughy interior clung to his mouth. He needed a cup of coffee, didn't have one. Sighing, he reached for the bourbon in his bottom drawer. The alcohol tasted sterile, didn't go with the bagel. With the residue in his mouth, he dialled Bernard Maloney's number and commiserated on the death of his wife.

Thirty minutes later, with Maloney's request to investigate the murder rather than a missing person, Mordent was back in his car, driving across town to call in a second favour.

It had begun raining as soon as he had left the office. On his drive through the city, the outside world bled against his car windows; fractured colours reflected in isolated water bubbles; tiny worlds were created and dissolved like miniature Victorian portraitures. His wipers swept these aside, like a burly man pushing through a crowd. The slick tarmac gleamed like liquorice; numerous potholes formed lakes with hidden depths. Mordent was cocooned within the car. He could himself be a bubble, just like all the other drivers on the teeming highway, all waiting for the wiper that might end their own existence.

Tessa Maloney's existence had terminated unexpectedly.

There was a thin line between life and death: not just the physicality of it, but a time line. Who wanted to know their own date or method of death? Life could be held in a tentative embrace due only to the fact that, while recognising its transience, one remained ignorant of the details of its ending. Mordent had met those with terminal illnesses, who had a greater certainty as to the date of their demise, and these were split into two camps: those who wished to cram everything into their last months or weeks and those who wished just to wait for the reaper. Mordent didn't envy either. Being able to block out death allowed for lives to be lived. And was it worse for a life to be cut short suddenly or for there to be a long, slow fade? Did it matter to the person who died, or only to those they left behind?

Death: the great divide.

Maloney had sniffled on the phone. He had been expecting the link with Cottingham – the abduction coincidence had been too great to ignore. Mordent did not consider the husband a suspect – this was no inside job. Yet in the time he had spent investigating Tessa's disappearance, there had been no indication as to why or where she had gone. Knowledge of murder didn't add motive. All it subtracted was that Tessa hadn't gone willingly.

A taxi cut a yellow path in front of Mordent and he leant on his horn. The sound was lost in the swish of rubber on water. The lights turned red and he reached into the bag on the passenger seat, pulled out his baguette. For some reason, hunger dogged him. He took a bite, and lettuce and tomato slid out of the sides and onto his trousers. He swore, lost some ham, then was pitched forward by the green light. He placed the baguette back onto the seat, braked, and watched it roll into the footwell. Sighing, he wiped traces of mayo off his mouth with the back of his hand, the greasy sheen a pallid smear as he returned his hand to the wheel.

In the rain, life was different: enclosed and personal. The sun expanded, was expansive. Open skies opened up universes, widened perspective. In rain, pedestrians kept their heads down, half-hidden by concave umbrellas, eyes peeled for puddles. If there was an analogy there, then Mordent didn't have the head for it. He preferred the noirish light of the rain, the way darkness became populated by diamonds in streetlights, the machine gun downpours that took no prisoners, the refraction of shadows, the distillation of life to each and every sodden step. In sunlight, the world was too much with you. Possibilities weren't narrowed. Focus was lost. It suited him as much as the suit he was wearing didn't.

Traffic thinned out the closer he came to his destination. So did the buildings, or at least their appearance. Cracks ran riot across disused shop fronts – windows etched with web-like trails of glass spiders. Soaked cardboard clung wetly. Rubbish collated in doorways, as though herded by sheep-dog wind. Grilles on some windows were rusted, their individual squares bent into rhombuses by street children with little else to do with their crowbars. It wasn't the most salubrious area, but Mordent's appointment wasn't with the most salubrious of people.

Hubie had a long connection with Mordent that was mixed up with gambling and girls. From his former prominence in the financial sector, his weakness for both had carved a channel that he had eventually slipped down like a greased pig on a waterslide. Now he operated an advisory service on the wrong side of the city, but his links to previous contacts in the industry and subsequent expansion into the lower echelons of society made him a prime source of information that Mordent was always quick to mine. Even if he had to wade through piles of rubbish and risk car damage to get there.

Mordent parked up. The street was deserted. Two nearby pizza parlours were boarded and closed. Hubie lived and worked in his office. Mordent imagined he didn't get out much. Pushing through the large creaking doors to the communal hallway, he ascended the piss-stained stairwell, fists clenched in case of trouble, until finally he was on Hubie's floor.

With Hubie, Mordent never rang ahead. There was an element to catching him off-guard that appealed. Not that

Hubie's information was ever wrong, but Mordent didn't want to place him in a situation where he might have the opportunity to think how it might be divulged.

He gave the door a series of quick knocks. Then waited.

There was movement within the room. A scraping sound like granite on a cold stone floor. Perhaps a sigh. A click as the connecting door to Hubie's bedroom was closed. Then the main door opened on a two-inch chain.

'Who is it?'

'Mordent. There's no need to be so careful.'

The door closed a fraction and Mordent heard the clink of the chain being removed before the gap widened enough for him to enter.

'Can't be too careful, though, Mordent. There's been trouble here recently. Riots, would you believe.'

Mordent edged his way into the room. The main office was as sparse as his own, although from previous visits he knew the bedroom was opulent, and a lady of the night might be languorously draped across the bed.

'Riots? Haven't heard anything on the news.'

'No-one cares about this side of the city anymore. They start a few fires, no-one puts them out. Didn't you see the smoke?'

Mordent gestured to the window. 'Didn't you see the rain?'

'Fair enough. Still, it's a worry. I can't afford to move out of here if the area gets any worse.'

'Maybe. But you couldn't afford to remain here if it got any better.'

Hubie wandered over to his desk, looked out of the window. 'Strange how you can get used to somewhere you decide to call home.'

Mordent nodded. People were like sediment; they settled at their own level.

'Well, you might as well sit down.' Hubie gestured Mordent to a chair opposite the desk. 'I'm guessing you're not here to enquire after my wellbeing.'

'Hardly.' Mordent shifted his bulk onto the chair, which squeaked as though stuffed with rodents. 'I need some information, Hubie. Although as of yet I'm not quite sure why.'

'Sounds intriguing.'

'Who knows?'

'So,' Hubie said. 'Hit me with it.'

Mordent leant backwards, trusting the wooden chair as much as he trusted Hubie.

'Tell me what you know about Reflective Tony.'

Hubie made a triangle with his fingers. A curlicue of a smile threatened to break across his face. 'Now there's a name to conjure with,' he said.

'It's not unknown to me,' said Mordent. 'I just want your take.'

'Small-time hood. Sometime fence, sometime dealer, sometime everything. A bit-part player in a wider criminal world. One time he fell into a bonfire and was found in his garage lying in a pool of kerosene. As a result he's slightly disfigured. You probably know that story. You probably also know he's called Reflective Tony because nothing seems to stick. The cops know he's part of stuff, but investigations always get deflected. Now, maybe he's got influence up high, but if he has, it doesn't reflect none on his lifestyle. He lives in a wood-built building out on the East side.'

'Everyone knows he's just lowlife,' Mordent growled. 'You got anything new on him?'

Hubie shrugged. 'Maybe he's on the up. I heard he's got a bodyguard. A hunk by the name of the Frame. Sounds like an ex-WWF guy to me, but more likely a bouncer who's got bounced around too often and has decided to move into the dodgy protection business.'

Mordent ran his tongue over his lips. It was dry in Hubie's office. The windows were closed and the atmosphere was stuffy, airtight and air tight. 'Any recent activity?'

'None that I know of. Maybe you should pay a visit to him, not me.'

'You know me, Hubie. I like to cover my bases.'

Mordent rose from the chair, turned to the door, then had a thought and turned back.

'How about Isabelle Silk? Does that name mean anything to you?'

Hubie shook his head. 'Sounds like a girl I'd like to get to know.'

'She'd eat you up, Hubie.'

'I could live with that.'

4
All Done With Mirrors

Mordent said his goodbyes to Hubie and returned to the street. Sat in his car eating the remains of his baguette, he watched the rain dry on the sidewalk. The surface was pitted and uneven. Puddles collected like street gangs, until the heat of the sun finally pierced the smog and evaporated them as effectively as a SWAT team.

Occasionally, with food in his mouth, he wondered if he wanted Silk to eat *him* up. Decided against it. Life was complicated enough.

It was a dry time for Mordent. Female company, usually transient in the best of circumstances, had been lacking of late. Like everyone, he had his peccadilloes, satisfied them occasionally with desultory encounters in backstreet bordellos, faces and names interchangeable, unnecessary. There had been a woman once, Maria, but long-term had been punctuated with the pressures of an on/off switch. Sometimes the hunger in his belly couldn't be filled by a baguette.

So he might toy with tawdry fantasies of his female clients expressing their gratitude, or the recently-widowed turning grief into solace, or jumped-up and overly-educated law students wanting a bit of genuine street-smartness. Or else phantasmal visions of half-remembered women hovering over his bed while he shook the covers and the bed springs played a disconsolate rusted tune. So he might.

How did that old English song go? *A policeman's lot is not a happy one.* True, he was no longer in the force, but being a PI wasn't all Tom Selleck and sunglasses. It wasn't even Jim Rockford living out of a trailer park. Being a PI was akin to being a writer. Women weren't interested. Didn't see the potential glamour, because there wasn't any. What they saw were long nights alone abandoned to the cause. It was like Woody Allen's character in *The Front*, turning one woman off when he says he's a writer, then turning the next one on when he lies about being a dentist. Mordent's hands weren't steady enough to be a writer or a dentist.

He released the handbrake and began the motions that would take him over to the East side.

Mordent was well aware of Reflective Tony, although previous encounters had been arbitrary. A face at the back of a crowd, an onlooker rather than a player. Yet in a world of ups and downs he was a constant: had avoided prison on the right side of the law and gangland conflict on the wrong side. He had something, Mordent wasn't sure what, that was akin to a badge of protection. If you fired a shot at his heart you could be sure the bullet would be stopped by a silver cigarette case in his top shirt pocket. Hubie was right; the *Reflective* moniker was apt, in the sense that you couldn't even look at him without your gaze being turned away. Sleight of hand, misdirection; Tony was hardly a magician, but he knew when to disappear. Mordent wondered what the connection would be with Isabelle Silk.

Again, he'd accepted a job without a proper briefing; had decided to run full throttle without a tank of gas.

As he approached the East side, the houses became movie sets. Not opulent and foreboding, but like those wooden-built structures that were all façade, propped up at the back by beams and rivets, temporary visions of grandeur that now looked abandoned and false. Tufts of grass forced their way upwards through the sidewalk like a bad haircut. The lots were large, unnecessarily so. Driveways were clogged with vehicles in various states of disrepair. Tyres lounged against fences, tools rusted in the sun, hoods propped open like lizard mouths, windscreens smashed and jagged. The area had more welfare per capita than the rest of the city put together. Mordent had once dated a girl who came from this area. She had worn braces and chewed gum, and the two didn't mix.

It was clear, as he cruised, that that day would be one of preliminary surveillance only. His car, as bruised and as battered as the best of them, still stuck out like a sore thumb. There wasn't a street corner he could hang by without it being obvious he was law enforcement. All those movie scenes of cops or PIs sliding down in their cars as pedestrians walked by, embedding themselves in upholstery, clenching paper cups of coffee and half-eaten hamburgers, were myths. As soon as word was on the street of an occupied car, Mordent could expect the surveillance tables turned, laced with potential violence. No, today was just to set the scene, determine how best to keep tabs on Mr Runcorn, perhaps to glimpse sight of the Frame.

Hubie hadn't needed to be explicit. The Frame would be built like a brick chicken house, arms as wide as Mordent's body, and a skull so thick you couldn't crack it with a sledgehammer. This was a fact. He wouldn't be called the Frame because he could hold a picture. He wouldn't fit in an art gallery, that was for sure.

Tony's property was like all the others, maybe a bit tidier out front, with his car resting in the garage, which seemed able to contain it, unlike the others on the block, which were filled with tools and parts. Mordent was guessing Tony wasn't the kind of guy who wanted his vehicle parked out on the street. He cruised past. The windows of the house were blank, and it was unclear whether or not he was being watched. At that moment he was torn between parking up and asking direct questions and leaving the job in its entirety. What was Silk doing around a guy like Reflective Tony? However far down the echelons of power he might be in her organisation. Maybe he needed to find out more about her organisation before he found out more about Tony.

Further down the street he passed a Buick containing a driver whose body was so thick he blocked out the view of the back seat.

Mordent nodded to himself. That would be the Frame.

He watched in his rear-view mirror as the car pulled into the drive, then he turned at the next junction, reverse spun and headed back, just in time to watch the Frame edge himself into Tony's property. Sideways. The door frame being too narrow to accommodate him.

Note to self, Mordent filed in a mental cabinet. *Don't anger that guy*.

Yet maybe that was also misdirection. Maybe the outside appearance was a subterfuge, a misnomer. Maybe the Frame was a kitten.

Maybe that was also Santa on Tony's roof, heaving a sackful of presents down the chimney.

Mordent decided to stick with his first impression. Make it count.

Later that afternoon, Mordent was nursing a glass in Morgan's Bar.

Alcohol was the great leveller. It reduced the human race to a pre-evolutionary state where employment status, class, race and even language became immaterial. Sure, there were those who became violent with alcohol, where each of the above distinctions was like a red rag to a bull; but even with the violence there was a babyish intensity, a naïve and basic misunderstanding that underneath it we are all the same. Within the alcoholic glow, mankind didn't need to be wife-beaters or carousers with strangers; the levelling was done deep inside the soul, an awareness that life might be tamed, that a fuzzy head brought down the shutters, enclosed us. On that level, we were all hiding away in the evolutionary soup, slightly raising our eyes out of the mud to look occasionally at the shore.

Mordent guessed that taking tentative steps on new legs toward land must have been akin to having several shots of bourbon. That same unsteadiness, that same numbness of spirit, yet also the embracing of the unknown without preconception or fear. And if there had been a bar supplying alcohol to our amphibian ancestors then Morgan would have had a hand in it somewhere. A consummate barman, Morgan knew when to talk and when to keep quiet. That afternoon, silence reigned.

Mordent had a newspaper in front of him on the bar, one corner wet and beer-stained, the other curling like a dry sandwich. Someone had half completed the crossword, indenting the paper through several pages, the writing a scrawl making some letters indistinguishable from others. It annoyed him. Not that he would have started or finished the crossword himself, but that it was despoiled. Some people couldn't stop imposing themselves on others, blundering through life without concerns of impact, rendering everything second-hand.

He shook his head, shook the dregs in his glass, then shook them into his mouth. Called Morgan over for another.

Morgan took the glass without a glance, replaced it full in a moment. Hung back.

Mordent looked up.

Morgan was looking at the paper.

'You want something?' The drink had dulled Mordent's senses. Or was it the crossword? Or the fact that he had taken on another case without getting the full facts? Or that his last missing person case had turned out to be a person missing body parts? Whatever. He wasn't usually this abrasive.

'Ten down.' Morgan said. 'It's *Continuum.*'

'You're kidding.'

'A continuous succession. *Continuum.*'

'I'm not doing the crossword, Morgan. It just happens to be open on the bar.'

Morgan shrugged and returned to wiping glasses.

Mordent shook his head. Downed more bourbon. Life had stalled.

Truth was, the crossword was open on the bar because he didn't want to turn the paper to the first page. He didn't want to be confronted by the torso of Tessa Maloney. He hadn't failed her. He hadn't even failed her husband. But at the end of the day a torso was a torso, and it knit itself inside him all the same.

His mind wandered over the magician analogy Hubie had mentioned when discussing Reflective Tony. Not that the cases were linked, but torsos seemed a by-product when sawing a woman in half. Maybe it was an act gone wrong. Maybe it was all done with mirrors. What did they say? Smoke and mirrors. Obfuscation and distraction. Yet maybe that was it. Maybe the spec mirrored that of Cottingham, the original Torso Killer, in order to deflect suspicion from the real murderer. Or maybe it *was* a copycat, plain and simple.

The maybes and possibilities increased the further Mordent's nose descended into the glass.

Despite the afternoon sun, Morgan's Bar rested within its own time zone. Here it was perpetually black, continuous night. To expand on Morgan's crossword answer, the room was a continuous extent where no part could be distinguished from neighbouring parts. A cocoon, sanctuary, home: call it what you will. No light came through the windowless exterior; just the dull glow of interior lighting illuminated the faces within.

In Morgan's Bar there were no romantic corners.

And the only mirror was the one behind the bar.

Mordent watched himself pick up his glass for another drink, changed his mind. Behind him, blurred shadows populated the black tables, shifts in darkness indicating a raised arm, a turn of the head. Just a few years back, those shadows would have been pinpricked with the tiny red glow of cigarette embers, like looking into a forest at night and seeing the eyes of a multitude of wildlife. Nowadays, smokers at Morgan's had to go out back, into a metal compound flanked by corrugated sheets and trashcans. It wasn't inviting, the light was too bright whatever the weather, and it was rare that anyone ventured outside. Doing so broke the atmosphere.

The absence of colour lent the mirror a tangible quality of otherness, as if, like Alice, or Jean Marais in Cocteau's *Orphée*, he might dive inside it, creating ripples that would lap at the edges of the frame. Briefly Mordent wondered what it might be like on the other side of the mirror, although his noirish mind suggested it would be a mirror image of his current view: his own face with the rest of the clientele behind him.

At that moment, like a silver fish shifting in a black pond, there was movement. As though she had emerged from the mirror, a woman appeared on the adjacent stool.

Mordent turned his head. Watching her reflection seemed more obvious, somehow. More perverse.

She was a brunette, curvy, about five-eight, maybe 28, eyes aglow, wearing a silver dress that looked like a glitter-ball rolled flat then rolled around her. It hung in all the right places, and some of the wrong ones. Mordent clocked his watch: it was a little after 4.00.

She noticed him watching. Held back her gaze. Morgan fixed her a glass; a screwdriver. She downed it in one.

'You look like the kind of man who'd be a good listener.'

Her voice was gutsy, with an underlying guttural growl. It wasn't the most attractive voice Mordent had ever heard, and she wasn't the most attractive woman. He wondered how much he wanted to listen.

He shrugged, but didn't look away.

She sighed. 'Look, humour me, buy me another drink. Do something, for God's sake.'

Mordent shrugged again. 'I'm no counsellor or councillor. You want my time, I charge for it.'

She raised a hand, beckoned Morgan over. 'Another one for me, and one for my friend here.'

'I didn't say I wanted a drink.'

'You're in a bar, aren't you? You're in *this* bar – the only bar worth being in.'

Mordent sipped his bourbon. 'If you're a regular, I haven't seen you here before.'

'I could say the same about you.'

Mordent shrugged once more. The alcohol was dimming his senses, his sense. It had been a while since he'd let himself be this affected, and he still wasn't sure quite what had prompted it.

'So, go ahead. Looks like you're going to tell me your story whether I want to hear it or not.'

He watched as she shifted her position on the stool, crossed a shapely leg and revealed a knee.

'My ex is stalking me.'

'Heard that one before. Some guys are difficult to shake off.'

'We were together four months. It got a little obsessive. *I* got a little obsessive. Then I decided I didn't want to be. Does that make sense?'

'Women blow hot and cold all the time. It's another familiar story.'

'I don't want you making assumptions about me, Mr ...?'

'Mordent. My name is Mordent.'

She reached out a hand. Her fingers were cold in his. Nails painted purple. 'I'm Jessica.'

He mumbled 'Nice to meet you'. Didn't mean it.

She left her hand in his for a little longer than was necessary.

'This isn't much of a story,' he said.

'There's more.' She withdrew her hand and clasped a handbag to her lap. Mordent hadn't noticed it before. Maybe because it was of the same material as her dress.

'Last night I went out for a few drinks with the girls. I was wearing this dress. It was his favourite.' She paused. 'He saw me out in it.'

'It might be a silver dress, but it's a red rag to that bull.'

'Exactly!' A smile spread across her face that looked wrong. Everything looked wrong. 'So he made a scene, stormed into the club – just like, as you said, just like a bull in a china shop.' Her voice was getting shrill, out of place in Morgan's Bar, with a Southern Belle edge to it. 'I had him thrown out, Mr Mordent, out on the street.'

'I'm guessing he's not there now.'

'Well, that's right. He wasn't there. But he was there when I got home. Mr Mordent, I've been trapped in my house since last night until a few hours ago, when he fell asleep and I managed to get away.'

'That sounds as plausible as the story that you've worn that dress all night.'

Jessica put on a sad pout. 'You don't believe me?'

'Hell I don't.'

She huffed. Finished her drink. Looked at the glass as though she expected it to become molten before her eyes. 'I guess you think I'm trying to pick you up.'

Mordent shook his head. 'You couldn't pick me up. I'm 180 pounds and all muscle under this fat. I don't know quite what you're doing, but what you're not doing is me.'

He disembarked from the stool. The floor reeled beneath him as though they were on a wooden sea. Just as he was about to say something, the entrance door to the bar was flung open and a half dozen teenagers fell in. One of them blu-tacked a poster to the back of the door, while another distributed leaflets to the disgruntled occupants at the tables. Morgan was trying to shoo them out, just as one of them was fobbing him off with flyers. Mordent hadn't seen anything like it. Not there, not in that sanctuary. He shook his head violently, and as though he was shaking the alcohol out of his mind, it began to clear. Grabbing hold of the collar of one of the youths, he hauled him out the door, just as Morgan frogmarched another.

Soon after, the bar regained itself, the incident forgotten.

Mordent glanced over to where Jessica had been sat, but she was gone. Presumably in the commotion. No loss.

He raised an arm in a Columbo-like motion to anyone who appreciated his effort and exited onto the street. The youths had disappeared. Maybe he had overreacted. He reached into his jacket pocket for his car keys and pulled out two folded pieces of paper.

One held a phone number and Jessica's name.

The other was a flyer for the Church of Wire.

5
Like Glue

After sleeping for the rest of the afternoon, Mordent woke with a headache and a hunger.

He had slept in his clothes, having returned to his apartment and fallen onto the bed with little memory of how he had arrived there and an internal reprimand for having driven the distance. His dreams had been mangled: car chases in tiny vehicles; gangsters with prohibition-era machine guns; masked ladies with elongated snouts; a figure always in shadow that turned his feet to stone.

His clothes clung and stank. Rivulets trickled under his armpits. When he sat up there was a pull from the bed, as though it was covered in glue or there was someone tugging him back. He turned around, saw the collar of his suit had got rucked in the bedclothes. Sighing, he disentangled himself, rose to his feet and leant unsteadily on the windowsill. Night was in the process of falling, slowly at this time of year, and the underside of the smog was lit with a rosy glow. It looked vaguely apocalyptic or romantic, depending on your disposition.

While waiting for the ready-meal that turned under a spotlight in the microwave like a particularly tacky showgirl, he reached into his pocket and pulled out the scrap of paper and the flyer. Even in his drunken state he had considered it odd that Jessica had been able to plant it on him in the time available. There was only one possibility: she had had her name and number pre-written. That struck him strange enough to retain it, although perhaps too strange to call her.

As for the flyer, he glanced at it again, crumpled it up, and placed it in the waste bin.

Religion didn't sit well with Mordent and never had. For him, it was all subterfuge; or, to continue the magician analogy that had tagged him most of the day, misdirection. If mankind wanted to kid itself that there was some importance to the world or significance after death, then that was fine with him, but he didn't need to be involved, or cajoled into taking part. As he saw it, as mankind had evolved, then so had its gods. From deities in every inanimate object and thenceforth a narrowing down to just one god, it was all so much bluster and balderdash. The sooner mankind admitted its own mortality then the sooner it would start to police itself. For Mordent, having no god did not equate to the anarchy and destruction of civilisation that those who held a religion tended to believe. In fact, the opposite was true.

So the flyer's tag line, 'Celebrate God's Seventh Day Creation', was as unappealing as the lasagne congealing in his microwave. But unlike religion, he would consume the lasagne half-heartedly, because at the very least it would assuage his hunger.

The microwave pinged and he removed the offending article and ate it out of the packaging at his table in front of his PC. Mordent didn't own a television: real life was too close in his day-to-day to watch it dramatised into something less authentic. Instead he accessed his news online, occasionally watched *The Simpsons*, and once in a while browsed jazz websites. Very occasionally he watched porn. But then, who didn't?

The final strip of pasta was firmly stuck to the bottom of the microwaveable container. He dug into it with his fork, dislodged it with a looping motion that saw it glide like a flying carpet and land on the floor.

Maybe it was divine intervention.

Mordent clocked his watch. If he got over to Tony's in an

hour, maybe he could cruise past and see if a light was on. But it was all a bit desultory. In fact, it felt like he was kicking around the traces of a fire long since burnt out, way before it was due to be relit. Reflective Tony, Isabelle Silk, a new Torso Killer – the disparate threads of the cases in front of him were nothing to get his teeth stuck into.

Instead, he ran his tongue around his mouth, removed lasagne residue, and went back to bed. Watched the cracks in his ceiling as they formed and reformed patterns on the peripheries of sleep.

6
Cold Light Of Day

Morning kicked Mordent in the stomach. He opened his eyes to an unfamiliar glare, the sun streaming through his window as though the smog had never existed, a blue patch of sky almost white in a retina burn, dehydrating him faster than the residual effects of the alcohol.

He got up and shook himself. Something was weighing him down and he wasn't sure what. A niggling in the back of his head. Then he remembered: all the pointing fingers of the victims he had been too late for or had let down had been pressing into the base of his skull all night. Dreams of lost causes, no hopers, losers, wasters in many cases, the dead and the dispossessed. If he were a TV show PI, these would be high-school debutantes, football coaches, high-standing businessmen, chat show hosts, trapeze artists, shrinks and pool attendants. Instead he had to deal with the humdrum everyday populace. Those whose disappearances weighed heavily only on family and friends – and sometimes not even on those.

He was getting to be a grumpy old man.

Outside his window the glare persisted, like the sun was a bad cop shining an unshaded lightbulb in his face. *Give me information and give it to me now.* There was some truth in the analogy – Mordent had found everyone was more pliant on a sunny day. Like flowers, people opened up when the weather was good and hunkered down when it was bad. That was human nature. It was also why, when he had been a cop, he had often interviewed people outside instead of in the cell. Not officially, of course, but in those days everything didn't need to be official. No-one knew their rights back then. And to be honest, no-one cared.

Part of him longed for the days of the long nights, the bright white light glinting off cold black stone, the brim of a hat, tilted, shadows delineated by sharp angles and odd corners, women with husky voices emerging from clouds of smoke, gunshots fired with accuracy and deliberate intent, brogues on wet pavements, the pressing down of the night onto everybody and everything – like a heavy blanket thrown over a wet dog.

The clear blue sky, the sunlight, the reflection of light from car windscreens way below, the colourful clothes of tourists and the casual attire of dressed-down office workers, these were all incongruous to his preferred PI way of thinking. It was an affectation, he was well aware of that, but for Mordent it added something to his chosen profession. At heart, he was a glamour-puss.

He performed his ablutions, drove to his office, walked the empty corridors, and spent thirty minutes looking out of *that* window at the traffic below.

Then his phone rang.

'Mordent.'

'It's Martens.'

Mordent glanced at his watch. It was after 10.30. 'You're working late this morning, Martens. Thought you were confined to the night shift.'

'I finished a couple of hours ago. I'm calling you from home.'

'From home?'

'That's what I said.'

'I love your dedication to duty, Martens.'

'Whatever. You can joke with me all you want, but I've got information. Couldn't call you from work, could I? Unless you're sleeping in your office, you wouldn't be there.'

Mordent opened his desk drawer and pulled out a notepad. One corner was decorated with a pink fairy waving a magic wand. A gift from a previous admirer, which he had thrown in the drawer and remembered only when he had to use it. Other than that, it held no memories.

'Okay Martens. Give me what you've got.'

There was a pause. 'Okay, but the trade off is that you don't get annoyed by what I'm about to tell you.'

'Maybe I'll decide that once you've told me what it is. Anyway, what is this? You're not a child.'

'Whatever.' Martens paused again. 'What I held back last time was the typewritten note stapled to Tessa Maloney's body. Well, I say a note, but it was a name: Richard Cottingham.'

Mordent laughed. 'So it was hardly Kovacs' powers of detection that made the link.'

'They wanted to hold it back.'

'I bet they did.'

'So, what's the rest of it? I'm betting you got another body.'

'That would be the case. Victim is African-American, male, mid-fifties, name of Kwamie Pettiford. Stabbed to death. His heart cut out.'

'That last bit sounds vaguely familiar. I take it there was another note? And I'm guessing not Richard Cottingham?'

'You'd be right. Does Joseph Christopher ring a bell?'

Mordent racked his brains for less than a second, gave up. What was the point of thinking it when Martens would tell him anyway?

'It doesn't.'

'Ah ... well Joseph Christopher was a serial killer active in the early '80s. He targeted African-American males, initially shooting them indiscriminately, but later using a knife. He cut out the heart of only two of his victims – I say only, because sometimes he killed up to five victims in one day. He became known as the Midtown Slasher. Died in jail in the mid-'90s with a rare form of male breast cancer.'

'And therefore not in line for Kwamie Pettiford's murder.'

'Exactly.'

'So it is a copycat killer. Of sorts.'

'You could say that.'

'Anything else?'

'Kovacs is investigating Kwamie's background, but this is recent and nothing's come of it yet.'

'When you say recent, you mean yesterday, right?'

'Yesterday is good enough.'

Mordent sighed. 'Just remember your job is in my hands Martens. Today is always better than yesterday.'

'Look, I gave you the info didn't I? After all this time they wouldn't listen to you anyway.'

'Do you want to chance it?' Mordent listened to the faint hiss on the line indicative of Martens' silence. 'Well then. Call me again when you've got more info. And call it as it happens, okay?'

He hung up.

Another serial killer on the loose. They say imitation is the greatest form of flattery, although he didn't think either Bernard Maloney or Pettiford's relatives would see it that way. Still, he had the information required. Investigating Tessa's death on the instructions of her husband had just got a little bit easier, or more intriguing, or more difficult. Take your pick.

In the cold light of day, a dead body was a dead body. Whether it was a torso or incomplete in other ways. They said dead men tell no tales, but that wasn't strictly correct. There was a lot you could glean from a dead body. It didn't have to have a voice to tell you how it had been killed. But there was no *life* in it; as obvious as it sounded. Mordent had witnessed a lot of grieving families in his time that would clasp dead relatives to them as though sheer love alone could reanimate them. At first – maybe at the *very* first – it had affected him, but less than a week later it had repulsed. Death needed getting shot of. Fast. And that included the grieving.

So it was with this in mind that he telephoned Bernard Maloney and updated him on his line of enquiry. Maloney wasn't as stoic as Mordent. He sniffed throughout the conversation, and Mordent guessed it wasn't from a cold. It was hard to tell whether Maloney found his wife's death easier to deal with, knowing it wasn't a one off, or whether this lack of uniqueness made it harder. Mordent wasn't sure how he would feel in a similar situation. Maybe he would feel nothing at all.

Meantime, he decided to do some poking around. Kovacs, chief of the homicide unit, was hardly his best friend. They had had more run-ins than Osama-Obama. But Kovacs would give him some information if he asked him nicely. And Mordent was prepared to ask nicely, because in this instance the police held all the cards.

Outside his office the sun was still lifting the tarmac from the road, divesting pedestrians of clothes, and had filled his car with a heat so thick that you could almost cut it with a knife. Mordent always wore a jacket. It was easier to conceal his gun that way and gave him the shabby authority that was necessary in his line of work. But the confines of the car caused him to throw it onto the passenger seat, where its torn lining splayed open as if he himself had been a victim of the Midtown Slasher.

He was vaguely aware of that case. Like most who had been on the force, he had an archival interest in crimes and criminals, and serial killers were often the most interesting. Not because of some Hollywood glamorisation, but because of the sheer number of people they killed. For Mordent, taking a life was something always regretted. However legitimate it might feel. Getting his head around someone who was a repeat offender was an interesting exercise. How the perp might circumnavigate their conscious objections, how they might need to justify their actions, how they could override their fear of entrapment and disgust; these were all questions he had mulled over.

The Midtown Slasher's murders had been racially motivated, but Mordent was sure that the killer of Kwamie Pettiford held a different angle. The link between Pettiford and Tessa Maloney was slim. Something was clear, but Mordent wasn't yet keen on entertaining it. Instead, he looked out of the window as he drove, regarded ostentatious human nature.

The heat had put smiles on the faces of the majority of the populace. As he passed by, his vision created a rictus effect due to his speed, but even so, it was evident that people were happy. Dogs strained leads, tails wagging. Lovers held hands. Potential lovers crossed eyes. Even the homeless, still wrapped in multiple layers of clothing as though they might tear like ages-old parchment should they attempt to remove them, had emerged from boarded-up shop doorways and were making their way toward the park.

Glinting off expansive shop windows, light reflected in turn off engagement rings, eternity rings, wedding rings, earrings. The sparkles with which people adorned themselves were more sparkly than ever. Jewellers' shop frontages burnt diamonds onto retinas. Even grocery stores with their wares out front were resplendent in colour bursts of reds, oranges and greens.

It was at times like these Mordent wished he wore sunglasses.

Or had tinted windows.

Or both.

He pulled up at the precinct and managed to get himself waved through into the parking lot. Despite increased security precautions his past carried a lot of weight. He parked up next to Kovacs' car, considered dragging the edge of a dime along the side of the vehicle, but after a glance at the security camera dropped the coin back in his pocket. He smiled instead, a rare crease on his face, which he then inverted and attributed to the weather.

The history of Mordent and Kovacs could fill several encyclopaedias. As it happened, Mordent's star was descending just as Kovacs' was ascending, and as those stars passed, their points rubbed each other up the wrong way. It came down to different styles of policing. Mordent was old school, Kovacs was by the book. Mordent saw nothing wrong in applying a little pressure in the interview room, Kovacs would have had video running as well as audiotape if he could. Mordent was comfortable mixing with low-life to gain information, Kovacs needed the internet. Truth was, Kovacs irritated the hell out of Mordent, and gradually – over a period of time – Kovacs came to realise it.

There was also the matter of some physical violence between

them, when Kovacs was being particularly an ass.

When Mordent left the force, Kovacs would have happily obliterated all traces of him from his fellow officers' memories. But they were individuals, not robots, and it was always to Kovacs' chagrin that whenever Mordent paid a call he was greeted with enthusiasm and even a little affection by the others. Sentiments of which Kovacs himself would never be either a supplier or a recipient. Banning Mordent from the precinct would have been churlish, so whenever he came calling they tolerated each other as civilly as possible; Kovacs having the upper hand of superiority in that he knew Mordent would only ever visit to glean information, while he would always be the one that held the cards.

Mordent headed up the stairwell, distrusting the elevator, until he reached Kovacs' floor. He pushed open both doors simultaneously, making a dramatic entrance. Then he stopped in his tracks: the familiar office space he knew and had inhabited for some years was deserted.

Sure, desks populated the floor space, but they were bare, without even a computer or a desk tidy atop them. A few broken chairs had been pushed into one corner, resembling modern art. A vacuum cleaner lay sideways on the floor, the flex extending to the socket, as though its operative had vanished on depressing the off switch. Mordent glanced over to Kovacs' office. The door was ajar and the interior as empty as the exterior.

He wandered through the space like a ghost from the past come to visit the future. It had been only recently vacated; the barest patina of dust adorned the desktops, apart from where equipment had stood, which silhouetted and delineated shapes like in a child's object-identification game. Water coolers were stagnant. A solitary jacket hung on a coat stand. In the desk drawers that Mordent pulled open, stationery lay patiently awaiting use, forgotten coins accumulated no interest, training manuals sat as pristine as the day they were first handed out, pens with chewed ends rolled like mutilated corpses and gum was wedged into the corners, easily traceable through fingerprint identification.

Mordent sat at the edge of one of the desks, looked around. He had once spent a lot of time here. Too much time, if truth be told. They weren't exactly happy memories. Yet seeing his past displaced was a little unnerving. Something inside him faded, winked out of existence. There was more to life than objects and memories, yet both created identity. While he returned here only infrequently, whenever he did he became rejuvenated, his current existence justified through the validation of his previous existence. Now that would never happen again.

He stood before he became too melancholic. Then entered Kovacs' old office.

Unsurprisingly, it was bare. There wasn't even a trace of dust. Kovacs left life with the same principles that he entered it.

For a second it crossed his mind: Kovacs left? Then he shook his head. It was fantasy. He exited through the main door and made his way downstairs. Bartholomew was on the public counter, a pencil behind his ear.

'Mordent! How the devil are you?'

'I'm good, Bartholomew. How's the wife and kids?'

Bartholomew smiled. 'They're good thanks.'

As a point of fact, Bartholomew had no wife, no kids. This was ritualistic banter that he and Mordent had always sparred with.

'So, where's Kovacs?'

'The whole department moved onto the eighth floor.'

'Penthouse, huh?'

'Sure. Some said that was the only way Kovacs could get any higher in the force.' Bartholomew laughed, his voice like a sledge on gravel. 'Of course,' he added, 'we know that ain't never gonna happen.'

Mordent allowed a smile. 'So why the change?'

'It's just as it is. New Commissioner, something new needs to happen. At the moment, it's just moving chess pieces on a board. Can't say there'll be any more to it than that.'

Mordent had read in the papers that Ormiston had been appointed the new Commissioner. Not that it made any difference to him. At that level it was all bureaucracy, and while a new appointment might be heralded with a fanfare and some cosmetic changes, ultimately once they had settled in, most Commissioners adopted an *If it ain't broke, don't fix it* policy. It was easier just to confirm business as usual and scoff canapés at high society functions, eyeing up waitresses and generally hoping nothing major would kick off while they were in charge.

'So, looks like I'm gonna have to take the elevator.' Despite his preference, Mordent didn't fancy that many stairs.

'Guess so, Mordent. What brings you here, anyway?'

'Information.' Mordent knew Bartholomew wouldn't know anything, but it paid to appear to take people into his confidence; just oiled the wheels a little, substantiated his reputation. 'You heard about the Maloney case? And Kwamie Pettiford?'

'Only what I read in the papers.' Bartholomew gesticulated to the rag splayed on the front desk. 'No-one up there tells me anything down here.'

'Have to see if my luck is in, then,' said Mordent. He wandered over to the elevator and pressed the button for the eighth floor.

It wasn't that he had ever been trapped in an elevator, but there was something in his mind that distrusted them. Maybe it was a concern about the reliability of a mechanism that could plunge him a fair drop at a whim, or the claustrophobia he would experience should it stop between floors. More likely it was the unawareness of who might be waiting once the doors opened, or the discomfort of sharing a ride with someone he wouldn't choose to. Solitariness and small places were fine when he was in control. But remove that control and the space wasn't that pleasant.

But he pressed the relevant buttons and rode the elevator all the same.

The eighth floor had had a makeover. He couldn't recall for sure who had inhabited it before, but he had to admit on first viewing it looked classy. For a moment his presence was lost between artificial plants and sterile workstations, until Jamieson spotted him and called him over, patted his back and swung out an arm, taking in the department in its entirety.

'Welcome to our new offices.'

'Yeah, right,' Mordent growled. 'All it needs now are new *officers*.'

Smiles were exchanged. His hand was pumped vigorously. Calls went out to the other regulars he had once worked with, and one side of the office became people-heavy. If it were a boat it would have listed, possibly sunk. Even the newbies crowded round, just in case they were missing something, although eventually they slipped away once they realised they hadn't a clue who Mordent was.

Mordent's skin shifted uncomfortable in his clothes. He didn't deserve the acclaim, had done nothing to merit it other than make the occasional good call and not mess anyone around. He was more than aware it wasn't necessarily himself they were welcoming, but a remembrance of times past, the way things used to be, the noirish sensibility that he coveted and that had never really existed but that both appealed and called to them. More than anything, he was being back-clapped and welcomed because he wasn't Kovacs. That much was clear. As it was also clear to Kovacs, who watched from the pristine area of his new office, a look of distaste on his features as though he'd popped a strip of Velcro into his mouth rather than bubblegum.

Mordent disengaged himself and wandered over, extended a hand. 'Kovacs.'

Kovacs shook the hand, briefly, a placebo of goodwill to keep him in with the men under his control, then nodded into the office and waited while Mordent sat down, before closing the door behind them and fixing the blind.

'What is it this time?' he asked. Impatient.

Mordent glanced around the office, biding his time. It was akin to shooting himself in the foot, but he couldn't help it. Everything was in order; there was barely a piece of paper to be seen. On a filing cabinet in the corner, a trio of cacti stood in a row, tallest to shortest. The walls were bereft of a calendar or noticeboard. There was nothing in the office that personalised it to Kovacs – no photos of wife or kids, no quirky desk toys, no doodles on a notepad. But then maybe that was it: the lack of anything was what personalised it for Kovacs. An empty office. An empty head.

Mordent couldn't deny that Kovacs knew his stuff, but he was entirely without empathy. As far as Mordent was concerned, that lessened Kovacs' intuitiveness as a police officer. As far as Kovacs was concerned, the lack of personal involvement enhanced it. Old school versus new school.

As Mordent ran these thoughts through his head he became aware of Kovacs irritably tapping a pencil on the side of his desk.

'When you're ready, Mordent.'

Mordent sighed. 'I've been employed by Bernard Maloney to investigate the murder of his wife, Tessa Maloney, on a private contract basis. I thought it might be worthwhile sharing the information that we have.'

Kovacs almost broke a smile. 'And you expect me to go first? After which, you'll tell me nothing I don't know already.'

Mordent shrugged. 'That's how it works.'

'How it works is that I have no obligation to tell you anything. I exercise a certain discretion when it comes to sharing information, and I appreciate you have a job to do. A job that is usually much more unsavoury than mine, but in this instance is on the face of it for a good cause. However, too many cooks spoil the broth. We're already on this one. All you're doing is taking money from some poor sap who doesn't have faith in us. Which ultimately undermines both the integrity of the police as viewed by Mr Bernard Maloney, and his bank balance. In this instance, Mordent: request for information is denied.'

Mordent leant back against the prefabricated wall. It gave a little.

'What you're saying, Kovacs, is that you don't have anything to give me.'

'That's not what I'm saying at all.'

'How about Kwamie Pettiford?'

'What's he got to do with it?'

'Everything?'

Kovacs paused. It was a brief pause. Probably less than a second. But Mordent noted it was a pause all the same.

Then he straightened his back. He had relaxed shortly after Mordent appeared in his office, but now he asserted his full height. All five foot six of him.

'If you want a fishing permit, those are issued on another floor,' Kovacs said. Now the smile played on his face like two kids in a paddling pool.

Mordent growled. 'There's a connection. You know it. I know it. More importantly, the killer knows it. We can work together on this one, Kovacs.'

'Mordent. You have nothing to give me. You were charged with finding Tessa Maloney and couldn't do it. What makes you think you can find her killer?'

'The edge. The edge that I have over you.'

'Over me? And over the other fine officers of this police force? Those that greeted you like the prodigal son just now? How would they like it to hear you doubt their abilities?'

'You know that's not what I'm saying.'

Kovacs folded his arms. 'It doesn't matter what you're saying, Mordent. What matters is that you have no information for me, and consequently I have no information for you. This is a closed investigation. If there is a link between those two murders, then the fewer people who know about it the better. We don't need the papers getting involved. You do your thing, I'll do my thing. That's how it goes.'

Mordent remained stationary. Thought for a moment. The only way to progress matters would be to beg. He wasn't going to beg. And Kovacs was right: he had nothing to bargain with. He had gone about it the wrong way. What was it with him recently? He just couldn't seem to get a handle on anything.

However, to leave without some kind of parting shot would be churlish. He turned his back on Kovacs, said something he wouldn't be able to hear.

'What was that?'

'Nothing Kovacs. You didn't want to know, so you don't want to know.'

Kovacs hesitated.

Mordent looked back. 'I'll tell you when you have something to tell me,' he said, then closed the door behind him.

Riding the elevator down to the ground floor, he mulled over what he had muttered under his breath: 'Church of Wire.' It had been the first thing that popped into his head.

7
Recap

An hour later and Mordent was out tailing a Buick in heavy traffic.

Reflective Tony was in the passenger seat. The Frame was driving. Mordent had picked them up at the bottom of Tony's road just as he had been turning into it. Fortuitous, maybe, although it had necessitated a surreptitious U-turn, and after five miles he couldn't be sure that they were unaware he was following.

If you dressed a block of concrete in an ill-fitting suit you would have the Frame.

If you made furniture flesh and put a wardrobe through boot camp you would have the Frame.

If you took a haulage truck and compacted it in a car crusher you would have the Frame.

If you took a mattress, righted it, then sprayed it with adhesive you would have the Frame.

The Frame tightened the grip on the collar. But then he got clever and began to lift Mordent off his feet. Mordent swung his legs either side of the Frame's body, and leant backwards fast, causing the Frame to overbalance and fall forward on top of him. Mordent locked his legs and rolled sideways, pinned the Frame down. Shook his arm free and connected – once, twice – with the Frame's face. The blows landed soft, as though he was hitting putty. Mordent wasn't sure whether it was his own strength at fault or the texture of the Frame's face. Either way, he had a fight on his hands.

Mordent sighed. Some days, everything seemed like flashback. As if he was getting hurt all over again.

He made his way back to his car. No point in hanging around. He drove slowly out of the compound, Tony and the Frame holding his gaze as he left. Mordent wasn't sure what he had achieved, other than drawing attention to himself. Again, he was moving ineffectually, doing a half-cocked job rather than getting to grips with things. As he turned out of the compound he glanced down at his suit, covered with a fine layer of dust and dirt. He was in no state to meet anyone, but there was tension that needed to be relieved. Heading out onto the main highway he made a decision, rejoined a familiar route to liaise with someone he knew.

8
The Call Of The Wild

He knew her only as Astrid.

She had been recommended by a previous call girl, Anna, who had earned enough to get out of the trade. Serving only specialist clients, Anna had offered to pass his details on. Mordent had sighed and agreed. Astrid came at a higher price than Anna, and previous to that Simone: but then he had killed Simone and had found Anna a poor imitation of a replacement. Astrid, thankfully, was less of a danger and more of a professional.

She worked from a brownstone in a mundane neighbourhood, cosy suburbia. Every woman in the area had the requisite 2.4 children, happy home life, gym schedule, a reliable husband, and did lunch with the others. That was where the similarity ended. Mordent was sure that while Astrid did indeed drop her kids off to school after sending her husband to work, none of the other residents in the brownstone – or indeed in the area – spent much of their spare time jacking off clients for money.

He parked down a side road, decided to remove his jacket and by necessity his gun. Placed them both on the passenger seat, one under the other. He got out and rubbed his hands over his trousers, trying to remove the dirt and dust. Finally, thinking he didn't look too shabby, he wandered around to

Astrid's apartment building and pressed her buzzer. After a short wait, she let him in.

He ascended the stairs to the third floor. Rapped on her door three times. Had the feeling of being regarded through her fisheye. Then the door opened and he stepped inside. His heart beating fast.

The apartment was tastefully furnished. Rows of family photographs lined a mantelpiece underneath a gilt-framed mirror that made the room feel twice as large. A polished circular table dominated the space, with a fruit bowl at its centre. The wooden floors were also polished, with no rugs as slip hazards. Light streamed through voile curtains, bathing the room a sumptuous pink. It was a picture postcard of domesticity. Astrid smiled as she closed the door behind him. She wore heels with rubber soles to avoid damaging the floor, and a short black dress that ended just above her knees.

They were cute knees.

She wore enough make-up to enhance her face without being tarty. Red lipstick clung fresh. When she smiled, her teeth were a perfect white. Her blue eyes sparkled beneath a tantalising fringe of naturally blonde hair. She was consummately beautiful. And for the next hour she would be his.

Mordent removed his shoes at the door. Allowed himself to be led into the main bedroom. The apartment wasn't big enough to allow for a separate room for clients, but what didn't bother her didn't bother him. He removed the rest of his clothes and allowed her to tie his hands in front of him with Japanese silk rope. Sitting down on the floor beside the bed, he then allowed his ankles to be cuffed. Lying prone on the floor, naked, he watched as Astrid opened the wardrobe and removed the bubble wrap.

Everyone had their peccadillo, their vice. Mordent defied anyone to be completely straight. This thought played at the edges of his mind as Astrid slipped off her rubber heels and selected new shoes with pointed spikes. He watched as she walked up and down over the stretch of bubble wrap, heard the *pop* as each pod was speared and then burst. The bottom of her dress rode up her thighs as she walked, but he was never afforded a glimpse of her panties. After a time that seemed much too quick but was probably much too slow, she stopped and entwined a section of the wrap around her left hand. Bending down on the floor beside him, she took hold of his erect penis and masturbated him to climax, the bubbles popping as she squeezed harder as he ejaculated. From her mouth spilled foul words that would have caused everyone in the surrounding neighbourhood to blush, but that took Mordent to the height of releasing the tension that had been building the past few days, fogging his senses and debilitating his concentration.

Astrid cleaned him up, untied him and retired to the kitchen, while he reassembled himself into his clothes. The whole affair had lasted no more than thirty minutes, which meant he could use the remainder of his time to discuss his cases with her.

This was unusual in her line of work and Mordent knew it. He also knew he could trust her to keep everything to herself. Her reputation as whore and confidante depended on it. And during those times when Mordent had no-one else to talk to – which was often, considering his on/off relationship with Maria – Astrid was becoming someone he could chew the fat with. Occasionally he even considered paying for that privilege alone.

There was only one thing out of bounds when it came to their conversations. Other than when he had explained his personal preferences at their first meeting, any talk of sex or the perfection of the act they performed was off limits. Surprisingly, Astrid was content to talk about her husband and children as she might to any of the ladies she lunched with. Probably more candidly. The connection worked both ways. The security of the situation kept them close for the moment. And a moment was all that was needed. Mordent had no delusions that she thought of him once he was gone. Yet while he was there, he was hers as much as she was his.

'Cappuccino?'

'Not today,' Mordent said. 'I need something a little

stronger.'

'I don't do liquor, as you know. Will espresso do?'

'Sure.'

'Milk? I don't suppose so. Nor sugar, of course.'

'That's right.'

Mordent pulled up one of the beautiful dining chairs and sat down. Watched as Astrid sorted his drink and made herbal tea for herself. Her body moved rhythmically beneath the dress. He had never seen her naked and never expected to.

She placed a coaster on the table before setting his drink in front of him. It featured one of her two children, the girl, hugging a guy in a Mickey Mouse suit with a Disneyland backdrop. The girl had Astrid's eyes and hair. Mordent wondered what she might think in later life if she got wind of her mother's profession.

Astrid's husband was in banking. Astrid had once said they both found humour in the fact that her occupation was just one letter removed from his. Investment banking, at that.

'So,' she said, her lipstick leaving a residue on the edge of her cup, like a potato print, 'how're things?'

Mordent ran a hand through his hair. 'I guess you saw in the papers that Tessa Maloney got found.'

Astrid nodded. It didn't matter whether she cared or not. Only that she listened.

'So I've been kicking around trying to find her killer, but I haven't. In this case, the police are best placed to deal with it, yet I'm taking money from her husband anyway.'

'A moral dilemma,' Astrid said, raising her eyebrows and taking a sip of tea.

'You could say that. Then I've another case. I'm asked to tail a known petty crook for no specific reason, and all I've had out of it is a beating.'

She smiled. 'Thought you looked rougher than usual.'

Mordent shrugged. 'Happened less than a couple of hours ago.'

'So, you came running to mother?' There was a twinkle in her eye as she said it. Mordent felt himself stir again, although he knew there would be no point in progressing that for at least 48 hours.

'You could say that,' he said, eventually.

There was some silence for a while. Then Astrid said, 'You know what you need? You need to focus. I do believe you're trying to ride two horses at once, but you're not even in the saddle. Leave the murder to the police. Make enquiries as to this other gentlemen you're tailing, and pursue that until you get enough information to feed back to your client. That's how I approach life: one thing at a time.'

Mordent drank half his coffee now it had cooled. In the same way that his activity with Astrid had cleared his head, the coffee heightened his senses. 'I guess you're right,' he said. Then, knowing that he didn't really have much more to say to her, he asked the usual questions about her husband and children, which she answered fully and with passion. As he left, he wondered what it might be like to live with such an attractive and understanding woman, and yet also to know about and accept her occupation. For the life of him he couldn't work her husband out.

'Oh, and Mordent,' Astrid said, hanging onto the door frame just as he was on the first step of the stairs. He turned back. Light from the apartment shone through her hair, making it glow. Her eyes seemed to sparkle even more intensely, as though her head were hollow and the sun was illuminating her face like a mask lit from behind.

He inclined his head by way of a reply.

'Come back soon,' she winked, and blew him a kiss.

Mordent descended each step as though it were made of sponge. His heart felt light. Just for a moment, he wondered if he was in love.

Yet by the time he reached his vehicle he knew he had had nothing else than an assignation with a beautiful and emotionally-manipulative female, and it was no more than that. As the money he had left beside his coffee cup attested.

9
Emergency Access

Come late afternoon, Mordent was back in his office, his PC powered up on the desk in front of him, a half-eaten meat pie going cold on a paper bag, and a tumbler of bourbon down to its last dregs by his mouse.

Light from the screen gave his face a pasty glow. Not for him the Hollywood sheen of Astrid; more a torchlight-under-the-chin Halloween effect. On the screen, he was scrolling through a street map of the business district, trying to determine where the disused car park had been situated, and from there which building Reflective Tony had entered.

It crossed his mind that they must have seen him pull up – they hadn't been in the building long enough to conduct any business. So either entering the building itself had been a ruse to flush him out, or they had continued doing what they needed to do after he left. What that meant was it was a fifty-fifty chance as to whether or not his research would lead to anything at all.

It didn't take him long to find the information that he needed. The car park was clear on the usual map, and clicking an aerial photographic view confirmed it. From there, the building Tony had entered was evident. Online, however, there was no identification as to what it was or had been. Mordent angled the view on screen in an attempt to get the number of the property or one of the adjacent ones, but again he came up blank. He sighed. He needed to go back there. Yet the whole thing could be completely pointless.

He had Isabelle Silk's number and deliberated phoning it. He couldn't follow Reflective Tony everywhere. There were any number of legitimate places he could go: the bank, the bathroom, a coffeehouse, a bar, a restaurant, his sick mother's retirement home, a boxing match, a clothing store; you name it, Tony could go there. While he knew Astrid was right about sticking to this case for the moment, he did need more information. It wouldn't just come to him all by itself.

Outside the window, the sun was on the way down. He wondered if the unseasonably temperate weather would last into the next day. Maybe that was the cause of his discomfort and restlessness. He couldn't slip into his preferred noir detective mode while the sun was blazing like a Miami summer scene. His kind of work needed the dark corners where the sun never shone, where he could pull his hat down over his eyes and remain anonymous. Now Tony and the Frame knew him by sight, tailing them would be far harder in the harsh light of the 15-million-degree-Celsius sun. While it was obviously not that hot on Earth, the unremitting light was like a beacon in the face. He wanted it dark, he wanted it miserable, he wanted to pull up his collar and imagine it was the '40s. Even if only for the duration of this job.

As the sun worked its way down the height of the skyscrapers and apartment buildings, a hundred shadows cast the street with sundial timings. Evening came faster here than it did down on the docks. A full hour quicker in some instances. Mordent nodded his approval. Some said that on certain days the sun lined up with the main streets – a modern Stonehenge. Car windshields glowed as though the vehicles had filled with golden syrup, and some people shielded their eyes against a false apocalypse; sunglasses before dark. Mordent was partial to a sunset, and whereas others drew the blinds at its descent, that was the signal for him to open them.

He turned back from the window and was powering down his PC when the phone rang. He lifted the receiver: 'Mordent.'

'Hey, Mordent. It's Hubie.'

'How the devil are you Hubie?'

'Huh?'

'Nothing. I just had an uncharacteristic moment of enthusiasm. What have you got for me?'

'I did some digging after you came to see me about Reflective Tony. Word on the street is that he's got a predilection for women of dubious character.'

Mordent fingered the meat pie on his desk. His hunger was coming back. 'In what way?' Surely that applies to every male?'

'He's dating a string of women currently in prison. Writing to them, making social visits, that kind of thing.'

'But that's all above board, isn't it?'

'Of course. There's even a website where lonely hearts banged up can promote themselves. But I thought you might be interested, particularly if you're thinking he might be involved in an activity that could upset this nameless organisation of yours.'

Mordent sucked in his lower lip. 'I guess you're right. Anything else?'

'Nope. That's just what I heard. Thought I'd pass it on. Help clear my slate, as it were.'

'Just out of interest: who gave you the info?'

Hubie laughed. 'You know I can't reveal my sources, Mordent. Just as I'd expect you not to mention me.'

That was true. Just as water babbled down a brook over various stones, weirs and waterfalls, so language and information cascaded from one informant to another. Just as long as it was accurate and Chinese Whispers didn't come into play, then everything was just kootchy.

'What I meant was, I'm curious as to how this came to light.'

There was a pause. 'Let's just say that these women eventually end up back on the streets. Some of them find out that Tony's been double, triple, quadruple dating. They're not gonna shoot him over it, but they might shoot off their mouths.'

'Hell hath no fury like a woman scorned.'

'Yeh. What you just said.'

'But you got no names for me, right?'

'Right. But you stick your PI hat on, Mordent, and I'm sure you'll come up with something. Anyways, gotta go. Gotta hot date with a girl and a horse.'

'Sounds illegal.'

'I wish.' Hubie laughed. It wasn't a clean laugh. Mordent had the feeling Hubie's mouth could do with washing out with soap.

By the time he put the phone down, darkness had fallen, as though the city itself were sleeping and its eyelids were closed.

He opened his desk drawer and poured a half-measure of bourbon into the glass. Downed it in one. Then turned off the lights and sat in the dark awhile, his office delineated by the glow of the buildings outside and a thin strip of light thrown by the corridor that sat like a piece of processed cheese under his door.

Despite the sounds of traffic filtering in from the street, like radio static, it was relatively quiet. Mordent closed his eyes, let the darkness swim over him, cleared his thoughts. He knew what he was going to do that evening: the parking lot beckoned. For no other reason than that it was there. If he shut his lids particularly tight he could almost imagine entering the building's dull interior, moving cautiously with a flashlight, traipsing through broken glass and litter and disturbing a group of homeless bums. But however hard he might imagine it, imagination wasn't enough. Imagination wasn't what Isabelle Silk wanted in respect of Reflective Tony. He was going to have to go there.

Mordent wasn't lazy. But sometimes the interior of his warm office, the sanctuary contained within a glass of bourbon, the holding qualities of the dark, these were difficult to emerge from. He was wombed there, cocooned there. And always, always, the birth was a difficult one.

Mordent knew a lot about difficult births, even if he had no memory of one. Like Macduff in the Scottish play, Mordent was not of woman born. His mother had intended him to be a home birth, but complications had arisen when the umbilical cord had wrapped around his neck. His mother had been rushed to hospital, and he had been born by caesarean section. Had another hour passed, he would have been dead. Had it given him a charmed life? Could he defeat all-comers conventionally born? Probably not. But at some level the darkness of the room reminded him of the calm before the storm. He paused life for a second, before snapping his eyes wide and leaving the office, descending the empty stairwell to his vehicle.

Before setting off, he opened up the trunk and retrieved his flashlight. Checked the batteries were working, then slung it on the passenger seat. Roared out of the car park. It was time for exploration.

Along his route, the surrounding buildings had pulled on their glad rags. Lights speckled, sparkled. Window displays were like theatre stages, surrounded by dark, lit by floodlights. Mannequins posed decorously. Multiple TVs played the same programmes, like life seen through a bee's eyes. Flashing neon enticed pedestrians into bars, clubs, hotels. Rolling LED screens advertised electrical stores, Coca-Cola, international phone cards. It seemed as though the lights were pushing against the dark, holding it at bay, like two boys under a collapsed tent, their flashlights multi-directionless as they flapped against fabric, struggled against suffocation.

Pedestrians had adopted glamour too. Especially as Mordent passed through the city's nightspot quarter. The clear skies had brought on a cold evening, but despite this, females paraded their legs in short skirts. Halter tops showcased their breasts. Males wore T-shirts and jeans, the material tight – in many instances, too tight. Bright colours were all the rage. He passed by in a blur, creating a rainbow effect. When he left the district and moved onto the business quarter, the lack of colour became reassuring.

The parking lot was easier to find than he had supposed it might be. The ins and outs of that morning were negated when there was less traffic, and strangely the night seemed to detract confusion rather than add to it. Mordent turned off his headlights as he turned into the lot. There was just enough illumination from the surrounding buildings and a circular moon to light the way. Save for those vehicles that were abandoned, the lot was deserted. He parked his car in an area where it wouldn't be seen from the road, and switched off the engine. It idled noisily in the dark. Outside, broken glass glittered the ground.

The building was dark. If it had showed no sign of occupancy during the day, then equally there was none at night. Mordent left his vehicle and locked it. Torch in hand, he advanced toward the building.

Steps led up to the main entrance, flanked on either side by metal handrails. Mordent trod carefully, waited at the top in the same position from which Reflective Tony had watched the shambolic fight, then surreptitiously turned the door handle. He was allowed into the building with nothing more than a squeak of protest, the dark inside deeper than that illuminated by the moon. As he slipped within, it absorbed him much like the La Brea Tar Pits might have absorbed a mastodon. Slowly and slickly.

In front of him was a reception area, but it didn't seem to have been used for some time. There was a PC on the desk that belonged to another era. Mordent imagined it captured information solely, provided a database and a calendar and little else. On the desk were some pieces of unused paper – once white, but now grey with dust, the edges curling. A swivel chair lay on its side. Mordent entered the reception area via a side door, rooted through the drawers, but if there was anything there once, it wasn't now. The only surprise was that the PC hadn't gone the way of the stationery.

There was a sign behind the main reception desk that stated 'Harvey Bearing & Associates'. The name meant nothing to Mordent, but he filed it away in his memory for later.

His flashlight played mini spotlights on the floor, walls, and surfaces. He was aware that with the open door anyone could be in the building, wasn't sure if it would be advisable to trip all the lights or even to announce his presence through a circular glow. He decided to stick with the flashlight temporarily, banished thoughts of hoods and drug-users hiding in the darkest corners. As he moved further into the building, multiple doors led off the main corridor, and each room was much the same as the last, his beam playing against worn tables, broken chairs, light fittings damaged and hanging recklessly from the ceiling. At the end of the corridor sat another stairwell. He went up, made the same journey but in reverse, one floor above. Again, nothing to see, no evidence of anything happening of any note.

On the uppermost floor he came to the conclusion he had been duped. It was clear-cut: the Frame had known he was being tailed and had pulled him in either to shake him off or to shake him about. There was no reason for Reflective Tony to have entered the building other than to watch him from the inside out. Another blank inserted into the barrel of the gun of life. He imagined Isabelle Silk stood in the darkness, her harsh features admonishing him for his stupidity. He would have to contact her and get further information. All this was leading nowhere. Astrid might have been right: concentrate on one thing at a time. But even following that advice, he was just finding dead ends.

Rather than leave the building the way he had come, he decided to make for the fire escape. At the end of the corridor on the fourth floor there was a door marked 'Emergency Access Only.' It seemed a misnomer. 'Emergency Exit' would surely have been more appropriate. But he could hardly charge the building's supervisor with poor English now that it was empty. He pushed open the door and found himself in a small area, no larger than an elevator, which acted like an airlock would on a spaceship before another door leading to the outside fire escape. As he angled his flashlight so that he might switch it off, the beam picked out a leaflet lying face up on the floor. Then the light went out.

Mordent shook the flashlight and the beam came on again. He stooped and picked up the leaflet.

It advertised the Church of Wire.

10
Re-Enter Jessica

Mordent slept deep.

His night was plagued with dreams.

A baby told him, 'You're not yellow.'

A small animal ran around his feet, but when he looked down, his legs stretched so far beneath him that he couldn't see the animal or the ground.

He was an author, and someone tried to buy a book he hadn't written.

Marina, a girl he once knew, was splayed across a bed with her hand outstretched.

He watched as night was personified. Ran toward him, smothered him with a black blanket, bundled him into the trunk of a car.

Another dream – or the same one – of a low humming in the dark.

Finally he awoke with a scream in his mouth and a half-open elevator door in front of him. Something unknown and terrifying had hidden there as he ran toward it. A moment more and the door would have closed with him inside.

Mordent wiped a hand over his forehead. It was cold and wet. He flung the covers off the bed and they landed in the dark like a soft gymnast. Moonlight illuminated his pale body: a ghost of itself. He held his right hand out in front of him and realised it was unsteady. His heart: pounding. He rubbed at his eyes with his index fingers, removed sleep that grated on his skin like wet sand. Blew air out of his mouth. Did it again. Sat up, his legs over the edge of the bed. Yawned.

That last dream was still inside him. He shivered. He hadn't known a dream to frighten him so intensely. He wondered if he had screamed aloud or if that had been just part of it. Wished there was someone there to hold, to hold him.

He reflected on the end of the dream. Running toward the elevator, into death. In the steady light of the approaching dawn he wondered how many people rushed headlong, unawares, to their demise. Those who raced traffic lights to make flights that subsequently crashed; those who squeezed into the closing train carriage containing a terrorist bomb; those who were simply quick their whole lives, not realising the faster they went, so did their internal clock, counting down the seconds that would have slowed should they have led slower lives.

And then he wondered how he would die.

But not for long. Early mornings were depressing enough without dragging himself down. He stood and looked out of the window. Again, clear blue skies. Unseasonal weather. Buildings blinked as sunlight hit each window, and as the sun rose, so each window glinted in turn, like watching the lights change as an elevator reached different floors. Down on the streets, commuter traffic in shadow was already thick, pushing out toward the business district like the elongated ash of an indoor firework. Mordent sighed, fixed himself some breakfast, deliberated what to do with the remainder of the day.

Coincidences were adding up.

He pulled out the leaflet for the Church of Wire from his jacket pocket overhanging a chair by his kitchen table. Then he reached into his waste bin and found the first leaflet he had discarded the previous day. The one given to him by the unsound Jessica, or inserted into his pocket by one of the zealous students he had hastened out of Morgan's Bar. They were identical: 'Celebrate God's Seventh Day Creation.' A congregation member beamed under the heading. It was all so genuine yet all so false. The genuine belief in a false deity, as

Mordent liked to call it. Other than that, there was simply a telephone number. Not even a website.

Mordent didn't know much about religion, but he knew enough to understand that according to the Old Testament, God created the Earth and all its inhabitants in six days and on the seventh day he rested. Presumably the Church of Wire thought otherwise.

He powered up his PC and ran a search online. There was no website for the Church itself, and the only references were vague mentions on a few message boards. Maybe it was a new construct. Religious groups shot up all the time. And as usual, Mordent's position was that he wouldn't want to belong to any club that would have him as a member.

What link – if any – there might be between the Church and Reflective Tony was another matter.

Unless.

And he drummed his fingers along the tabletop.

Unless the Church of Wire was the organisation that Isabelle Silk worked for. The one she didn't want Reflective Tony to infect. Now that would make sense.

What if you were starting up a brand new business, one that had to be squeaky clean in order to draw in the faithful, and then you discovered one of your business companions held a dodgy background? You'd want him investigated, quietly, before you decided what to do. Suddenly it was all clear. Although, even as Mordent thought it, he wondered how many mental hoops he had jumped through for that conclusion to be reached. Finding one leaflet in an abandoned building and having another slipped into his pocket within the space of a few days …

He scratched his head. Deliberated calling Isabelle Silk and quizzing her on the Church of Wire, but realised that in doing so he would have to admit that he had no information on Reflective Tony other than what she probably already knew. So, the alternative was another woman, the one who might have dropped that first leaflet in his pocket, however kooky and false she appeared to be: Jessica.

He still had her number somewhere.

He recalled her figure: curvy, five-eight, late twenties. Brunette. On the face of it, tempting. But then he recalled her story: the jilted lover, the stalker, the implausibility. He wondered if she was a front for the Church of Wire, tasked with casing a joint before the young people with their leaflets leafleted. However implausible that seemed, it was certainly more plausible than her story had been. Maybe she was a pick-up in more ways than one.

Wasn't religion supposed to pick up fallen women?

He rooted around in his wallet and found her number. Dialled it.

It rang seven times before it was answered.

The voice was female and hesitant: 'Hello?'

'Jessica?'

'Who wants her?'

'Name is Mordent. You slipped your phone number in my pocket over at Morgan's Bar.'

'Did I? I did, didn't I.' Her voice softened. 'Why, Mr Mordent. I didn't think it likely I would hear from you again.'

Mordent bit back a 'Neither did I'. Instead he said, 'Can we meet?'

'Oh my! Can we meet? Well, *should* we meet, Mr Mordent. What do you think?'

Mordent sighed. Did anyone really talk like that anymore? She was like a Southern Belle. Without the Southern. And with a Belle that had been rung on more than one bicycle and was no doubt getting a little rusty. Regardless, he played along.

'I would suggest that meeting would be very fortuitous, Jessica.'

'Oh my, again! Well, if *you* think it's best Mr Mordent. If you really think it's for the best.'

'Absolutely. Unless, of course, you're still being tailed by that ex of yours …?'

There was an almost audible pause. Then: 'Why, Mr Mordent, you didn't fall for that old pick-up line did you?'

Mordent coughed, intending it to sound like he was

embarrassed, when in truth he had no more fallen for her story than for that of Adam and Eve. 'Well, no, not really,' he said.

'Bless!' Her voice was high, spirited. 'Bless you, Mr Mordent. Well I will meet you. I *will*.'

Under the circumstances, Mordent decided Morgan's Bar wasn't the best venue. Besides, he wanted it over and done with, and it was not yet ten in the morning.

'Do you know Bukowski's, the deli store just up from Morgan's Bar? They do sit-down coffee, bagels, lunches there. Could you be there around 11.30?'

'Well, I do have to prepare myself, Mr Mordent. I surely do. But an hour and a half is more than enough time for me. I will see you there then. I will.'

'See you then, Jessica.' Mordent disliked the way her name left his tongue, as though it were an assignation rather than a job.

'See *you*, Mr Mordent.'

He waited, but she didn't hang up. So he did.

There had been the intimation of a blown kiss at the end of the call.

Mordent wiped his hand over his forehead. It came away wet. There was something about Jessica that he vehemently disliked. Maybe it was all of her. His estranged wife had once said that he was scared of women. He had denied it. Yet the knowledge that his dealings with most of them involved money seemed to substantiate it. Who knew? Women were strange creatures at the best of times, with different views and motivations than all of the men he had encountered. Generally, the only differences he concerned himself with were the ones that were biological.

Had Jessica come into Morgan's just for a pick-up? A desperate housewife? Or had she entered as a precursor to the leaflet-distributing youngsters? If she *had* no involvement with them, then the meeting was going to be pointless yet interesting.

Either way, he really didn't want to go to bed with her.

Still, he spent the next hour shifting things around his apartment. Not tidying as such, but reshuffling, making the appearance of having made an effort. He washed the microwaveable dishes littering the armchair in front of the television, gathered up – with increasing clinks – various glasses containing alcohol sediment, kicked unidentifiable crumbs under the fridge, and forced his dirty laundry into the washing machine. Under his breath, he muttered that it needed doing anyway.

Mordent didn't discriminate when it came to female company. He fell into relationships haphazardly, through more luck than judgment. Fell out of them the same way. Other than Maria, who remained his wife despite his not having seen her for some while, the women he encountered were all transitory. When he was on the force, he had put this down to the nature of the job. Few women wanted a man they couldn't count on to be at a certain place at a certain time. Since leaving the force, he had blamed the sporadic nature of his work. Specifically, his income. Again, the women he knew wanted more than it might appear on the surface. Underneath the crawling desperation of sex lay the nebulous concepts of security – both financial and physical – coupled with longevity, and ultimately – particularly for women of a certain age, an age not a few years younger than his own – his suitability for fatherhood.

Mordent never wanted nor needed a clingy female desperate for a child. Nor, indeed, that child itself. That left him without many options, but there weren't too many nights when he didn't want to come home to Maria, and ultimately held a hope that she might come back to him again.

The traffic was light as he drove downtown to Bukowski's, the sun refracting off the dirt on his windscreen, which his screen wash couldn't shift. At some angles, he was fogged. The interior of the car was warmer than the air outside, despite the late presence of the sun. He wiped the back of the windscreen, smeared a view to look through. Wound down the window to clear it better. Fuel fumes and hotdog smells commingled. Despite the minimal traffic, car horns raised a cacophony that was almost an orchestration. Weaving in and out of both the traffic and the symphony, the sirens of a police car added to the show.

There was something homely, something wholesome about it that Mordent loved.

He slowed up outside Bukowski's, turned and parked down the adjacent side street. Sat in his car awhile wondering what he was doing, before making his way around to the storefront and popping himself inside.

It was 11.20. He imagined Jessica would be fashionably late, if she arrived at all. He was somehow reminded of the Pedro Almovodar movie *Women on the Verge of a Nervous Breakdown*. He glanced at the menu, ordered a coffee, espresso. Sat on a stool at the long window table overlooking the street. He was comfortable with stools, uneasy in chairs. If he closed his eyes he might imagine the light through the window was the reflection of the mirror behind Morgan's Bar, the stool identical, with only the contents of the beverage making the difference. It comforted him.

Outside, the world ran by the window. When he was moving with the traffic flow his senses amalgamated with the vehicles and were therefore part of one great machine, yet here his view was syncopated, like watching a single frame of film repeatedly flicker-booked in front of him. On the road, cars were distinct, pedestrians a blur; here, as voyeur at the window, the opposite was true. Cars flashed by like a painter's streaks on a clear polypropylene sheet, pedestrians were the detail. Some passers-by stopped outside the window, fixed shoelaces, consulted newspapers, maps or the weather before taking another step. Some stood and looked directly at him, or so it seemed, their gaze searching for a menu, or the prices, or a friend. Everything was in flux, Mordent mused. The entirety of life and all its ramifications and meanings spun around each individual in a separate orbit. All of them distinct and different, with conflicting motivations and ideals. You could take this view and replicate it out of café windows in Paris, Brazzaville, Tripoli, London, Islamabad, Lima, Ho Chi Minh City, Ankara, Harare, Ottawa and Beijing. Plus any others that you cared to think of. That view might well be similar, but the individuals would change. And it was the individuals that mattered.

This reverie played on his mind until he was snapped out of it by a familiar face pressed close to the glass: Jessica. A smile split her mouth, pristine white teeth set between two deep red lips; like a bloodied hot dog with the meat bleached by the sun. He forced a smile back. Despite his mental state, his eyes were drawn to her curves like a car round a racing track. Without the subdued lighting from Morgan's Bar, she had aged a few years: mid-thirties rather than late-twenties. But it was all just perception. Maybe it was the sun that was wrong and the dark that was right. Mordent preferred the dark without question.

As if her face on the glass wasn't enough, she rapped on the window and waved. She wore a lime green woollen dress. Inappropriate for her age; inappropriate for any age – historical or physical. Mordent hid a grimace behind a cough and waited for her to locate the entrance, shifting sideways on his stool so he might face her full on. Wondering just how long the coming afternoon might last.

'Why, Mr Mordent. Here you are. Just as you said you would be.'

Her voice was loud. Mordent noticed a few patrons glance up and then look away. A couple of them didn't look away. One of them looked her up and down, until finally he too looked away.

'What can I get you?'

'Coffee. Milky and sweet. Are you eating here, Mr Mordent. Or are we eating later?'

'Eating here would be fine, don't you think?' The intimation of *later* curled his toes.

'Well,' she said, without a hint of anything in her voice, 'I think I'll have one of those little pasta salads. Do they do those little pasta salads here?'

Mordent nodded. Passed her the menu. He waited for what seemed like ten minutes while she scanned it, then he got up to the counter. For himself, he ordered ham on rye. For the lady, the little pasta salad.

While they waited for their food, her voice quietened. She

drooped her eyelashes. They were long and thick. Trying to be all little girl and looking up from underneath them, she asked him why he had called her.

'Can't we just drop the charade for a minute?' Mordent felt this had gone on too long. 'The first time we meet, you spin me the story of an ex gone wrong, then drop your number and a religious flyer into my pocket. Now you go all flirty as if we're best buddies and you're stuck in the Southern states, just as my detractors think I'm stuck in the '40s. Even if that were the case, I'm all hard and noir and you're all soft and beguiling. It's not a match made in heaven. But maybe heaven is what you're aiming for if all you really want to do is pitch this.'

He pulled the flyer for the Church of Wire out of his pocket. Back at his apartment, he had had a choice between the one dirtied on the floor of the abandoned building or the one he had screwed into a ball and thrown in the bin. Ultimately he had decided on return to sender. He smoothed the leaflet out on the counter, its crisscross lines giving it the impression of unfolded origami, although what it might fold into was anyone's guess: a church, maybe, or the curvy, shapely creature that was looking at him with offended water droplets in her eyes.

'Mr Mordent, I don't think that's fair. Do you?' She opened a clutch bag, as lime as the dress, which had sat chameleon-like in her lap, and pulled out a white handkerchief, which she dabbed at the corners of her eyes.

'Whatever it is, lady, it doesn't smell right to me. Suppose you start at the beginning. Like what were you doing at Morgan's Bar in the first place? And no more stories about that mysterious ex.'

She nodded. Seemed to compose herself. Mordent suspected it would be more country than jazz. Another mismatch. Still, he sat back, waited, got interrupted when their food arrived and found himself watching her eat that little pasta salad, slowly, as if each mouthful delayed the inevitable telling of her story, while his own mouth exploded with flavour from his simple meal, reminding him why he was drawn to Bukowski's again and again and again.

Finally, that handkerchief came out once more, but this time dabbed at the corners of Jessica's mouth rather than at her eyes.

'Okay, Mr Mordent,' she said. 'Let me tell you all about it.'

11
The Church of Wire

Jessica sat up straight, as if it would bolster the veracity of her story. Mordent couldn't help but notice the motion accentuate her curves. He might just have to re-evaluate his reluctance to sleep with her after all.

'I found my salvation,' she began, 'during my time in state prison, Mr Mordent. Yes, I can tell you are shocked. But in my youth I wasn't the demure woman you see sat here before you. I fell into bad ways. I'm sure you can guess the kind of thing. I don't need to go into details, now do I? So, while I was there, I had plenty of time for reflection. That's what they say, isn't it: reflection? And while I reflected, I found myself, as though I were looking into a mirror. I do like that analogy, but it was true, Mr Mordent. I saw myself while looking in a mirror.'

Mordent nodded. Wondered how many times a woman might look into a mirror. Knew that mostly they didn't see what everyone else saw. Usually they just saw what they didn't want to see.

Jessica took his nod as a desire for her to continue.

'I took to reading the Bible, Mr Mordent. Of course, I'd read it before. In Sunday school in the little old town where I grew up. But I'd lapsed. You know how it is. You know how easy it is for a girl to lapse nowadays. And lapse I did. So I started reading it again, and you know what? Something was missing. I couldn't put my finger on it, but something wasn't quite right with it. I thought it would plug that hole in my life, but I still seemed to be draining all the same.'

'That doesn't surprise me.' Mordent raised a hand and called for a refill of his espresso. 'Religion is an empty experience, but for some, as empty experiences go, it's one of the best.'

Jessica frowned, bit her bottom lip. For the life of him Mordent couldn't work how much of it was an act and how much might be her backwoods education. It mattered only in as much as that act might conceal a real intention, but for the moment he was content to take the ride to discover more about the Church.

'You're not making fun of me, are you, Mr Mordent? I wouldn't like that.'

Mordent shrugged. 'I'm here to hear your story and you're here to tell it. Tell it.'

She sighed. It sounded like she often sighed, and just for a moment Mordent felt the hard knot inside him soften.

'Well, a while passed, and then I got to corresponding with someone. Someone from outside. It was a little delicate. For a moment, Mr Mordent, I believed I was actually in *love!*' She gave a nervous laugh. Damaged goods. Mordent could see that now. 'Yet through that relationship, if you could call it that, I discovered a new Church. One I hadn't heard of before. That explains what I was doing in Morgan's Bar, Mr Mordent. I was canvassing – is that the right word? – I was canvassing for the Church, and so I slipped that flyer into your pocket.'

'Along with your telephone number.'

'Well, I'm still confused. Everything isn't always black and white, is it, even if you want – even if you *need* – it to be.'

Mordent shifted on the stool. It wasn't as comfortable as that at Morgan's Bar and the espresso wasn't as comforting as bourbon.

'I'm confused too, Miss Jessica, because you never had time to write your name and number on that paper. Do you always carry that around with you? I'm not that special, am I?'

Mordent thought he might have seen her blush under the rouge. She opened the lime bag again, unpopped one section and pulled out a handful of papers with her name and phone number handwritten on them.

'You may think I'm a desperate woman. Well, perhaps I am. Perhaps all I need – all anyone needs – is someone to hold at night. Someone to wake up to in the early hours and know they are there even if they're sleeping. Someone to come home to.'

'And sometimes it doesn't matter who that someone might be?'

'Sometimes,' she said.

There was a pause, just for a moment. Long enough for both of them to reflect on what both of them had said.

'So.' Mordent took a sip of his fresh espresso, the bitter taste almost recoiling on his tongue. 'The Church of Wire. Does that plug your gap?'

Jessica smiled, wanly. 'I believe so, Mr Mordent. You see, it's not like a regular church. It's more a state of mind.'

If it was anything like Jessica's state of mind, Mordent wondered how long the Church would last. He said nothing.

'Do you know the Bible?' she continued. 'There was a time when I knew it inside out and upside down, but there's only one thing I need to know now. Do you know what that one thing is?'

Mordent shook his head.

Jessica shifted on her stool. 'Well ...'

She paused. Suddenly her eyes fell on the multitudinous pieces of paper lying on the top of the counter. She swept them to the edge with one hand, then collated them and popped them back in her purse. 'Really, Mr Mordent,' she said, 'I'm forgetting myself. I'm not supposed to divulge the secrets of the Church. That would be bad form. They might kick me out. It's happened before. So they said. You wouldn't want to be the one to discharge my happiness, would you?'

She looked around. As if even talking to him was a cardinal sin.

'I do forget myself sometimes. I really *do*. There's the conflict, you see; the conflict between finding the right man and following the right path. You can understand that, can't you?

We all have that conflict don't we? I imagine you're sitting there right now wondering, *Is Jessica the right woman for me?* I think I'm going to have to answer that question for you, Mr Mordent. I think I'm going to have to say no.'

She slipped off the stool, her dress riding up her thighs. She unselfconsciously pulled the hem down with one hand, glanced over to Mordent, then ran her fingers through her brunette hair as if she had just come out of the shower.

'I have a habit of saying too much about myself. But you haven't told me anything about you.'

Mordent shrugged. 'There's never much to say.' He also stood. Resisted the urge to grab her wrist, slap her, shake her from side to side. Resisted the urge to kiss her. 'Can we speak again, another time?'

He imagined taking her clutch bag, opening it, removing the other pieces of paper and putting them in his pocket. He imagined saying, *You won't be needing these now.* He imagined her falling into him, falling for him. He imagined mind-fucking her, knowing he would break her heart just to get some information about some cult church she had got involved with, just to satisfy his own curiosity. He didn't do it. But he knew he could have done it. Instead he said, 'You know, if you want to, that is.'

The Southern Belle persona slipped back into place. She lowered her head and raised her eyelashes, almost spoke through them. 'Why, Mr Mordent, I'd love to. If you would have me, that is.'

Mordent flipped his mind over the double entendre. The woman was too complex. He would be shouldered with all her hang-ups as cleanly as if she put a cape on him. A moment on the lips and a lifetime on the hips. But he needed her in other ways, so he gave his best smile and said, 'Of course. I have your number.'

As she left, he was sure he caught a whisper: *See you in church.*

12
Decision-Making Is A Man's Best Friend

Mordent waited a couple of days.

The sun's hold on the weather started to fade. Nights encroached like a creeping glacier, bringing the cold and the dark to the city. Mornings were crisper; frozen star-shapes tessellated the corners of his apartment windows; and within the trees, silver-threaded spider's webs hung like complex diamond necklaces. He made the usual trips from home to office to bar to home. Waiting for something to happen. Maybe for someone to call. And when no-one did, Mordent knew what he had to do. He had to make those calls himself.

As Astrid had suggested, the police could keep looking for the possible serial killer. Mordent could cream off their results and pass those to Maloney, and half that work would be done and all of it would be paid for. That left Isabelle Silk and Reflective Tony. Mordent didn't fancy another run-in with the Frame – at least, not without preparation. So it was time for those calls to establish his next step – even if it was only down the yellow brick road to a fictitious Wizard of Oz.

He had his feet up on his desk. The old-fashioned Bakelite receiver in his hand. A list of the nearest and dearest state prisons on the desk in front of him. A few calls yielded little. His authority to request information was challenged. He couldn't argue with that. Being a PI was much different from being in the force; something that clients often didn't appreciate. You couldn't just ask for information from the authorities and get it. Nowadays it was all *data protected* – he had either to establish a *need to know* or get someone on the other end of the line who didn't give a damn. It was the latter where he expected most success. And that didn't fail him now.

Jessica's last name turned out to be Boothby. She had done seven years in the can for attempted armed robbery. Had claimed diminished responsibility, and this had been accepted to the extent that a few years had been shaved off her sentence. The robbery had been carried out with two accomplices: both guys; both, it appeared, guys Jessica had been in relationships with. Either singularly or simultaneously. The words *vulnerable adult* featured a lot in the conversation. Yet there had been sufficient grounds for a proper sentence, and the reduction in term seemed to have been more of a nod to a prolonged campaign than any evidence of a genuine attempt to understand her. The word *manipulative* came up twice.

Mordent got all of this from a female who just wanted to talk, although she stressed that everything she was telling him was in the newspapers anyway. Later – now knowing Jessica's surname – Mordent would be able to check the veracity of her account and take in the lurid headlines. But what wouldn't be in the newspapers was the information Mordent was really after. Had his source heard anything about the Church of Wire or the person Jessica had been in communication with?

'I can't say as I know anything about that Church, although she did express an interest in the Bible and spent some time with the chaplain. Way I see it, she was just flexing her options, making herself look good. I saw her twice, personally, and she came on to me both times. *Even* me. Not that I would. And I didn't. But I tended to believe those stories that accentuated her involvement rather than lessened it. Course, that's only my personal opinion, you hear.'

Mordent reassured her that none of the information was going anywhere other than inside his head. He asked about any letters Jessica had received.

There was a sigh. 'Well, there's some in here that get fan mail and some that don't. She got a few, early on, when the case was still fresh and everyone local knew all about her. Some of the other officers here reckoned she revelled in it. But that died out, as it does, so then she racked up more attention by courting the outside world. I can't say I agree with it, but the prison allows certain inmates some time on the internet to create profiles to attract partners. It *can* get lonely in here, we all know that, and I see it can work as a release, but the way I feel, it's just not right. But sure, she had her fair share of admirers. Some might say she's a bit of a looker. I would have a list of those who contacted her, somewhere. Did you want me to give you that?'

Mordent wasn't sure of her intentions: jealousy, the annoyance of being hit upon, or just a home-grown willingness to be friendly despite the rules, but he confirmed that yes – *certainly* – he would be interested in the names of Jessica Boothby's potential online suitors.

And he wasn't surprised when one of the names came back as Tony Runcorn.

'Just one more thing Tracey – may I call you Tracey? – just one more thing. Are you able to tell me the names of any other inmates who were contacted by the same males who contacted Jessica.'

'Not without the names of the inmates, and not without some digging.'

'And I don't suppose you have copies of the letters?'

'Nope. They would have been opened and read for security purposes, but once cleared, we just passed them on.'

Mordent thanked her, repeatedly and profusely. It always paid to keep someone sweet who was generous with information that should have been prohibited. Then he hung up and leant a little further back in his chair, the edge of it nudging the wall behind him. Another coincidence. One he had anticipated. But a coincidence all the same.

He had two other numbers written on his scribble pad. One

was that from the flyer for the Church of Wire, and the other was that of Isabelle Silk. Already it was clear to him that they must be one and the same. It was just how he handled it that was the question. Some part of him resisted revealing to Isabelle that he knew her organisation. She hadn't wanted to tell him, and it hadn't been in his remit to find out. Yet he *had* to call the number on the flyer, and if he had already called Silk, that might be awkward if it happened to be she who answered the phone. Best bet was to call the Church first, then call her. So, after taking a bite of a ham and cheese baguette he had picked up from the deli, he did.

'Hullo?'

Not the greatest welcome you might expect from an organisation dedicated to spreading the message of love and happiness from our Lord.

'I've got a flyer,' Mordent said. 'Is that the Church of Wire?'

The voice on the other end, muffled, possibly disguised, asked him to describe the flyer. Once satisfied, the tone became lighter. It was only then that Mordent recognised it as male.

'How can I help?'

'I'm just curious,' began Mordent, 'as to what you might offer.'

'We're a church that believes in one singular aspect of the Bible,' said the voice. 'That aspect governs everything that we strive for. Whatever you are looking for will be found within that aspect.'

'I am ...' Mordent paused '... a little lost at the moment.'

'Lost, found, we take all types here.'

'So how do I get involved?'

'We're having a new members' meeting in a couple of nights' time. We don't meet traditionally. There's no physical church building. But there's an address I can give you. Just turn up with an open heart and an open mind.'

The voice gave him the address. Mordent knew where it was. But it wasn't the deserted office building where he had found the flyer.

'One more thing,' Mordent continued. 'This *aspect* that you spoke of. Can you give me an idea of what it is?'

'We don't divulge the nature of the Church until you've attended the first meeting,' the voice said.

'It's just that,' Mordent allowed a quaver into his voice, 'well, I mean, it's not Satanic is it? In any way?'

The voice laughed, but it wasn't an unkind laugh. Humour reverberated down the line. 'No, it's not Satanic. Different, maybe. But not that.'

Mordent returned the laugh. 'That's good.'

'Well, we'll see you there, shall we? Then you can find out all about us. Goodbye for now.'

The line clicked dead without the opportunity for more questions.

Mordent had a heap of questions. Considered waiting a while and calling back. Maybe using a different voice. But he didn't. Instead he called Isabelle Silk.

'Ms Silk?'

'Who is this?'

'Mordent.'

'Ah, my PI. Well, Mordent, what do you have for me?'

'Tony Runcorn is a little shady in the underground business world, Ms Silk. He has ties to some minor hoods, has a heavy who knows how to swing a punch, and has been running some kind of racket when it comes to picking up fallen women. I suppose whether or not that information's of any use to you will depend on the nature of the organisation.'

'Tell me more about that *racket* you mentioned.'

'He writes to women in prison, gains their confidence and then breaks their hearts.'

There was a strangled cry on the end of the phone, suddenly caught short, as though Silk had pulled it out of her own throat and then killed it.

'Ms Silk?'

Her voice came back, by degrees. Initially shaky and then back to full, hard form. 'How does he break their hearts, Mordent?'

'The women find out about each other.'

'I see.'

There was another pause. Mordent wasn't sure how to fill it. 'Is that the end of my duties,' he finally said.

'Hmmm?' Her voice came from far away, as though she was at the end of a long tunnel; which, considering Mordent's understanding of telecommunications, he considered could be literal. 'Oh no. No, Mordent. That is not the end of the investigation. There's something missing, isn't there? The reason he is befriending these women.'

'Money?' Mordent guessed.

'That sounds like an assumption rather than a fact, Mordent. And I need facts.'

'It would help if I knew what organisation you were concerned he might soil the reputation of.'

'I'm not sure that would help, Mordent.' Her voice had returned to the core of her personality. 'The essence of my organisation has no bearing on Tony's activities. It's the other way around that the problem arises. Hence, the problem is with Tony.'

'Sounds to me it might be more personal.'

'Sounds to me, Mordent, that you're thinking in a different direction from how you're being paid to think. What I need is some hard facts as to how Tony is using these women. Once I have those, I can release both you and your cheque.'

'I might need a little more danger money,' Mordent pushed. 'Tony has a heavy that I've already had a scramble with.'

The sigh that came down the phone could have frosted his office windows. 'I don't pay you to be obvious, Mordent. I thought you worked on the sly.'

'Sometimes working on the sly needs a bit of luck.'

'I'm tempted to decrease your fee rather than increase it under the circumstances, but give me your information and then I'll see what I can do.'

There were no pleasantries at the end of the call. Silk hung up.

13
Out Of The Frame

That evening found Mordent loitering in the vicinity of Reflective Tony's abode.

Night had fallen chill. The faint heat that had gradually permeated into the afternoon had dissipated through the lack of cloud cover. There was a bite in the air: a sign to the homeless that the balmy summer nights were over; a warning to the elderly of an increase in fuel bills. Mordent sat in a rented car that he hoped he could add to his expenses, the window wound down to avoid the windscreen collecting steam like breath on a mirror, his arm on the sill, the brim of his hat pulled over his eyes, dark pooling inside the vehicle like blood.

Twenty minutes earlier the Frame had pulled up at Tony's and gone inside. Mordent was waiting for them both to come out. He was up for some illicit breaking and entering. Information tended to fall into your possession that way. Unlike through questioning. Questioning only raised more questions than answers. And questioning revealed your hand.

The area appeared even less salubrious in the dark. Hulking ironwork shapes resembled shadowy sculptures on battered lawns; interior lights illuminated what couldn't be seen during the day: living areas with peeling wallpaper, floors littered with beer cans, the latest widescreen TV's on the walls, women – mostly wearing skinny tees and jogging bottoms – ironing, exercising, or on the phone making hand signals to imaginary observers. Other occupants were heavier, pound for pound, slumped on stained sofas, beer in one grip, remote in the other. And in a couple of windows groups folded over makeshift card tables, large men, skinny men, all in off-white vests and shorts, cigarettes behind ears or dangling like bent wire from the edges of hard, desperate mouths.

Mordent held no judgments. A view into his window would yield just such a caricatured existence. Caricatures were like similes: they were as they were because they embodied the perfect. The window tableaux reflecting contemporary life. Seen between blinks as static imagery they were snapshots, dirty postcards of subliminal messages. On the move they were movies. All life as art.

And – Mordent was reminded – within each window was a microcosm that could only hint at the vastness of life. Everywhere – right through the city and right across the globe – families, individuals and couples played out their roles in similar boxes. It was staggering. Mind-bending. Impossible. That was it. That was the crux of it. It was impossible but it was also true.

Yet in the car, alone, huddled, coat pulled around him, hat down over his eyes, he could make a reasonable argument that there was only himself in the world. It was only his breathing he could hear, after all.

Then there was another sound.

Heels clicked along the pavement. A tall woman with a blonde wig. Her skirt might have been round her waist. Drunk, not cruising. Talking to herself. Mordent couldn't make out the words. She passed him and continued ahead, fumbled with a key at the property next to Reflective Tony's, then let herself inside, light spilling from her window as the house came alive, spotlighting on the front lawn an area of grass burnt dead by a diesel spillage.

As if it had been a signal, the lights in Tony's property went out, and shortly afterwards his front door opened. The Frame edged his way through and over to his vehicle. Tony was just behind. They populated the vehicle, which itself then came alive in a blaze of noise and light. Moments later, it pulled away from the kerb, passed Mordent with his hat down, and disappeared into the distance, the red taillights finally winking out like the eyes of a dying rat.

Mordent waited ten minutes, then left his vehicle and wandered over to Reflective Tony's property.

The street was quiet. It was close to midnight. He sneaked a glance at Tony's neighbour and found her slouched on the sofa wearing a dressing gown, with a towel over her head. He looked no further, headed up to Tony's door and gave it a tug. As expected, it held solid. He wandered around back, mindful of dog shit and broken glass. At worst, both. At the rear there was a window partly ajar. He slipped out the crowbar that he'd concealed in his pocket and halfway up his right sleeve and levered the window open. The wood creaked and splintered, but it pushed upwards against the catch and broke it. So Reflective Tony might work out he had had a visitor, but Mordent was going to be careful to ensure that he wouldn't know who that was.

There was an old milk crate conveniently placed near the base of the window. Mordent stood on it and swung his leg into the room, followed it with the other. A stale smell of cannabis and body odour was partly masked by newly-sprayed deodorant. Mordent wasn't of the flashlight brigade when it came to housebreaking, found that it raised more suspicions than the actual house lights. So he manoeuvred his way to a door and felt around for a switch. Clicking it immersed the room in light, as if it had fallen into the sun. Immediately he saw that Tony's taste in furniture matched his taste in women. Everything was second-hand.

Yet, as though a woman lived there, everything was tidy.

There was no clutter. No beer cans, no plastic bags, no signs that Tony lived off microwaveable meals or takeaways. In Mordent's experience, this was unusual for a single male. But at the same time there were no signs of life: no family photographs of estranged children or ex-partners, no knickknacks picked up in foreign places or received as other people's souvenirs, nothing indicative of a private existence. It was almost a showroom – albeit for those on welfare. Its décor was that advised by realtors when putting a property up for sale.

In some ways, this made Mordent's evening easier. There was no rubbish to search through, nothing to declare. Yet also it made it difficult to hide his tracks. Broken window aside, even the slightest disruption of the interior of the house would be obvious to Tony.

He pulled his gloves on tight, opened several drawers in a cabinet underneath the television. Stacks of DVDs were in alphabetical order – the usual array of heist flicks and action movies. Mordent opened a handful, checked the contents were as they said on the packaging, then replaced them as carefully as he had found them. He continued a sweep of the living area, finding nothing of interest, then moved into the kitchen. Here, two beer cans stood beside each other on the drainer, like a robot couple. Again, the remainder of the room was clean if not sparkling. Opening a few cupboards revealed pulses, beans, a well-stocked spice rack, bags of rice: basmati, long grain, Thai. Vegetable compartments held ginger, galangal, lemon grass, pak choi, zucchini, two varieties of mushroom, garlic, carrot, potatoes.

Mordent scratched his head. Opened the fridge. Packets of diced pork and beef were still within their use-by dates, as were the containers of milk – both skimmed and Soya – half-opened tubs and tubes of tahini, tomato puree, chilli paste, Thai green curry, Mexican salsa. If nothing else, Tony was a surprisingly diverse cook. Mordent wondered if he had underestimated him. If he didn't know better, he might have been forgiven for thinking he had stepped inside the wrong house: that of an upwardly-mobile businesswoman with a new beau and a little too much time on her hands.

However, on the kitchen table sat the reminder of what he was there for. A stack of flyers for the Church of Wire.

He picked one up. It was identical to those beneath and to the two he'd seen previously. Not that he needed to have his suspicions verified, but for once it was reassuring to touch a cold, hard fact.

The Church had to be a scam. There could be no other reason for Reflective Tony's involvement; and presumably his courting of female prisoners was with a view to enlisting them in the organisation. For what purpose, Mordent didn't know. Prisoners didn't usually have a lot of money. And what was Ms Silk's role in this? If she thought Tony was bringing the Church down, then maybe it wasn't a scam after all. Maybe he was running a scam alongside the Church, using it as a convenient front? That seemed much more likely. He could run with that. Even if he couldn't run that far.

Also on the table was a laptop. Mordent deliberated starting it, but he hadn't brought a memory stick and he didn't want to hang around too long. Stealing it wasn't beneath him, but if it were password-protected all he would achieve would be to alert Tony to the fact that someone was onto him. Instead Mordent checked out a few more cupboards, then moved across the hallway and into the bedroom.

Again: clean, tidy. The bed was made. Either Tony was a woman in disguise or he was expecting one. It wasn't natural for a single male to live that way. Then Mordent remembered that Tony's front yard was tidier than the others he had passed in the daytime. Maybe he was obsessive-compulsive?

Mordent rummaged through closets and drawers, finding nothing suspicious. A niggle ran through his mind that the Church was legit and that Tony was turning over a new leaf, but that thought was quickly negated by the memory of the Frame advancing toward him across the parking lot while Tony watched with a cool detachment.

He sat on the bed. The mattress was firm, possibly new. He looked under the bed. There was no porn stash, no love letters from criminals. No sense.

He felt around the carpet: no bulges, nothing but floorboards. He stood up.

Mordent had discovered something amid the nothing: Tony had such a big secret to hide that he couldn't risk concealing it within his home.

He left the way he had come, pulled down hard on the window and left the same gap as before. If Tony noticed it was broken, he might well believe he'd done it himself. Then he walked back around to the front of the property, no longer worried about stepping on broken glass, dog shit or both. There just wouldn't be any. He could see that now.

He glanced through the lighted window at Tony's neighbour. She was asleep on the sofa, and the towel had slipped from her hair and lay languorously alongside her, like the ghost of a lover. Under the blonde wig she was a short-haired brunette. Despite her white trash look, he considered knocking on the door, introducing himself, working his way inside. He imagined her cooking him up a meal, eating it in front of the TV, maybe sharing a joke and then later sharing a bed. Sometimes the pull of a woman ran deep, usurped his inherent loneliness, his willingness to remain alone, his need. But then he projected the scenario, played it out widescreen with all the arguments and fertility and money worries. Leaving before the credits, he pulled his hat down over his eyes, wandered over to his car. Unlocked it. Sat inside. Drove.

He wasn't that far out into the suburbs, but the city was still a distant beast, illuminated like the interior of Aladdin's Cave, the slight rise of a hill giving him an elevated view as it spread out before him. A pocket of civilisation: plugged in. He gunned the engine, revelled in the dark. Night pressed on all sides, threatened to envelop the car like a black mass. As he stepped on the gas, he felt taken up by the tarmac, swept down toward the city on an overflowing river of molasses, melded and melted as one. His headlights picked out unidentifiable wildlife; eyes bored white, cheap Photoshopped effects. Other cars were like radar blips, head and tail lights delineating their presence as they roved on unseen roads, UFO-like by perspective, the night suffocating individuality, wrapping them all in the same blanket, bearing down on him just as he bore down on the city.

Then, somewhat unexpectedly, the number of lights increased, a plethora of cars emerged as if from nowhere. He snarled, slowed, re-entered the main traffic stream, and then instead of molasses he was riding a silver sea, the wet tarmac as bright as underfloor lighting. Cars pressed on either side instead of the dark; a coruscating melange of metal and flesh. He followed his route like a salmon returning to spawn, an evolutionary pawn, taking him, his spiritual home, parking in the side road nearest to Morgan's Bar.

14
Just One More Drink

It was after 3.00 in the morning. Mordent sat and watched his reflection. Or was it his reflection looking back? Which was the more permanent? For his reflection, the clear image within the mirror behind the bar was home. Sure, it followed Mordent around other places – car wing mirrors, shop windows, pedestrians' spectacles, the convex curve of a kettle, the concave burrow of a spoon – but it was here in the bar that it was the most prominent, that it existed most fully. So who was Mordent to speculate that he was the more solid, when he lived a life in fluidity? Maybe his reflection was always there, waiting for him to sit down and reinstate the connection. Or maybe it was indicative of the drink and the hour that he was having these thoughts at all.

Also reflected in the mirror were the other clientele. A disparate group of ne'er-do-wells or respectable businessmen? At this hour, who could tell? Whether they had previously sat together or not, the party was over. Each individual cradled a glass, nursing demons. It was as if Mordent's reflection had become fractured and reflected through time as well as space. At each table was a version of himself. Sorrowful. Sad. Alone.

He took another shot. Beckoned to Morgan, who refilled his glass without comment. Mordent wondered if he needed a comment, a connection. He thought about Astrid: no doubt sleeping, an arm draped around her husband, maybe with a facemask maintaining her almost untouchable beauty. Then he thought of Jessica: spreadeagled, tied to a bed, taunting him in that stupid Southern accent. And finally he thought of Maria, his estranged wife. And his fingers tightened further around the glass.

Regrets, he'd had a few.

A few too many.

He pulled himself up from being maudlin. It was no way to behave. Raising an arm, he signalled Morgan to come over. Morgan placed down a glass he had been cleaning and leant across the bar.

'Another drink?'

'I haven't started this one.'

'What do you want?'

Mordent wondered why Morgan didn't employ any barmaids. Shouldn't he be spilling his heart out to them? Counselling at the most, listening at the least, was the heart of their job. Instead he regarded Morgan's grizzled face. 'Do you remember the other day,' he said, 'those kids with the flyers? You seen them before?'

Morgan shook his head. 'Thanks for helping me out there.'

'No problem. And the flyers, for the Church of Wire. You heard of that?'

Another shake of the head. Morgan stood back from the bar. He wanted to get away, Mordent could tell. Making small talk wasn't his forte. Placing drinks on a smooth bar, cleaning glasses, keeping the place in check: that was what he did best. Most days, that was all Mordent wanted.

The barmaid thought flitted through his head again. They weren't needed here. Would be only a distraction. But then Morgan never had any other staff. At whatever hour of the day. Through the soft fuzz of the drink – which would turn hard come morning - Mordent wondered how he did it. Wondered if he could do it himself. Knew that he couldn't.

Knew that he was treading water.

Knew that he had to get to bed.

He downed the glass. Stood. Tottered. Watched as the room

swam in and out of focus, the mirror behind the bar giving funhouse reflections until he settled in his new position. He walked to the door, each step treacled. He was dimly aware of his empty glass being collected and rinsed, returned to a family of similar glasses, waiting for the next customer. The circle of life. As he pushed the door open, cold air drenched his face, sank into his skin. Sobered him with the knowledge of how drunk he had become.

It had been raining. Any residual heat gained during the day had long gone. The streets were slick with moisture, streetlights illuminating pockets of speckled tarmac as though he were lying on his back looking up at the stars. There was a sudden shift in his perspective, a soft folding, a clump. He was exhausted. He closed his eyes. Sounds reverberated as though through a tunnel, a sweat broke on his forehead and kaleidoscopic lights patterned the back of his eyelids. Vibrations juddered his skull. Something wet seeped into his clothing.

He became aware incrementally. A pair of heels on the pavement, that paused before walking on. A swish of tyres: looping surface water. A swirling blackness, forming indistinct shapes at the back of his vision. A voice – hollow, resonant – words unknown.

Something prodded him in the stomach. He opened his eyes. Saw the moon's reflection on the tarmac. The perspective was all wrong. Buildings were suspended in the air, rain soared upwards, a policeman's face hung upside-down as though suspended from monkey bars. As though a monkey. As though.

As though.

Rain wetted his face. He turned. He was on the floor.

'Get up.'

He recognised the words as soon as he heard them. As though their previously indistinct tones had been translated, or, like someone banging on a balsawood door, they had broken through with easy persistence. He pushed himself with one hand into a seated position. The ground righted itself with him. Then he reached out another hand, and the cop must have known him, because he was gripped and pulled to his feet.

Mordent wiped water out of his eyes.

'Thurlow.'

'That's me, Mordent. Can't say I welcome seeing you there in the gutter.'

The brim of Thurlow's hat maintained a skein of surface water that – if frozen – would have made a perfectly circular ice rink.

Mordent shrugged. His head pounded. He wondered if he'd banged it on the way down. He wondered how long he had *been* down. The fabric on the entire right-hand side of his jacket was sodden.

Thurlow gesticulated. 'I take it you've a licence for that piece?'

Mordent glanced down. His gun was on show; the holster he had been wearing had twisted as he fell. There was also a dull ache against his ribcage. He wondered if the image of the gun was imprinted on his skin, like some 21st Century brass-rubbing.

'Not on me,' he said.

'Perhaps we can let that one go,' Thurlow nodded. 'I'm not sure about the drinking. You know, when you were on the force, you were quite the teetotaller.'

Mordent could remember. But you couldn't live in the past.

'Things change,' he said.

'There's plenty still see you as a role model.'

'Either me or Kovacs,' Mordent managed a grin. 'I know who I'd choose.'

Thurlow smiled. 'Even so,' he said, 'if this is regular I'd suggest the AA. They helped my sister-in-law. She never touches the juice now.'

Mordent held back from commenting on Thurlow's sister-in-law.

'So, I'm free to go?' he asked.

'As I say, I guess so. And we'll keep it between you and me. One off, though, right?'

'Definitely.'

Mordent began to scan the street for a taxi. He couldn't be

seen getting into his car. He still wasn't steady.

'As I say, we'll keep it quiet.' Thurlow seemed reluctant to leave. 'Can't give Kovacs any ammunition, can I? Not that he'd stoop to name-calling I guess, although I know you guys have some history. Not that he'd have time with all that. He's pretty tied up with these murders right now.'

Mordent raised an eyebrow. It seemed to balance him.

'The Torso Killer,' he said.

'And the rest,' Thurlow smiled. 'There's another body found this evening. He's headed that way now.'

'Oh yes?' Mordent tried to keep his enthusiasm as damp as his jacket.

'Who knows if there's a connection. Bit of a weird set-up. Weird enough to send Kovacs scampering over there, anyways. It's gone round like wildfire.' Thurlow patted his police radio.

Mordent was glad it hadn't made the press. As casually as possible he asked where it was at. Then bade Thurlow farewell and resumed looking for a taxi.

But he didn't take a taxi. He waited for Thurlow to turn the corner and then made for his car, stopping at Bukowski's for some strong black coffee on the way.

He would need it.

He knew the location where the body had been found.

A disused parking lot.

Surrounded by trees.

15
History Repeats Itself

Police tape stretched like the arms of Mr Fantastic around the parking lot.

Mordent pulled up some distance away. The flashing lights of two cop cars strobed the scene in red and blue, blocking the entrance physically and spectrally. He sat in the car awhile, wondered how he was going to play this. Thurlow had indicated the murder was linked to those of Maloney and Pettiford, but Mordent's personal link was to Maloney only. Whether or not he could ease his way into the picture on that nebulous connection was anyone's guess. And probably unlikely if Kovacs was intent on keeping the lid on things.

Sometimes his reputation went only so far.

He could taste alcohol in his mouth. Knew it was on his breath. Couldn't risk getting breathalysed. The journey to the lot had been a miasma of neon lights and wet streets, reflections looming from the pavement like rainbow creatures intent on destroying his vehicle in 3D Technicolor; an amalgam of gritty black and white and cartoonish celluloid. He had opened both car windows wide, the cold air swirling like a vortex around his head, in an attempt to clear it. Now he had two headaches, one fuelled by alcohol the other by cold. He flipped open the glove compartment and searched for mints. None were forthcoming. The remnants of a pastrami sandwich were on the back seat. He sniffed it. Ate it. Wasn't too bad. Effectively it staunched his breath. Who knew what it might do to his stomach?

Locking the vehicle, he wandered over to the scene of the crime.

He recognised a cop resting against one of the cars. Marsham stood six foot plus, lanky, shaven head under his cap. He leant nonchalantly, toying with his nightstick. Pun intended.

'Hey Mordent.' He stuck out an arm. The hand at the end was large and it gripped Mordent's tight. 'Long time no see.'

Mordent nodded. Glanced over at the rookie he didn't know. The rookie wasn't bothered, just kept looking over his shoulder into the lot behind them. Arc lights had been set up, illuminating the area like a basketball court. Mordent could see various officers in uniform meandering about, a couple others wearing fetching all-in-one white suits, and Kovacs with his ear to a cell.

He could just make out a body on the ground. At angles, four or five small trees were poised over the corpse. Almost protecting it, in a conical fashion, like a tepee.

'Can you give me any information about that?' Mordent gesticulated into the lot.

Marsham was loud, opinionated and never gave much of a damn who he spoke to or what he said. 'Dead prostitute. Probably. Knocking on a bit. Maybe late forties. Tarted up. Looks like she was tied, raped and stabbed.'

'Bit of an out-of-the-way spot to be turning tricks, isn't it?'

'I dunno. Looks ideal to me. Isolated. Quiet this time of evening. Probably was killed in the building then brought outside. Me and Barker here were first on the scene. Anonymous call. I reckon the killer phoned this one in himself.'

'What's the significance of the trees?'

Marsham shrugged. 'You tell me. Probably why Kovacs is down here. Would be something out of nothing otherwise.'

'And the chances of me getting in?'

'I dunno about that, pal.' Marsham looked around. As though for a sign. 'I let you slip through here and there's gonna be questions asked. You know what I mean?'

Mordent nodded. He could wait. If he pushed himself onto Kovacs' turf that would only annoy him. If he waited politely, he could quiz him later. It still wasn't obviously anything to do with his working case. And he needed convincing that there would be enough of an information exchange for him to tell Kovacs of a possible link between the murder scene and Reflective Tony.

Also, the trees intrigued him.

He reached into his pocket and pulled out a cigarette. It wasn't often he smoked, and usually cigars, but he always had a stash on him, and on a cold night waiting for a corpse to tell a tale, it seemed reasonable to still the waiting time with some nicotine.

Mordent jerked the packet toward Marsham, knowing he couldn't take one but realising the offer lubed the gears.

They exchanged a manly conversation about their love lives. Both of them exaggerated. Leant against the other side of the car, Barker was jittery. Maybe it was the cold, but he couldn't keep still.

'What's the matter with him?' Mordent said, soft and low.

Marsham glanced. 'Either he needs a piss or he's got a girl he wants to get back to. We should have finished an hour ago. I don't get to talk to him much, even when we're in the same car.'

Mordent remembered a stakeout he had taken part in with Kovacs long ago. He knew what Marsham meant.

'I saw Thurlow earlier,' he said. 'He seemed to think this murder was linked to that of Tessa Maloney and Kwamie Pettiford. Not least because Kovacs is down here. What do you think?'

Marsham shrugged. He regarded the end of Mordent's cigarette. 'Rumour has it,' he said carefully, 'that we've got a serial killer on our hands.'

Mordent was about to open his mouth, but Barker spoke up: 'Who is this guy?'

'Name is Mordent,' Marsham answered, rolling his eyes. 'Used to work on the force. One of the good guys.'

Barker shrugged. 'So does data protection mean nothing to

you?'

Marsham laughed. 'He's not getting nuthin' that won't be in the papers tomorrow.'

Barker stood away from the car, inflated his chest. He was all of five foot five and a half. 'It's not tomorrow,' he said.

'Technically, it is tomorrow,' insisted Marsham. 'It's way after midnight. We hang around another hour and the sun will start to push its way up like a young girl's tits.'

Distaste wrought its way across Barker's face like a desultory sunrise on a cold winter morning. Mordent listened to them bicker. Marsham might as well have been himself, with Barker as Kovacs. The parallels were there. One guy sticking to the rules, the other flouting them. Did it really matter to Barker if Mordent got the information he was after? Apparently so. Would Barker be the one rising through the ranks, rather than Marsham? Apparently yes. Should Mordent tell Marsham this? The answer was no.

'Listen,' Marsham was saying, 'this guy is sound. He's not just some pedestrian being nosey. He's here for a reason and I'm sure it's legitimate. I'm not gonna be telling him to move along.'

'Kovacs would.' Barker's face held a smirk. He knew he was right. Revelled in it. 'Besides, I've been listening, and you haven't asked if he has any connection to this case. You're speculating.'

The word *speculating* came out with an intonation that would have accompanied the word *masturbating*.

'Look,' said Mordent, 'I'm privately engaged on the Maloney case. That's my point of interest. But I don't want to cause problems for you, buddy,' he slapped Marsham on the back. 'I'll pick up the scraps from the papers.'

Marsham took him to one side. 'Don't worry about him,' he said, with a jerk toward the jerk. 'He's just a pain in the ass. Hates being out on the street yet loves the paperwork. He's got his values upside-down. Give me your number and I'll fill you in later, once these guys have cleared up and gone home.'

Mordent handed over one of his business cards. Touched his nose. 'Thanks buddy.' He began to walk away and shouted over his shoulder at Barker: 'Goodnight officer.' He heard Barker mutter something under his breath.

The night wasn't lost. Marsham would give him as much info as he could, just to spite Barker. That was fine and dandy. It always paid to have someone on the inside. Marsham. Hubie. Martens. His network was building.

He sat in the car. Waited a while, just to annoy Barker further. Then started the engine and became absorbed by the dark.

16
The Molalla Forest Murderer

Mordent awoke in bed fully dressed with a headache. The headache wasn't dressed. It was bare and throbbing and hard.

He sat up. Made his way to the bathroom and clinked a couple of paracetamol into a dirty glass that he filled with cloudy water and downed in one. Then went searching for food.

Food shopping wasn't something he did on a regular basis, but there were eggs that he hadn't had for too long, so he ran up an omelette together with some defrosted hash browns. Breakfast rarely tasted so good.

He hadn't been up long before the call from Marsham came through. Good to his word, he had information. Hot before the press.

'Hey Mordent, how's it going?'

'I'm just up. How's Barker?'

Marsham laughed. 'I imagine Barker is just peachy.'

'So, what have you got for me?'

'Corpse is Loretta Gidney. Originally from Oregon. Late forties, as I'd guessed. Currently single. One child, a daughter, whereabouts is unknown. As I said last night, she'd been beaten, tied, raped and then stabbed.'

'Nasty.'

'Not the way I'd choose to go.'

'And the other stuff. The trees?'

'Yeah, this is what has got Kovacs all worked up. Five small trees, about three metres tall, placed like a shrine over the body.'

'Hiding it in plain sight?'

'You could say that. But meant to be found, right? And here's another thing. There was a small bottle found in her handbag. Like one of those bottles you get on airplanes. Lab have already done a test on it. Vodka and orange. A screwdriver.'

'I don't get it.'

'Neither did I.' There was a pause, as if Marsham was preparing for a big reveal. 'But you've got to give it to Kovacs. He knows his stuff. You ever hear of the Molalla Forest Murderer?'

Mordent racked his brains, but Molalla didn't shake out.

'Can't say that I have.'

'Me neither, but Kovacs, he's walking up and down, pacing the car lot when that bottle came out. Muttering to himself, you know, like when he's stuck on a crossword clue. You must have seen him. He was onto it straightaway, and we all got briefed this morning, just before I finished my shift.'

Mordent stood. Walked over to his window. No strong sunshine that day. The sky was grey, like washed out old clothes. Like a decomposed corpse. Mordent knew it was a day for hearing what Marsham was going to tell him.

'Go ahead,' he said.

'There's a guy called Dayton Leroy Rogers, was known as the Molalla Forest Murderer, as you've probably guessed. Currently residing in the Oregon State Penitentiary on death row for six murders. Suggestion is he killed at least seven, but one of the bodies remains unidentified. Those six bodies were found within the Molalla Forest, a national park in Oregon. They were all street women – prostitutes, addicts, runaways or a mixture of all three. Apprehended in 1987, so quite some time ago. Obviously this perp isn't him, but the specs are the same. What linked Rogers to the bodies was the screwdriver and those small bottles. Habits die hard. All this is public knowledge, of course, so we've a copycat on our hands.'

'Like Tessa Maloney and Richard Cottingham?'

'Right.'

'Like Kwamie Pettiford and Joseph Christopher?'

'Maybe. Kovacs is still working on that one.'

'Maloney's husband said Tessa believed she was a victim of Cottingham, but had managed to escape death. You're gonna tell me there's a similar link with Loretta?'

'Spot on. It's tenuous, but DNA links her to having worked as a prostitute under another name in the late '90s. Here in this city. She had reported a rape. During the interview she mentioned another rape she had suffered, that went unreported, when she was living in Oregon in the mid-'80s. No DNA evidence there, of course; too early for that. But the record states she believed it could have been Dayton Leroy Rogers. Anyway, she didn't pursue it, and Rogers was locked up anyway, so we didn't pass the info onto Oregon. Maybe, just maybe, like Maloney, she was a survivor of a serial killer.'

'Who has just been murdered with the same specs as the original perp.'

'Just like Maloney, and probably just like Pettiford.'

'So,' Mordent said, 'we've got a serial killer on our hands who's taking out the survivors of previously failed serial killer attacks?'

'Magic, isn't it!' Marsham was almost jubilant. 'That takes some beating.'

'I can see how Kovacs is all worked up.'

'You *should* see him. Doesn't know whether to rub his hands or curl up and die.'

'It's a hot potato.'

'It sure is. And you won't be seeing this in the press, not yet.'

Mordent ran his mind over the possibilities. There was one thing Marsham hadn't voiced, but from what he had said it was clear as day. And a brighter day than the one that poured dismally over the horizon. The killer worked in the force, or had worked in the force. The information about Loretta's previous rape was a clincher. Unless that *had* made the papers. Mordent would need to find out.

But would he? This wasn't his case, not really. Who was

going to pay him for this work? Bernard Maloney wanted him to nail his wife's killer, but with the police going all out on the case, it was a tab Bernard would likely not pick up. But then he remembered Reflective Tony and his link to that parking lot. Another coincidence? Unlikely. Astrid had told him to concentrate on one case at a time, but it seemed the paths were converging. Should he tell Kovacs about his encounter with Tony? Not until he'd checked out the Church of Wire. He had cards, and he wanted them kept close to his chest.

'Say, Marsham.'

'Yeah?'

'Thanks for this, buddy.'

'No problem. A problem shared is a problem halved, right? Way I see it, you'll come in at a different angle from Kovacs, won't be so analytical. Besides, if you're working for Maloney, then he has a right to know. Can't see Kovacs getting all sentimental over him.'

You don't know me that well either, thought Mordent, but didn't voice it. 'If you hear anything else, Marsham, you know where to find me.'

'As I say, no problem. And I trust you, man. Don't reveal your source.'

'I won't.'

Mordent hung up. He sat back in his kitchen chair, felt the wood keen against his skin. He let out a breath he hadn't realised he had been holding.

Serial killers – real fucked-up serial killers – were the stuff of movies. When they bled into real life it was usually as disparate individuals. Maybe cold. Maybe calculating. But frequently just obsessive-compulsives driven by goals that the rest of us understand, but can't *comprehend*. Experience of dealing with serial killers was slim – right across the board. Most cops would never encounter one, at any level. For some, drawing inspiration from the movies was an angle into the case – looking for some psychological clue that would pin down the identity of the killer, and make them a hero in the process. Truth be told, however, most serial killers were caught by chance. Numerous kills invoked the law of diminishing returns – the longer it went on, the more mistakes were likely to be made; the closer the net would draw. Yet ultimately few cops caught a serial killer – they caught a murderer and subsequently found out they were a serial killer. A cinematic trail of clues was just that. Few killers wanted to tease the cops into finding them, because few killers wanted to be caught. It all came down to luck and chance.

One thing Mordent was sure of was that Reflective Tony was no serial killer.

Yet there was still a link.

Mordent powered up his PC. Checked out the information Marsham had given him on Dayton Leroy Rogers. It all matched. He wondered about the trees. The killer had wanted the body found, conspicuously. Had Tony been scouting for locations when he'd followed him to the lot? Was this a movie, after all?

More questions. He put his hands behind his head. He itched to phone Kovacs. Wondered about his way of thinking. It was a puzzle, and Kovacs loved puzzles. But Kovacs also loved his job, and all the trappings that came with it. Kovacs could lose his job over a high-profile case if he made mistakes and didn't act fast. If he could shadow Kovacs it would make interesting viewing.

Then again – he moved his hands, crossed his arms over his chest – what did this have to do with him? Take Maloney out of the equation and it was nothing. Even if Tony was involved, Mordent's remit was just to report back to Silk. Unless he excused his interest as public duty – *unpaid* public duty – he should hang fire and let them get on with it themselves.

He decided to take a shower. Undressing in front of his window, he regarded the buildings opposite, wondered who might be interested in perusing his aged and naked body. Assumed it would be no-one he wanted to know. In the mirror in the bathroom he regarded his face. It had aged slowly, almost on tiptoe over the years, yet suddenly he regarded the visage of an old man. A tired old man. If he rubbed the top of his head, it wrinkled.

How had it come to this? Suddenly, so fast, despite it being slow. The years telescoped inside him. He was reminded of seeing a cousin grow up – one who had seemed to mature at great speed because of the sporadic times Mordent saw him. It all came down to perspective. Age was like watching the minute hand on the clock: if you turned your gaze it sped up, watched it close and changes were incremental. He wasn't *overly* old, he wasn't near death old, but he was getting old. Getting older. Getting to the point where he knew that there were experiences he would never have. That there were experiences he had missed.

He wanted to slap himself for getting maudlin. Didn't.

He'd never had a child. He'd never travelled much. He'd never done a dangerous sport or gone hunting. He hadn't read enough books or seen enough movies. He hadn't seen enough movies with enough women. He'd married only once, and wasn't sure if he wanted to be divorced and married again. He hadn't played bass guitar in a rock band in his younger days and was unlikely to play anything in a jazz band now. He wasn't going to be growing his hair back or reclaiming all the dead skin cells that had fallen from his body. He wouldn't be regaining the kisses of women he should have loved harder and faster, and he wouldn't be gaining many more kisses from women who wanted him hard and fast.

He *had* done stuff. Of course he had.

But some days it wasn't enough.

He stepped into the shower. Let the water wash over him. His body wasn't too bad. He recognised parts of it from his youth, but then there were parts of him he had never seen. He wondered how a man could inhabit a skin without being fully cognisant of its workings. Maybe the brain was the motor and the mind was the driver. If so, evolution was all about autopilot. No one actually *chose* to mutate, regenerate, get old. We just inhabited a space, decked it out as best we could, approved of our decisions, and finally had it all taken away by a sneak thief. Ageing by degrees, slow theft of youth, mental capabilities, years. And no-one did anything about it.

Sure, product manufacturers were producing creams and unguents constantly to make you *appear* young. But to his knowledge there was no investment to actually *prevent* the ageing process. He'd had some brushes with death, didn't like it; his approaching mortality was something he didn't want to consider. Yet somehow, on grey mornings like this, reminded of the corporeal nature of the body by a murder, those thoughts rushed to the front of his mind like elderly women at a garage sale. And however much he shook his head, even under the shower, they remained there; only being dislodged to the back of his brain to resurface when the time wasn't right.

He sighed. Watched hair disappear down the plughole.

It was almost enough to turn anyone to religion: that great placebo in the sky.

It would be the following night, however, that he would attend church. It would be interesting to see what the Wireists had to offer.

Until then …?

He didn't know.

And then he did. He decided to take a walk.

17
Ground Level

When there wasn't much to do – when he needed time to think – Mordent turned gumshoe.

Gumshoe was synonymous with *detective*, although its usage was increasingly archaic. Derived from a waterproof overshoe that protected normal footwear during wet weather and also softened footfall – giving anyone who desired it the ability to sneak up behind someone with the minimum of noise. Sneaking around was a detective's speciality, hence the term. Not that it applied literally, although Mordent was aware that Gummo Marx – one of the Marx Brothers – had been given his nickname due to his habit of wearing those shoes. But he liked the term; it held the appropriate noir overtones, and for him implied the constancy of walking: if not physically looking for clues then a metaphor for the machinations of his brain.

Walking also bought time to think that driving never did. More time, in fact, than doing nothing achieved. It bundled vestiges of boredom into a cupboard, tied and gaffer-taped, allowing freedom of thought to emerge. It was therapeutic, healthy and put a different slant on the world. Mordent might not do it often, but always wished he did it more.

All those questions scurrying through his head needed filing, sorting, answering. It wasn't the type of fog that ejaculation relieved, however tempting another visit to Astrid might be; more the job of a secretary. If he had had a confidante in his office that would have been swell, but the only staff he had ever been able to afford had been elderly and ineffective. His mind wandered to the agency girls he often watched flitting down the corridor, all heels and tan stockings, slim-line pencil skirts and sharp jackets. His income wouldn't stretch to them, and even if it did, he wouldn't find a Girl Friday. Those days were long gone. The archetype of a wisecracking PI with a smouldering secretary had been negated by equal opportunities and harassment-at-work lawsuits. Maybe it wasn't a bad thing, considering. But some days, when the bottle in his desk drawer didn't provide enough company, Mordent could have benefited from a partner in anti-crime to bolster his ego.

Walking, then, was – if not a close substitute – close enough.

He left his office building and hit the street. His jacket staved off a hint of cold; the sun was firmly behind cloud, an intimation of fall kicking in with a probable vengeance. Mordent liked the darker nights, duller mornings, but was less keen on the chills. What he did appreciate was living in a city that went through the seasons – people needed that rotation to mutate and evolve. Otherwise it was just running to stand still. A physical manifestation of the passage of time gave humanity the edge, in his occasionally humble opinion. A reminder that after life there came death, and that after death there might be a semblance of life, rejuvenation, regardless of mankind's capacity to understand it.

So he pulled his jacket tight, trod the sidewalk. Mid-morning, pedestrian traffic had lulled, he wasn't jostled or cut up in a manner that car drivers would have been sued over. His neighbourhood was more neighbour than hood. Not in the sugar-borrowing sense, but also not in the exchange-of-other-white materials sense. He hadn't chosen carefully – his place of abode had been more luck than judgment, harnessed to what he could afford – but around there his fellow residents were more likely to attend a drive-in than a drive-by shooting, and that was good enough for him.

If he recognised any of them he didn't show it, didn't know

any names. He varied his gaze from sidewalk to side, avoiding chewing gum and focusing on the stuff that he rarely saw when driving. The mock-art-deco refurbishment of the small library across the street; the change in fashions from summer to fall; the shop-window displays at the deli, with a mixture of genuine and plastic foods; the bakery with tiered wedding cakes; the condition of the steps leading up to various brownstone apartment blocks, scoured by generations of shoes.

He recalled an image once seen in a magazine. The atomic burn post-Hiroshima of a figure scorched through concrete: a stick shadow only vaguely human, a reminder that mankind's capacity for desolation could be as effective as it was potentially heartbreaking. He imagined *those* accusing fingers pointing toward the authorities, the warmongers, reminded himself that in days gone by, the causes for fighting were just as tenuous and illegitimate as they were nowadays – specifically where members of the public were concerned. There could *never* be any justification for mass destruction of a population – yet it seemed that it was perpetually the winners of a war that wrote that history, *rewrote* the moral code by which they had achieved it.

Yet, on a micro level, Mordent was aware that the divisions between criminals and cops were also subjective. Along the lines of one man's freedom-fighter being another man's terrorist, society did dictate rules, and he had signed up to abide by them: to enforce them. Occasionally, and usually with clarity dulled by the clear mist of alcohol, it bothered him. But now, out on the street, amongst people, the evidence that law was required was obvious. People might not have the right to live their lives as they chose – for some, choice was a fiction pre-determined before their births by their parentage, location and status – but they should be given the opportunity to live in a way where they wouldn't be harmed or would wish to harm others. If he had a role to protect that virtue, then he was glad of it. Despite the inherent contradictions that he knew ran riot in his head, ultimately Mordent considered himself one of the good guys.

He turned a corner onto more of a major thoroughfare. Yellow taxi cabs flashed by the edge of his vision, like canaries in flight. The sidewalk heaved with discharged office workers on early lunch breaks. Steam rose from a motorised van masquerading as a coffee shop. An upmarket hot dog vendor stood with peaked cap, turning sausages with tongs. Across to his right, what passed for parkland was inhabited by couples on benches snuggled together for warmth, one pair surreptitiously throwing illegal breadcrumbs to pigeons. Overhead the drone of a plane reverberated downward on a steady route to the airport. Underfoot the hum of traffic vibrated the sidewalk. Machines and machinery dominated the landscape, from those that had constructed these buildings to the tiny communication devices held to almost every ear. Progress was a juggernaut with which Mordent held a hate/love relationship. The pull of the past a vortex against the push of the future.

Truth was, he liked how it *had* been but didn't want to fall behind. If evolution was the survival of the fittest, then he was reluctant to be the slowest bison on the prairie. He *had* technology, embraced the internet and owned a cell phone, acknowledged them as useful tools. But it was the perpetual redundancy of many applications that abhorred him; the fact that big companies released new products piecemeal, with upgrades already waiting in the wings. This, mapped with the unconscious consumer drive religiously lapping up each new device, struck him as unnecessary waste. The travesty of capitalism was that it always had to prove itself; the comfort of communism was that it needed to do that only once.

He continued to walk. Each tread of each foot spooled ideas into his head. It had been a while since he'd allowed himself to think. Wrapped up in his cases, the unremitting compactness of his lifestyle, it was easy to lose perspective, to lose the ability to think. Here at ground level everything was even. Just as each step followed on from another, so he reverted to the A-Z. Taking one thing at a time.

His stomach growled.

He stopped off at a small café, ordered a latte and a turkey club sandwich and sat by the window. The sandwich was traditional, three pieces of toasted bread cut into quarters with turkey at the bottom and bacon, lettuce and tomato on top. For Mordent it was soul food. Whenever he had been on a stakeout he had always tried to eschew the burgers and doughnuts that other cops had scoffed. Real food always tasted better to him, although aside from that he couldn't claim to be a health freak, as the contents of his refrigerator would prove.

Outside the window life moved at a regular pace. Females' skirts were longer than he had seen a few days earlier, boots had replaced heels, and jackets were wrapped around both simple and ample frames. Men, whose fashion sense stumbled, were still sparsely-dressed and suffered from the increase in cold. Mordent rarely took his jacket off – all the better to conceal his weapon – so for him it was the hot days when he faltered rather than the chill.

As he sat, as his gaze turned inward rather than outward, he wondered about the mentality of the serial killer.

Assuming his connections were sound, someone had decided to pick off the survivors of previous serial killer attacks. If nothing else, it was a limited exercise, constrained by the availability of information, the possibility of locating the victims and the paucity of potential kills. But then Mordent presumed serial killers weren't logical people. Their choice of victims could be just as random as they might be specific, and what he had to remind himself time and again was that this was a real situation, not a movie where clues were laid by a cunning supervillain with too much time on his hands. And the choosing of *modus operandi* based on those of previous killers didn't necessarily smack of a lack of imagination, but possibly a stroke of genius.

In short, he was back where he started.

He finished the sandwich, drained the latte and beckoned for a refill. The coffee was smooth and sweet. Outside, it had begun to rain. Fat slugs smashed against the window, trailing downward in a swift movement indicating the strength of the shower. Umbrellas and collars went up, the drops bouncing off the top of stretched fabric like kids on a trampoline. Mordent shivered. Either the temperature had dropped or his aversion to water had kicked in. He had almost drowned once. Almost *been* drowned, that was. He moved his feet against the ridge of the footstool, not quite subconsciously, as if to reassure himself they weren't encased in concrete.

Clouds darkened further, as though cotton wool dipped in ink, a slow progression. Spray from car wheels almost reached the café window due to puddles created by dips in the road. Mordent watched pedestrians jig to one side, dance-stepping with the spray as partners, attempting not to touch each other's toes. Wind was channelled down the funnel of streets flanked by buildings, whipped around corners, dislodged hats. A sudden, violent storm.

On his side of the window, all was calm. Diners ate their food, drank their coffees, commented on the weather. All it took for the difference was a sheet of glass and some bricks. While the wolf raged outside, huffing and puffing, the little pigs were safe. If there was an analogy between those untouched by crime and those affected by crime, Mordent choose to push it to one side. Instead, he watched the show, until, after ten minutes, areas of blue were revealed between the clouds, which gradually broke up like dissolving soap suds and finally let through some warmth that began to work the sidewalk dry.

Pedestrians who had milled in the café doorway without actually crossing the threshold to become customers returned to the street. Mordent paid up and joined them. The air felt washed clean, the odour of fresh grass from the nearby park wafted over him like fabric softener, although soon it was replaced by the danker smells of wet newspaper and garbage from drains that now chugged down the remnants of water, releasing smells as blockages cleared from the weight of the downpour.

If there were a thousand stories in the naked city, this was but one of them.

Mordent continued his gumshoe walk uptown. Gradually, the neighbourhood changed, became less residential and more commercial. Not like the financial district, with its skyscrapers and banks, but more traditional, with boutique stores, non-chain food stores, alternative clothing shops and a smattering of art galleries. On one corner sat an independent cinema. Mordent remembered raiding it many years ago when the type of pornography it was showing was illegal. Now, maybe ironically, it was tarted up, had added additional screens. He scanned the frontage. In addition to recent low-budget fare, it was currently running a series of French new wave movies. Mordent was familiar with the genre, but not with that day's movie: *Lift to the Scaffold*, directed by Louis Malle and starring Jeanne Moreau and Maurice Ronet. Mordent glanced at his watch. The afternoon matinee would begin in thirty minutes. He considered the brightness beginning to consume the remainder of the afternoon and headed into the dark, an appointment with noir leading him by the elbow.

The foyer was pristine, not the area of scrubby carpet fused with cigarette burns and stubs as he remembered it. Behind a desk – unusually not encased within a bubble of plastic – sat a tall, thin young man with a goatee, shuffling cards. Mordent nodded and spoke the name of the film. Took the proffered ticket, together with a movie information sheet, then walked less than ten feet to hand the ticket to a young girl who tore it in half and opened the door to the auditorium.

It was quiet inside. Mordent wouldn't have been surprised if he was the only patron, and certainly this was true when he entered. The lights were down low, illuminating each seat-back but not each seat, giving the impression that they were floating in gloom. The screen was small by chain cinema comparisons, but big enough. A dull maroon curtain hung over the white expanse. Mordent took a seat dead centre, his eyes level with the middle of the screen. He wondered about popcorn.

Closer to the start, the cinema began to fill. From habit he glanced at each newcomer, paying more attention to the females than the males. Many of the clientele were solo, with only a few couples amongst them and one group of three students. Like most humans taking seats, all parties situated themselves at least four spaces from each other. Then the lights darkened further, so that only green emergency exit lights showed at the fringes of the room. The curtains drew open and, without any adverts or preamble, the movie began.

Mordent became engrossed. A simple murder, a love triangle, succinct black and white photography, Jeanne Moreau in close up and frequently in natural light without make-up, the accentuation of existence, and – especially pertinent for him – an improvised score by Miles Davis. For 88 minutes Mordent was held enchanted, lulled by the comfort of cinema, oblivious to serial killers and psycho-cats, rain and shine.

You see, madam, there are always several photos in a camera.

Mordent remained still at the end of the picture, heard others leaving around him, stayed within the cinematic bubble, his life turning on a film spool as he settled back into the real world, wished himself into the late '50s – a time of budding sexuality and fresh ideas.

Then he became aware of someone seating themselves behind him.

'Why, Mr Mordent. I would put my hands over your eyes and say *Guess who?*, but I wouldn't want you startled enough to shoot me.'

Jessica?

'And Mr Mordent, if I wanted to read I'd pick up a book, not visit the cinema.'

He turned his head. It was indeed Jessica. She was smiling, and in the subdued light he could almost mistake her for Jeanne Moreau.

Almost.

That illusion lasted for more than a second. Long enough for Mordent to twist in his seat and kiss her.

As the bubble burst, so the regret set in. And he knew she would be taking him home.

19
Danger Zone

Her apartment felt clandestine.

The curtains were drawn. The bed had been made. Subdued lighting suffused everything but the corners. It was as though she had been expecting someone. As though she had been expecting him.

They had taken a bus from the cinema. It was large, almost predatory, and dominated the traffic with hisses and creaks. Mordent hadn't ridden a bus for several years, and the journey didn't fuel his inclination to do it again. They stood, each with a hand raised clasping a leather strap. Jessica's body knocked into his, the intimation of what was to come. Mordent felt anxious, almost schoolboy-ish, for reasons he couldn't exactly define. Perhaps because he knew it was wrong.

Not wrong in the conventional moral sense. Both of them were adults. But one of them was vulnerable. And it wasn't Mordent.

The axiom that came to mind was never to mix work with pleasure. It was an axiom he frequently disregarded.

According to Jessica she had seen him enter the cinema as she had passed by in a bus. The mischievous Southern Belle side of her had decided to disembark at the next stop and follow him. Mordent wondered what the criminal side of her had thought. Nevertheless, he bought the story with what spare change he had.

When he told her he had contacted the Church of Wire and would be attending their next meeting the following evening, she positively glowed.

'Why Mr Mordent. It would be so good to welcome you into the fold.'

He took that with a pinch of salt.

Her apartment was similar to his, in a similar brownstone but a less salubrious district. He felt the urge to turn up his collar as he entered, but instead just kept his gaze low. Low enough, as it happened, to regard the heels of Jessica's shoes as she ascended the stairs to the first floor. They were black and high, with a shiny metallic heel that clicked like an old-fashioned typewriter as she walked. Her legs were encased in black, her skirt just above the knee. She wore a flouncy blouse that didn't delineate her breasts.

Her sofa was worn, as were the remainder of her belongings. The kind of stuff easily cobbled together by someone recently out of jail. There were no photographs adorning the walls or surfaces. Mordent wondered if she had children, decided she probably did. Knew that she didn't see them.

From the sofa he could see into the bedroom, the fresh bed dominating the space. Jessica was in the kitchen, which he could also view from where he sat. It was as though the sofa was deliberately positioned in the best place for reconnaissance. From there his retinas held a clear view of Jessica as she boiled some water and removed two cups from a shaky cupboard. He would bet the cups were chipped, and when she brought them over a few minutes later, he wasn't proven wrong.

'Well,' she said.

'Well,' he said.

Their drinks went cold.

Ten minutes later, Mordent was flat on his back in the now dishevelled bed, apologising.

'There's no need,' Jessica said, naked and bent over a cabinet, rummaging in a drawer. 'It can happen to anyone.'

Mordent stared down at his flaccid penis. It had been over far too quickly, and his fleeting desire to pleasure Jessica had deflated simultaneously, the evolutionary zeitgeist extinguished.

Maybe, Mordent thought, he had spent too long associating with prostitutes, where the impetus for gratification was one-sided.

During coitus he had had a vision of himself as a bison. Mounting Jessica with as much tact as a car might mount the kerb.

'Maybe I should go?'

'Hmmm? What? Ah, here it is.' Jessica moved back onto the bed, her body resplendent in all its shortcomings now that he was spent. 'No, of course you shouldn't go. You've got work to do first.'

She held up a slim vibrator.

'It's only fair, after all, wouldn't you say so, Mr Mordent?'

Twenty-five minutes later, Mordent was buttoning his shirt, his bare feet flat to the floor, his back to Jessica. Her left hand moved slowly up and down his spine, gently caressing him through the shirt. He took it as a thank you, even though he had done nothing to merit it. The dull light from the bedside lamps now seemed sordid rather than romantic. The push of the moment had gone.

He bent to pick up a discarded sock, felt her hand move from his back. As he straightened, he felt something cold and hard through the material. It was clear what it was. The barrel of a gun.

He decided against turning around.

They spoke simultaneously: 'What are you doing?' 'Why do you have this?'

Mordent's muscles eased. 'Have I not told you I'm a PI? I carry a piece because it's part of the trade.'

He risked turning to look at her, kept his arms by his side. Wondered just how easy it would be for her to shoot him, and how simply his life might end. In essence: not very. And they both knew it.

She lowered both the gun and her eyes.

'Are you investigating me, Mr Mordent?'

She was still naked. Her breasts were a pale simulacrum of what Mordent imagined they had been in her youth. He understood the cruelties inherent in observation, those details that had been shouldered aside during the heat of the moment. As if sensing his regard, she pulled a bed sheet around her before passing him the gun.

'No, I'm not investigating you. Should I be? Is there something to investigate?'

She shook her head. The false youth of her Southern Belle persona had been picked up along with the bed sheet. 'Why? Do you think I would tell you if there was?'

Mordent shrugged. Placed the gun on the floor beside his shoes. Without meaning to, he kissed her roughly on the mouth.

'It doesn't matter,' she said. 'It doesn't have to be perfect.' She paused, bit her lower lip. 'It very rarely is.'

Mordent knew he should leave. Didn't. Instead, with one sock on, he lay back on the bed as she loomed over him. Her hand slid over his underpants. Not that she could raise him from the dead. But she knew that. It was just a tender gesture. A gesture to be tendered against future encounters.

'I haven't had the easiest life,' she said. 'Sometimes you have to grab what chance of happiness you can. However illusory it might be.'

'Is that why you're with the Church of Wire?'

She shrugged, the sheet dropped. She made no attempt to pull it back. 'We're all looking for something, aren't we?'

Mordent wondered. Some people looked harder than others.

He didn't have any of the answers. Certainly none of *her* answers. Any answers that might have been found within the sheets simply raised more questions.

He looked toward the closed curtains. It was clear that the sun had begun to set. He needed to get home. Staying the night wasn't an option. While it was evident in his mind that getting into Jessica's bed had been a bad idea, he was unsure what she had made of it. Of what she wanted to make of it. He sat up again.

'I have to be going.'

She didn't disagree.

'But tomorrow night,' he said, 'can we meet for a coffee before attending church?'

A smile grew across her face. Naturally. 'Yes. I would like that.'

Mordent pulled on the second sock. Then his trousers. Then shoes. Holster. Jacket.

'Thank you,' he said.

'Thank *you*, Mr Mordent. You may see yourself out.'

Jessica rolled the sheets around her, faced the window.

He left. Not quite sure what they had been thanking each other for.

20
When A Man Won't Listen To His Conscience, It's Usually Because He Doesn't Want Advice From A Total Stranger

Mordent wasn't in the mood to go home. Outside the warmth of Jessica's apartment the evening had taken on a chill that hit deep inside him. As if together they had broken an antiquated contraption powered by coal. He wasn't sure what they had achieved. It hadn't been love-making, and it hadn't even been sex. If there was some other kind of word for it, then that would have been what it was.

Astrid beckoned. But the late hour and the fact he was spent negated her possibility. There were a few others he could turn to. Then again, there weren't. Other than the constant beckoning found within Morgan's Bar, the only other person he could see sober might be Hubie.

Hubie. Mordent had mixed feelings about him. As a source of information he was useful. As a person, he could be likeable. But as a friend – that would be questionable.

While in the force, Mordent had manoeuvred Hubie into a position where he would always be willing to do a deal for him.

Unlike Martens in the morgue, where the advice was accompanied by a great deal of reluctance, the situation with Hubie worked both ways. But even so, information gleaned by coercion came at a price: the person giving that information couldn't always be trusted. And no matter the camaraderie between them, Hubie was not a friend.

Mordent could count the number of his friends on the fingers of one hand maimed in a chainsaw accident.

Frankly, he had not one.

Those in the force that admired him didn't know him. Their template was built out of story and substance, an equal mix of fiction and fact. But being admired didn't mean that you had to be liked. Mordent had a few acquaintances but no close friends. That was the fact as he had to deal with it.

Still, Hubie would be home. He was always home. Mordent surveyed the streets slick with dark. At the bottom of Jessica's road, the lights of cars penetrated the gloom. His feet hurt. His morning walk had taken a turn unappreciated by his soles. He headed toward the traffic, toward the lights, then hailed a cab touting for fares and gave the driver Hubie's address.

Being footloose in the city had its disadvantages. Within moments, Mordent was missing the privacy of his car. The driver's radio station pounded out a rap track that was anathema to Mordent's ears. The driver drummed his fingers on the steering wheel, sang snatches of lyrics that he couldn't quite remember, meaning that a low monotone accompanied the beat discordantly. Mordent tried looking out the side window, but the fug inside the vehicle steamed the glass. The view out front was obscured by the driver's dreadlocks and a selection of dangly talismans hung from the rear-view mirror. There was little he could do but sit back and assume the driver knew where he was going. It wasn't late: somewhere past seven o'clock. Although Mordent knew getting a cab back from Hubie's neighbourhood wouldn't be easy if it happened that he wasn't in.

But he would be in. Hubie's two loves were horses and girls. No races ran that time of day, and when it came to girls, they usually ran to him.

Mordent could well understand Hubie's attraction to the female sex, but was more puzzled by their attraction to him. Maybe he had a certain charm that Mordent couldn't identify. But then Hubie wasn't fussy. And money had a habit of keeping its mouth shut.

They had gone another block before Mordent realised the driver was talking.

'I said man, hey man.'

Mordent motioned for the radio to be turned down. He wasn't sure what would be worse, the music or the conversation. It was a gamble.

'I was talking to you about the serial killer. You read about that?'

Mordent shook his head. It was always best to withhold information in order to gain it.

'No? It's all over the news, man. Where you been today?'

'With a girl.'

Mordent smiled, and it was returned wide.

'Maybe you didn't miss anything. Maybe you gained. Anyhow. The news. They found a body in the financial district. Covered in trees and leaves and shit. Serial killer city.'

'I wouldn't say one body makes a serial killer.'

The driver took a right then a left. 'It ain't the *number*, it's the *circumstances*. You ever hear about that?'

Mordent knew Kovacs had managed to keep stuff out of the press. The driver was all talk and no facts. Despite the leak.

Did it matter though? Surely those with anything to fear were few and far between.

'*Modus operandi*,' the driver said, almost in a whisper, conspiratorially. 'The method in the madness.'

'Right.'

Mordent settled back. Turned his head to the window, despite not having a view. After a few moments the rap music played louder.

Shortly the driver pulled up outside Hubie's apartment block.

'You sure this is the place?'

Mordent nodded. He knew what the driver meant. If he were the cabbie he might expect a call from the police the following day, asking where he had dropped off a slightly dishevelled, square-built gentleman with a turned-up collar and no desire to talk. Reason: body found amongst the garbage in an alley.

He paid up and left the vehicle.

Falling rain pierced by streetlights resembled needles. The cold similarly pricked. Mordent ducked his head down and made a few quick steps to the building entrance as the cab wheels washed the kerb in a spin. He pushed on the double doors and entered.

The interior was lit by a flickering strip light. In one corner a drunk was out cold with a bottle by his side. Another corner contained a pool of piss. Mordent grimaced, screwed up his nose and hefted his way upstairs. Hubie's taste in residence was not dissimilar to his predilection for horses and women. Rundown, but still fit for purpose.

He arrived on Hubie's floor. Rapped on the door. There was a strip of light glowing the floorboards like new.

'Who is it?' The voice sounded slept in.

'Mordent.'

'Bit late for a social call.'

'It might be in the circles you move, Hubie, but it's only a little after eight. Hep cats like me are just hitting the tiles.' Mordent leant against the door jamb. 'You gonna let me in?'

He wouldn't have been able to hear a sigh from the other side of the door, but knew there was one.

'Just a minute.'

Mordent ticked the seconds off in his head. Hubie came through before the minute was up: just as Mordent imagined he did with women and only occasionally with horses.

In the competition of the dishevelled, Hubie won with Mordent a close second. Despite the light in the room haloing stray tufts of hair, Hubie appeared as though he had dressed in the dark. One collar of his shirt was up, the other down. He wore pyjama bottoms. A tie hung lopsided and loose; no doubt it had been still attached to the shirt when he picked it up. His feet were bare.

Mordent wasn't keen on feet unless they were female and hidden, calves accentuated by heels. Hubie could have done with a chiropodist. Elongated toenails stuck out at weird angles, yellowed and sharp. Mordent realised the middle toes were webbed; their separation ended halfway along the joint in thick skin. When the floods came to the city, Hubie would hold the advantage.

'Come on in. I would say it's a pleasure to see you, but I'm sure you're here for unpleasurable reasons.'

'Bit of both, Hubie. Bit of both.'

Instinctively Mordent looked to his left as he entered Hubie's office-cum-apartment. The bedroom was frequently occupied by someone of the female persuasion. Hubie being easily persuaded. But it was bare. The state of the bed indicated Hubie wasn't expecting anyone anytime soon.

'Vacancy?'

'Funny.'

Mordent sat on one side of the desk, Hubie the other. However informal the evening might become, the delineation was too established to differ from the norm.

Hubie sat back, the buttons on his shirt straining in some places, creases gaping in others. 'So, what can I do for you?'

'Not interrupting anything, was I?'

Hubie shrugged. 'Can't a man spend a night alone?'

'A man is never alone,' Mordent said. 'He always has himself with him.'

'What's with the existentialism? You been reading too much literature, Mordent? You need to stick to the pulps.'

'As if you know anything about literature, Hubie. You wouldn't know Jean Genet from Jean Genie.'

Hubie shrugged again. 'Anyway, as I say, what brings you here?'

It was then that Mordent realised he wasn't sure. To say he needed someone to talk to would have seemed trite. Instead, he said: 'I ran into one of those women Reflective Tony was contacting in prison.'

Hubie's smile was just two train stops short of lascivious. 'Ran into, or ploughed into?'

'Use your imagination. I'm sure you will later.'

'And?'

'And I'm finding my moral compass has shifted.'

Hubie laughed. 'Can't say I knew you had one. Nevertheless, this calls for a drink.' He opened his desk cabinet and brought out a bottle of bourbon, two thirds full. He held it up to the light. 'Looks golden, doesn't it? Just like honey. How appropriate for someone who's fallen into the honey trap.' He fished around for some glasses, found one and blew into it. Poured a shot.

'I'll have another glass, Hubie.'

'So you *do* have standards.' Hubie stood and looked around. Picked up a glass from the windowsill – dried watermarks etched the sides – and entered the tiny kitchen on the left. Mordent heard the sound of the glass being washed. Didn't want to envisage the state of the cleaning product being used. Decided to risk it for the alcohol blast.

'So.' Hubie filled Mordent's glass and handed it to him. The outside was wet. 'Here's to fallen women.'

'To fallen women,' echoed Mordent, although he wasn't keen on the toast.

Women were there to be used and abused. Theoretically, at least. It didn't have to be a one-sided or mutually exclusive partnership. Dames were required to be as malicious and manipulative as males. Broads were there to be smacked around. Mordent recalled a judge once telling him you couldn't legislate for a woman who was prepared to be knocked about. He had done some of that knocking about himself. Wouldn't admit it, except in the wee small hours. And might not have been proud of it: but it was part of his make-up. That hard edge of noir that ran round his psyche like the silver lining delineating a cloud in a photonegative image.

But that was only how it *should* be. How it was portrayed in the various forms of media. Reality told him otherwise. A woman was as complex as a Chinese tangram puzzle. She might contain dames, broads, little girls, her own mother. What face she showed depended on which way you turned her. Fallen women, in Mordent's experience, fell only to be caught.

Hubie was licking his lips in a way that Mordent found disconcerting.

'If you're waiting for the details,' Mordent said, 'you won't get them.'

'I'm still waiting for the reason you're here. Presumably it's not to celebrate getting laid.'

Mordent sighed. 'I was going to offer you a conundrum. You've got an element of professionalism in your role giving business advice. Neither of us is a doctor flouting a code of conduct by sleeping with patients. But if you were aware of someone who was vulnerable, who had proven herself susceptible to influence, would you go there for the kick, or hang back?'

Hubie steepled his fingers, as though he were in thought. Mordent was well aware there was nothing to think about.

'It would depend on the comedown, wouldn't it?' Hubie said.

'You mean it would depend on whether or not you could get away with it.'

Hubie smiled. 'In my role, I'd be more likely to consider bleeding some of her cash for the horses than entering into a sticky partnership. What can this woman offer you other than her body?'

Mordent thought. 'She's a gateway into an investigation.'

'So you need her onside. And quiet. Lubing her defences could help with that, couldn't it? Until she finds out what you're up to. Once she does that, the steel doors close down. Or worse. She makes a ruckus.'

'I guess she could do that even now.'

'Particularly if you've already parted those curtains and taken a peak as to what's on offer.'

The size of Hubie's smile told Mordent that it might take a

while for him to live it down.

'The other thing,' Hubie said, 'which I'm sure you've given thought to, is Reflective Tony. She's his girl, right?'

'She was; the way I see it. To what extent, I haven't asked.'

'No surprises there.' Hubie poured them another shot, then downed his in one. 'You're in quicksand, Mordent. Each step you make takes you further, but also deeper. You've got to make sure you get to the other side before your head goes under.'

'Tell me about it. Say, Hubie, you ever hear of the Church of Wire?'

'Of Wire? Can't say I have. Why?'

'Let's just say I'm expecting they'll have an interesting congregation.'

'You're expecting? So, entering religion is now on the cards?'

'Religion and cards don't mix. Religion is no sport for a gambler.'

Hubie laughed. 'You know what I say Mordent. Odds are always the same. Fifty-fifty. You'll either win or you won't. There's either a God or there isn't.'

'If that's how you play the horses, then I'm not surprised you're still renting this dump.'

'I'm serious. Another thing: anything is possible given time.'

Mordent downed his bourbon. He could do with another. Perhaps just the one.

'You're full of soundbites this evening, Hubie. I'm expecting to find a spin doctor hiding in your bedroom. Fill this for me.'

The chink of glass on glass confirmed Hubie had done so.

'I'm going to bring something else into the equation. Something you're gonna need to keep quiet. You hear anything about a murder last night?'

Hubie shrugged. 'Was there just the one?'

'There was just the one that you would have heard about. If you've heard about any. Due to the, er, *circumstances*.'

'If you're talking about the corpse under the trees then I don't know anything about it.'

'Is there anything else in relation to that that you don't

know?'

'Well, let me see ...' Hubie steepled his fingers again. Mordent found it an annoying trait. An annoying *new* trait. He wondered where Hubie had picked it up. 'To be honest, I haven't. Kovacs and his department seem to be keeping that under wraps.'

'But it's in the papers, right? All over the news?'

'You could say so. But the details are obscured. Dunno whether you create more rumour that way or less.'

'I guess it could go either way. Fifty-fifty, right?'

'Right,' Hubie grinned. 'You're getting it now. Fifty-fifty.'

21
Sunday Best

Mordent woke with another hangover and only a mild recollection of how he had made it back to his apartment.

Had the dream of Hubie riding a hobbyhorse really been only a dream?

He damn well hoped so.

They had shot a few more glasses and exchanged a few anecdotes. That much was evident. Had it done the trick? Probably. Sometimes he needed more than to drink alone.

He ran a hand over the stubble on his chin. When had he last shaved? As a cop, he had kept certain standards. Even if they fell way short of Kovacs'. But in retirement – if he could call it that – each day tended to roll into one. It wasn't a Sunday, he knew that, but he did need to put on his Sunday best if he was going to church escorting Miss Jessica on his arm.

He hadn't quizzed Jessica further about the Church. It would have been incongruous considering the circumstances of the previous day's encounter. But as he lay in bed he thought about it hard. No pun intended.

He was pulling on a string. That string was attached to other strings. Sooner or later, whatever was at the ends of those strings was going to come together. And – if he thought about it – the result was likely to be incendiary.

Amongst the congregation that evening he might expect to see Jessica, Reflective Tony, the Frame, and – if his hunch was correct – Isabelle Silk. Safety in numbers? Possibly. Relevant to both clients? A slim connection with Tessa Maloney, but almost flying in the face of Silk's instructions. He shrugged, rubbed his stubble again to relieve an itch in his palm. If he was going to stir things, he might as well do it big time.

With time on his mind he glanced at his watch. He might just catch Martens at the mortuary if he was lucky. Picking up his phone he gave him a call.

'Yeh?'

'Nice professional way of answering the phone, Martens.'

'Who is this? Oh wait, don't tell me. Mordent.'

'That's the guy.'

'Bit late for calls.'

'Early, I'd say.'

'I'm just finishing my shift. Got to head home and catch some zees.'

'You should be careful you don't catch anything else, down there in the morgue.'

'Yeh, right. Same old same old. Look, you interrupted me pushing a stiff into the back of my van for some lovey dovey. *Not.* What do you want?'

'Tell me about the note.'

'The note? Yeh, the note. Well, you probably know it anyway. The trees were a big enough giveaway if you were of a mind to find out. The name on the note was Dayton Leroy Rogers.'

'Killer's making it a bit easy for us, isn't he?'

There was a pause. 'Well, yeah, I guess so. If you happen to know your serial killers.'

Mordent smiled. 'And you wouldn't know Jeffrey Dahmer from the Dalai Lama. That's where me and Kovacs step in.'

'Just 'cos I work in the morgue doesn't mean I'm stupid.'

'Did I say I was comparing you to shift workers at a meat factory?'

There was another pause. Then Martens seemed to brighten:

'Hey, you realise Kovacs has being going ape shit over this one? He wants someone to jump on.'

'Plenty of options where you are.'

'Can it, Mordent. That joke's going stale. And you can let that one pass too. I'm just saying, he reckons when this blows it'll blow. Papers have got a sniff, but only because he fed them the smell. They're holding back out of a sense of public duty.' He laughed.

'So what more can you give me? Same manner of death as the Rogers killings. I've heard that much.'

'Well, there's a bit more to it. She was tarted up before she was killed. I mean, it's been disclosed she once worked as a prostitute, but that was many years ago. Certainly not now. From our investigations here at the morgue, her make-up was applied with a shaky hand. Under duress. Overly decorative. The clothes she was wearing don't appear to have been her own. The skirt is one size too tight. We think he dressed her up so she fit the role. Once she was dressed, he killed her.'

'And where would that have been?'

'Not where we found her, that's for sure. Not enough blood.'

'But that blood's gotta be somewhere, right?'

'Right. Finding it, though, well, that's another matter.'

Mordent scratched his palm with his stubble again. What did an itchy palm signify? Coming into money? Pregnancy? But then didn't scratching the palm negate the fortune? Maybe it depended which hand. Either way, it wasn't the pregnancy.

'You got anything else for me?'

'Nope. Not that I can think of. You got anything for me?'

Mordent thought. 'I got a joke.'

'It'll be one I've heard.'

'Well, hear me out. It's an Irish joke. You got any Irish in you, Marten's?'

'Not to my knowledge.'

'Here it is then. A gift from me. Paddy dies in a fire and is burnt up bad. The morgue needs identification so his two best friends, Seamus and Sean, are sent for. They go in and the mortician pulls back the sheet. The stiff's's burnt so bad they can't identify him, so the friends both suggest he's rolled over. The mortician shrugs, but does it anyway. Seamus looks and says, "Nope, it ain't Paddy." Sean agrees. This puzzles the mortician, so he asks them how they know. "Well," Sean says, "Paddy had two arseholes." "What, he had two arseholes?" says the mortician. "Yup," says Seamus. "Everyone knows he had two arseholes. Every time we went into town, people would say, 'Here comes Paddy with them two arseholes.'"

'That's not funny, Mordent. Besides, I heard it before.'

'I guess it's about as funny as being dobbed in for what you once did. Right? Any more bodies coming into that morgue with notes attached, I wanna know. Straightaway. Not a day later.'

Mordent hung up. It always paid to keep Martens on his toes. And being on his toes was best for tiptoeing around looking for information.

Was it that time already? He got up, shaved and made breakfast. Eggs over easy.

He'd been to his office, shuffled a few e-mails, opened and closed a drawer containing a bottle of bourbon, considered heading down to Morgan's Bar, ordered a pastrami sandwich that now sat curling on the edge of his desk, stood at the window, listened for the click-clack of agency girl heels in the corridor, and plucked out three nostril hairs before he decided that he might as well be at home.

An influx of cash was a requirement, and at the forefront of his mind. He couldn't lean on Bernard Maloney, and Isabelle's second injection of funds wouldn't be coming through until he'd pinned something definitive on Tony. While that might be coming to a head that evening, two unopened bills sat on his desk where he had placed them that morning.

They had lain there while he shuffled the e-mails, opened and closed the drawer, didn't go to Morgan's Bar or eat that sandwich. They had burned into his back as he had stood by the window, agitated his mind as he had listened for the agency girls, and accentuated the pain as he had removed those nose hairs. He didn't need to open them; he knew what they were. One: a reminder about the rent for his office. Two: utilities.

He was also pretty sure that any money he did receive from Maloney or Silk wouldn't cover them.

Thing was: you couldn't just create a client.

At one point he found himself steepling his fingers together, and he shook them apart in a frenzy. Then he remembered creating a church from his hands when he was a kid. Tried to do it again. On the fifth attempt, not only had he succeeded, but he had recalled the accompanying rhyme. *Here's the church, here's the steeple, look inside, see all the people.*

Surely there were better things he could do.

Religion was a subterfuge. His feelings about the coming evening were mixed. His curiosity had been piqued beyond the necessities of the case. It could get messy. Things tended to get messy when he was involved. He could make the simplest things difficult.

Should there be a God, he imagined hordes of the dead in Heaven all facing that deity and pointing accusing fingers.

He remembered a quote from Woody Allen's *Annie Hall*. About life being full of misery, pain and tremendous suffering, and over much too quickly. Stan Laurel had also mistakenly said *Life's not short enough*, in *Sons of the Desert*. Things like that played on his mind: mankind being preoccupied with death yet doing nothing except talk about it. Even given hard, fatal realities, death was often personified or glamorised, or life became the focus instead. Take any funeral: the service was a celebration of a life, not the *black, empty nothingness* – to quote Allen again – that awaited them all.

He couldn't imagine there would be anything said at the meeting of the Church of Wire to persuade him otherwise.

He exhaled, long and low. It was depressing. This waiting for something to happen. Even when he was busy, when work pressed down upon him like an anvil, when his mind was distracted and strayed from the inevitability of his demise, he was always just waiting for something to happen.

Waiting.

For.

Something.

To.

Happen.

Had there been a God, at those thoughts his telephone would have rung or there'd have been a knock at the door. But instead he just continued, waiting for that something to happen. Just like the Sundays in his youth when the hours had stretched away and there had been nothing he was allowed to do to fill them. It hadn't been for the best.

22
Lights! Camel! Action!

Night had shouldered its way past day like a bouncer by the time Mordent left his office. He had fallen asleep in his chair; woken feeling attacked. His back ached, and his foot had become twisted under one of the chair legs. Awaking had spun the swivel, furthering that twist. He had extricated himself with difficulty, like a lover easing from a sleeping partner, then hobbled down to his vehicle, launching into traffic knowing he might be unfit to drive. Yet doing so cocooned by the belief that he was invincible and nothing could happen to him.

The evening was cold and dry. The dark populated with lights both static and in motion, buildings and cars co-operating in colour to stave off the edges of the night. Mordent recalled a water light show he had seen as a child, synchronised jets of water flashing red, white and blue in a star-spangled display. It had moved him, deep down, the water almost personified. His palms had hurt with the clapping as the final jets died down. But that was a long time ago, and magic moments were now few and far between. In fact, he couldn't remember the last time he had heard applause, never mind given it.

No doubt there would be some applause in church. They enjoyed that happy clappy stuff.

He needed to return to his apartment before hitching up with Jessica. A shower was on the cards. Traffic was light. It was Thursday, that post-midweek evening when nine-to-fivers could almost sniff the weekend, but for him meant no more than any other day. He recalled an insurance salesman once telling him that Thursdays were statistically the worst day for making sales; that, in all honesty, it would be pointless even attempting those calls. But then what did he know? Mordent had spent that day interviewing him over a desk, questioning why a dead body had been in the trunk of his car.

Looking at all the trunks around him, Mordent wondered over the possibility of any of them containing bodies, decided that he didn't need to care. He eased his car amongst the others, parked when he reached his apartment, and within the interstices of consecutive movements found himself in the shower with water cascading over his body, into each fold and crevice, his eyes squeezed tight and his ankle still throbbing, only slightly eased by the warmth.

Another time slip and he was back in his car, conservatively dressed in his suit and hat, his gun nudging his fourth rib tight against his body. A freshly-pressed shirt matched the cleanliness of his skin. He wondered how clean both would be by evening's end.

He waited for Jessica at kerbside. She fairly skipped her way down the steps of her brownstone. She wore a white, '50s rock 'n' roll dress, patterned with large red cherries and green stalks. She had her hair up in a bouffant. A lime green handbag hung off the crook of her arm. She looked incongruous for church, but Mordent wasn't surprised. He hadn't expected this to be a run-of-the-mill gathering, and it seemed he wouldn't be disappointed.

He was leant against the hood of his car, and she bent him further backwards with her kiss. Slipping a tissue out of her bag, she wiped lipstick from one side of his smile. 'My apologies, Mr Mordent. I'm all fresh.'

'All dressed up with somewhere to go?'

'That's right.' She clutched his hand. 'Excited?'

'Should I be?'

She smiled. 'I think so, Mr Mordent. I think so.'

While he drove she placed her hand on his knee.

They ducked and dived through traffic. Mordent had checked out the address on the internet before he left. That evening's meeting was to be in a warehouse near the docks that had previously held art exhibitions. He quizzed Jessica as they drove.

'I've been to five or six meetings, Mr Mordent, and they have all been in different locations. When you're celebrating the expansiveness of the Lord you don't want to restrict yourself to one building. Look around you: signs of his work are everywhere. It is *everywhere*, therefore, that we should rejoice.'

Mordent knew he would become less keen on the evening and his choice of chaperone whenever the words 'Lord' and 'rejoice' were used next to one another.

'You're still not gonna fill me in on what the big deal is with this Church?'

'Not until we get there.' She was beaming, her teeth not as white as they needed to be set against the redness of her lipstick. 'I'm sure you'll be converted. I could almost guarantee it.'

Mordent was far more likely to bet on one of Hubie's horses than on conversion to the faith, but he kept quiet and focused on the road.

It was a cool, dry night. He was surprised Jessica wasn't cold, but he said nothing about it, just as he did nothing about her hand on his knee. As though she were a puppeteer, her fingers pulled strings inside him. The slightest graze reminded him of his confused feelings, but also the embarrassment of the unreciprocated sex. Car taillights crisscrossed his vision as traffic changed lanes. They remained in silence for a while, the dark enveloping them, cocooning them, expectant of the relationship to blossom.

Jessica was the first to speak.

'I'm not sure what you think of me. Not really. Not deep down. But look out of the window and tell me what you see.'

Mordent glanced left and right. 'Cars. Pedestrians. Buildings. The dark.'

'Look again, Mr Mordent. And use your imagination.'

He took another look. Added detail: 'I can name the make of

each and every one of those cars, should you wish. I can describe each of the pedestrians. I can name the buildings, describe the shops and their contents. The dark will remain the dark.'

'But there's more, Mr Mordent.' She extended a finger toward the windscreen. 'Every occupant of every car, everyone in those buildings, every pedestrian, they all inhabit their own individual lives. There will be some overlap, but each is independent of all the others. When you take just one of those lives and delve into all the details, the personal relationships, the effects of their work, their ancestral history, their future history ... why isn't that just impossible to conceive? And there are more of them, more than just one, or two or twenty or fifteen-hundred. Do you know the estimate of the world's population? It's approaching seven billion people. Just think, Mr Mordent, *seven billion* individuals with separate yet interlocking lives. How can that be?'

Mordent grunted. 'It just is.'

'No. It can't be. It can't be possible, can it, because we can't imagine it. Therefore it just *can't* be.'

'But still, it is.'

'You will see.'

Mordent braked as the car in front broke, as did the car ahead of them both. A whole chain of braking cars affecting each other.

'You don't know what's ahead,' Jessica said. 'You're imagining a red light, or maybe an accident, or maybe just the accumulation of traffic. You can only imagine it, because by the time you get to where the first car stopped, the reason will no longer be there. Have you ever been on the freeway when there are bottlenecks, huge delays? The traffic crawls. Almost at a standstill. Suddenly, the whole expanse opens up and the clogged traffic disappears. Well, that's what the Church of Wire is to me. It clears up everything, stops me from worrying. Because the reasons for why we are here aren't here. We can stop looking for something that doesn't exist.'

'I'm not sure that I'm following.'

'It doesn't matter. You will see for yourself, and you'll take something from it, I guarantee. It might be different from how I see it. In fact, it almost certainly will be.'

'Who's running this show?'

'There's a Mr Francisco Carmide who conducts many of the services. But I'm letting this run away from me. I made a promise not to tell you more than you already know.' She stopped speaking, looked silently out of her passenger window.

'Who made you promise not to tell me anything?'

She sighed. 'Not just *you*, Mr Mordent. Anyone. *Anyone* who asks me these kinds of questions.'

The traffic thinned ahead. Mordent cruised for two blocks then headed left down toward the docks. He'd had an unpleasant experience there once. Actually, twice. The first time he'd taken a swim with concrete blocks as buoyancy aids, the second time he'd been chasing a composite missing person and ended up trapped with five or six women, one of whom held a grudge. Those weren't good memories. He wondered if he'd bump into the Frame that evening. It wouldn't be a happy coincidence.

But this side of the docks had undergone renovation since he had last been there. Old warehouses opened front-side, revealing fancy bars lit by glittering faux gas lanterns and buzzing with chit-chat from the young, moneyed and beautiful. Two art galleries were positioned side by side, one of them bearing a banner stating *C.O.W.*. Mordent wondered at the wisdom of the abbreviation. A parking lot serviced several of these establishments, and it was close to full. He swung inside, found a vacant spot and switched off his engine. Then he turned to face Jessica.

'I might know a few of the clientele here tonight. If you want a lift home, stick with me, even if what I say or do distresses you.'

'Oh.' Her lipsticked mouth might have held a hula-hoop.

'Nothing to worry about, I'm sure.' He patted her knee, experienced a frisson of desire that poked his insides.

Her smile belied her worry. 'Okay, Mr Mordent. But

remember you're amongst friends here. Shall we go?'

He nodded, got out of the vehicle, then realised she was waiting for him to be a gentleman. He ran around the front – wanting her to extend her smile, curiously desiring to impress her – and pulled open her door.

'Thank you,' she said. 'I've always relied on the comfort of strangers.'

Mordent knew the reference. Decided to ignore it. She might be the streetcar he desired, but they were on the waterfront, after all. Besides, he might have some method acting to do that evening, particularly if he was right and Reflective Tony was in attendance. He didn't rely on the comfort of strangers himself. His comforter sat in a holster under his left armpit. It was cleaned and loaded and – if necessary – ready for action.

Much – if he thought about it – like himself.

And possibly – if he thought further – like Jessica.

She extended her arm and he took it. They walked together like a familiar couple; although, with the few years between them, and his '40s attire coupled with her '50s get-up, they made a very *odd* couple. A few others were filtering ahead of them into the gallery where the Church of Wire was holding its meeting. The clientele were mixed. Male, female, singles, couples, some same sex; old, young, rich and poor. It seemed the church was broad. If there was anything linking any of them it was that none of them looked like they were actually going to church. Which – for Mordent – could only be a good thing.

The frontage to the gallery was glass, but visibility of the interior from the street was obstructed by a large sheet of plasterboard placed immediately beyond the doors. Mordent and Jessica entered and walked around the right-hand side of the plasterboard. Any preconceptions that Mordent had about the Church of Wire were immediately subverted.

The space inside the warehouse extended back at least a hundred feet. Apart from several dozen participants, the floor space was clear until about half-way down the structure. From where he stood, Mordent thought he could see the outline of a camel, however his view was obscured both by people and by the dull lighting.

There were no seats, no pews. Nothing on the walls – no stained glass or slogans. Beyond the camel silhouette there was a splash of red that he couldn't quite make out, and beyond that there seemed to be a rostrum from which he imagined the service would be given. If there was to be a service.

He glanced left and right. While there was an usher showing people to the back of the auditorium, there were no signs of any heavies. Certainly no sign of the Frame or Reflective Tony. Nor of Isabelle Silk.

They walked forward as others entered through the door behind them. Jessica's grip on Mordent's arm tightened. 'Exciting, isn't it?' she breathed. He wasn't sure he could concur.

The further they walked toward the camel, the more obvious it was what it was. Steps rose either side of it, and people were queuing to go up and down, stooping at the top before descending. The camel had one hump. Mordent couldn't remember if that meant it was Bactrian or Arabian. Wasn't an Arabian called a dromedary? He couldn't rely on recollections of Sinbad movies. In fact, the camel's posture resembled that pictured on a packet of cigarettes. It was then that an inkling of what he might be about to see filtered into his mind. He had read of an exhibition of the work of Salvador Dali somewhere in Spain, maybe at Dali's own museum. Wasn't there a work of art that could be viewed only by looking through a distorted mirror hung underneath a plastic camel? He couldn't recall the details, but this seemed similar enough for there to be more connection than coincidence.

Curiouser and curiouser.

Of course the camel wasn't real. But it wasn't plastic either. At first Mordent thought it might be stuffed, but as they got closer he realised it was a child's toy. Perhaps a big child's toy, but a toy all the same.

'What is that?' he couldn't help but ask Jessica.

'It could be anything,' she said. 'I haven't seen it before. They like to surprise us.'

The crowd moved in an orderly fashion, and they joined the

queue to the steps. As they ascended, it became possible to see beyond the camel. Two photographs hung on the back wall, either side of the rostrum. Before the rostrum a pale pink sofa was unoccupied. None of it seemed to make sense.

As he reached the camel on top of the steps, Mordent had to bend his head to look at the same scene through an oval mirror. The images resolved themselves, with the rostrum becoming a nose, the paintings eyes and the sofa lips. He shrugged and moved away, hearing Jessica gasp in awe behind him. As they descended from the camel they were directed to a space between it and the sofa. Chairs had been set out, so they sat and waited.

The place filled up. Jessica started talking animatedly to the woman next to them. Mordent didn't bother to listen.

There was a reason for the camel that he was yet to understand. It bugged him. As the numbers increased, so did the chatter, but like any kind of hubbub it was background noise and nothing discernible. He looked around once more for either Tony or Isabelle, but neither was in sight. He was seated sufficiently far back from the rostrum and the lights on the audience were dim enough for him not to be noticed should either of them appear on stage. By the time the chatter died down and became replaced by applause as a tall man walked toward the sofa, Mordent estimated there were between one and two hundred members of the congregation of the Church of Wire. He also realised the face of the man on stage resembled the one he had viewed from under the dromedary. The composite image of lips, rostrum and eyes was evident.

The man must have been pushing six feet plus. He was dressed in a black suit, white shirt, black tie. He could have passed for a Mormon, and Mordent wondered if the churches were linked. No hair featured on his head, and the scalp was spattered with liver spots. Age? Probably early seventies. Yet there was a strength to be had, an urgency that emanated from him, that was undeniable and belied his years. From Mordent's distance his eyes seemed blue, and no doubt they sparkled. His lips, like the sofa, were thin. His skin was as tanned as if he were of Mediterranean origin, or Mexican, but Mordent suspected the former.

'That's Mr Francisco Carmide,' Jessica whispered. Mordent nodded.

The man reclined on the sofa, to yet more – unfathomable - applause. Then he stood again and approached the rostrum. As the lights around them dimmed, Jessica reached out for Mordent's hand. He gave it a squeeze just so she knew he was paying attention. As he did so he noticed movement behind the curtain at the edge of the stage. A face came into view and, despite the low lighting, Mordent recognised Ms Isabelle Silk. She had on a suit similar to that worn by the man, who raised his hands to quieten the applause as she walked into full view and lay on the sofa in front of him.

As the man spoke, Mordent noticed Isabelle close her eyes. She slept.

23
The Salamander of Doubt

'Friends, newcomers and subversives. Welcome to the Church of Wire.'

Francisco's smile was wide and bright. Mordent had trouble identifying whether it was true or false.

'Some of you will have realised that this evening there is a Salvador Dali theme. Perhaps by way of initiation for those new who are present, it might be pertinent to quote from the self-appointed genius himself.'

Francisco pulled some papers from his inside jacket pocket. Cleared his throat. '"One day it will have to be officially admitted that what we have christened reality is an even greater illusion than the world of dreams."

'Now, I'm not professing that Dali would have been interested in our little Church, but acknowledging the world of dreams would be an intrinsic requirement for admission. I'd like to reiterate our manifesto: *Celebrate God's Seventh Day Creation!* We all know from the Bible that God created the world in six days and then he rested. But all of you regulars – and now our newcomers – will realise that here at the Church of Wire we *also* believe that He *created* on the seventh day. That He created when He was resting, through His *dreams*.

'For some of you this will be a new interpretation of the Bible. For those who find it too radical, you may go. For those who remain, we would like you to join us in celebrating the spiritual nature of the insane, of the gossamer-thin reality of dreams, of the interstices in-between, and of the knowledge that all is never quite what it seems.

'And here I draw your attention to the dromedary and our little tableaux this evening. Again, I will read from a work on Dali about the subject: "Dali's fetishisation of the lips would culminate in the artwork *Face of Mae West (Useable As A Surrealist Apartment)*, which in turn gave rise to the remarkable Mae West-lips sofa, and finally to the Mae West Hall in the Dali-Theatre Museum in Figueras, the most elaborate of Dali's face-to-space dreams-come-true. In the Mae West Hall the installation of a lip-shaped sofa, paired with giant nostrils and two retouched pointillist views of Paris, is resolved into a *trompe l'oeil* face only when the visitor ascends a flight of steps, stoops underneath a plastic dromedary appropriated from the Camel cigarette company, and gazes through a reductive lens."

'As you will see. Through the support of some of our student artists at the Church of Wire, we have recreated this illusion, albeit with myself instead of Mae West as the subject. I hope you don't think this egotistical of me; it was their idea, after all.

'However, my point is that the bland acceptance of what is in front of our eyes is not what the Lord meant when he wanted us to be sheep. In some respects, he might wish us to *become* sheep. In other respects it might be the opposite. You see, everything and nothing are true simultaneously.'

There was a ripple of applause throughout the audience. Mordent couldn't quite understand why. He followed the thread, that much was clear, but as to how it might impact on each and every one of them he was mystified. He guessed that new doctrines had to be bled from something, even stone. If nothing else, Francisco was entertaining, but even then Mordent didn't want the evening to drag. Isabelle still seemed to be sleeping. From her posture on the sofa, Mordent could have sworn that she was pregnant.

Francisco raised his arms again, to quieten the crowd. 'One final quote from Dali before we leave him: "Give me two hours

166

a day of activity, and I'll take the other 22 in dreams."

'Now, for a song ...'

The curtain backdrop behind him fell and a band started playing a song that – from the chorus – Mordent assumed was 'Walking on Sunshine'. The entire congregation got to their feet and in the limited space began dancing to the music. Mordent recognised a couple of the band members from those he had ejected from Morgan's Bar. Jessica cajoled him along, but at best Mordent's dancing amounted to shuffling from one foot to the other, like a child wanting the toilet but adamant not to admit it, and he restricted his movements to being jostled by the others. Jessica pouted and swung herself around, taking the hands of the woman next to her. Mordent scanned the room once more, trying without success to locate Reflective Tony. Meanwhile, Isabelle slept on.

When the music finished, Francisco regained the audience's attention.

'Friends, newcomers and subversives. Welcome back to the Church of Wire.'

Mordent wondered if Francisco had once been a TV evangelist. The sensation was that of returning from an ad break.

'Surrealism in all its forms is not something that we embrace, yet today's display is simply an example of what we can do if we use our imagination. Put simply: our manifesto is simple. *Celebrate God's Seventh Day Creation!* What elements of life might have been created through dream? How can we embrace them? How can we banish the salamanders of doubt and strengthen the lions of certainties? These are our goals.

'Other churches hold strict doctrine. We do not. This is a church that we can adapt to each of our own individual circumstances and beliefs. Consider our name: the Church of Wire. Wire is flexible; it can bend, encircle, hold. It is strong, yet supple. It can conduct electricity. It can form sculpture. We didn't choose the name lightly, and yet we might have chosen it at random. Anything and everything is possible.'

Mordent lost interest. The Church of Wire seemed so broad

that it might encompass every conceivable idea and belief. For him, there seemed to be only one reason for this: to create as large a congregation as possible. The more members, the more money. He was sure that either a hat or a silver platter, or – to follow the surrealist theme – the hollowed out underbelly of a frog, would be handed round at the conclusion of the event. Francisco was creating a feel-good factor, but there had to be a hidden agenda. And if Reflective Tony was involved, then it was bound to be sinister.

If he hadn't been hemmed within the congregation, Mordent would have taken his leave to find a toilet and snout about the warehouse. Maybe there would be nothing. This wasn't a headquarters, just a public-facing front. Temporary at that. He imagined the gallery itself would be independently owned.

Francisco had finished whatever sermon he was hoping to give and the band played again. Mordent recognised it as 'I'm A Believer'. He yawned, failed to put a hand over his mouth, and got a dig in the ribs from Jessica as a result. He wondered if he would be invited back into her apartment later. Wondered if he wanted to be. Decided it would be a decision made of the moment – perhaps attributable to the principles of the Church of Wire. At that thought, a half-smile crept across his face – but it was like a shadow across the sun.

Once again, following the cessation of the music, Francisco Carmide repeated his greeting: 'Friends, newcomers and subversives. Welcome back to the Church of Wire.'

Mordent believed subversion no longer existed. Everything taboo had already been absorbed into the mainstream. It was just a buzzword that would appeal to certain members of society, even if society as a whole rejected it as a concept.

'For the final part of this evening's service I wish to draw your attention to our lady sleeping on my lips: Miss Isabelle Silk.' Francisco gesticulated to her prone form. The audience roared their approval. 'Isabelle is a living example of creation: both of herself and in herself. For the duration of this service, Isabelle has been dreaming, and those dreams are both her creations and the creations of our Lord. Many of you might articulate meaning into dreams. Here at the Church of Wire we believe they have no meaning, but are simply the purest thoughts of God; undistilled and untainted from even His universal plan. In a moment, we shall wake her, and discover her creations.

'Some of you, quite rightly, might believe us to be shamans. Our beliefs an amalgamation of religion, surrealism and the teachings of Freud. Previously I have been attacked for pronouncing principles of the ego, the superego and the id, for equating them to the Christian doctrine of the Trinity: that of the Father, the Son and the Holy Ghost. I do not renounce those principles. God is in all of us and all of us are in God.

'According to the Christian doctrine, God exists as three persons but is one God. These persons are distinct, yet coexist in unity and are co-equal, co-eternal and consubstantial. I see no difference between this Holy Trinity and that expounded by Freud, of the ego, the superego and the id. We are, therefore, and in considerable brief, each individually equal to God. We each have the power of creation, of determining our paths, thus proving that our paths are not predetermined. Our dreams are an integral part of this process. They are unfettered, unconstrained by the shackles that the umbrella of society proposes, and – just as God's dreams – are the purest creation we can obtain. It is a crime not to embrace these dreams, to run with them, to let them dance with us, to embroil us within their meaning. Yet also to remember that they have no meaning other than for us to follow them. To revert to our true selves as human beings, as we would be in the wild, before we became domesticated. In short, the primal urge to return to the Garden of Eden.'

Mordent leant back in his seat, closed his eyes. In some respects, he understood what Francisco was saying. That if mankind followed its subconscious it might lead a purer life. He could equate that to *instinct*. Yet he could also equate it to anarchy. Nevertheless, despite grains of truth, he also found much of what Francisco was spouting to be contradictory nonsense. There was theory, there was exposition, but there was nothing concrete. It was a speech to inspire people without understanding. Most would leave the event feeling empowered, on a high, but Francisco's words were vacuous. You couldn't escape society or the rules it imposed. As a religion, a doctrine, a set of principles, or as a way of living, the Church of Wire was ineffective. But for those who craved guidance, who needed a placebo for something they might then control, then like all the other religions, it offered hope in an unforgiving world. Harmless, for sure; but again Mordent was drawn to what must be the underlying impetus for the Church's creation. Where was the money being made, and for what purpose?

Francisco continued: 'Let us wake our sleeping beauty and see what gems she has.'

It crossed Mordent's mind that Isabelle had been drugged, probably willingly. It would have taken a lot to sleep through the proceedings. He had kept a close eye on her and it hadn't appeared to be faked.

From the wings walked a second camel, essentially one suit and two men. It meandered its way across to the sofa, and with one front hoof lifted, gently tapped Isabelle on the shoulder. Twice, then three times. Her eyelids fluttered. She stifled a yawn. Then she sat, straight up, in the centre of the lips. Mordent noticed a small microphone pinned to the lapel of her suit. In a low voice, a soft voice, contrary to his previous experience of her, she began to relate a dream.

'I was in a supermarket, but all of the labels of the tins on the shelves had been removed. I was looking for something I can no longer remember. Several purchases were made. At my home – which wasn't really my home – I opened the contents. Some were fish, some were foul. Some were sticks of chalk. I remember putting a stick of chalk in my mouth, and although it was white it tasted of liquorice.

'Then I was outside. I was naked, running through woodland. I remember looking at the leaves and twigs on the ground and realising that, although I was barefoot, the soles of my feet felt nothing.

'Finally, I heard music. The dreaming felt lucid. I could hear myself singing along to "I'm A Believer" but my lips didn't move. The sofa lips spoke for me. I could hear Francisco speaking but I couldn't wake. I no longer remember his words. Were they indeed the words that he spoke to all of you, or were they alternatives created by my imagination? I suspect I shall never know.'

She stopped speaking, bowed her head. There was a ripple of applause. Mordent wasn't sure if this was out of respect or confusion. Even so, he realised, no-one had left the congregation throughout the entirety of the service. Like most religions, the Church of Wire seemed to be preaching to the converted.

Francisco spoke again. 'We must be wary not to interpret her dreams. They are pure creations, without needing to be fixed to reality. Some might say that the absence of labels on the tins refers to consumer confusion, others that the strangeness of contents relates to the subversion of expectation. Some could interpret Ms Silk's nudity as a return to the wild, others that her lack of physical feeling equates to being distanced from that experience. Some could determine that the hearing of our song confirms her belief in the Church, others that the possible mishearing of my speech means that she is open to the babble of others. But none of this would reflect Isabelle's direct experience, which is that before she slept she did not have these creations, and that these creations are solely the product of her imagination; that she created – just as did our Lord – while she slept.

'To conclude our evening, therefore, another song.'

Mordent shrugged and stood with the others. For him, the dreams were as meaningless as the entirety of life. Francisco seemed to be playing his cards far from his chest. To preach that there was no meaning, and yet then to proffer suggestions of meaning, was once again contradictory. There was little about the Church of Wire that might be pinned down. But what was evident, as the crowd sang and danced to the Rolling Stones' 'Start Me Up', was the physical nature of the collection tin being passed from congregation member to congregation member. Mordent couldn't discern any loose change being deposited;

notes held sway.

He watched Jessica search in her bag, felt tempted to stay her hand. But there was a radiant expression on her face that he didn't want to dispel, that he might benefit from later that evening. As for himself, he reached into his pockets and found the leaflet for the Church itself. He folded it out of sight, and slipped it through the slot as the tin passed by. It was easier than a camel entering heaven through the eye of a needle. If the Church of Wire wanted to mix their metaphors then that was a bandwagon he was content to jump upon.

The song ended. Francisco again raised his hands, and the faithful became quiet. 'Go in peace,' he said.

He left the rostrum and returned to the sofa, where he sat next to Isabelle and took her hand in his. It was a friendly gesture, without a suggestion of romanticism. The crowd began to disperse, and once more they were led up the steps to the belly of the dromedary and down again. Mordent hoped to catch Isabelle's eye as he left the seating area, but her gaze remained at her feet. At the top of the steps he crouched and looked through the lens. The couple looked like two piercings on Francisco's lips, or – perhaps more pertinently – like ants.

24

A Warm Embrace In The Cold Night Air

As they left the gallery, Jessica pressed her body against his, walked him over to stand by the river and pulled herself toward him in a kiss.

Her lipstick had faded during the ninety-minute service, but he could taste its chemical residue over the coolness of her skin. Desire ignited. He held her close for more. Their tongues engaged, she pressed into him hard and fast, flutterings of adrenalin coursed through his body. The softness of her folds, the proximity of her warmth, the femininity of her perfume: all these factors combined to subvert his senses, to pull the rug out from underneath him, to pump the button of manhood that was plugged into the concept of evolution.

They separated. Slowly.

Jessica raised a hand to her head and held it, as if to stop it from blowing away into the river. Mordent felt light-headed too.

'Oh my,' she said, resonating with her Southern Belle persona. 'That was unexpected.'

It was engineered, thought Mordent, but wasn't cruel enough to suggest it.

Beyond them, the river rolled by in an inky blackness,

accentuated by the night and populated in places by the coloured lights of riverboats and reflections from the quay. Sounds of the congregation carried over the water – an indistinguishable amalgamation of noise. The other waterfront bars were fit to bursting. Some of the churchgoers disappeared into them, proving that this religion wasn't averse to having its ideas lubricated by alcohol. Mordent felt himself swaying – whether in the light breeze or as an aftereffect of the kiss he couldn't be sure. There was something wanton about Jessica that somehow gave him a desire to mingle with her, even to make her happy; but he also knew it was dangerous, she was a loose cannon, the Jessica she projected was hiding a basic, fragile need. Getting involved would be far easier then extricating himself. And Mordent knew as surely as he believed the Church of Wire to be a scam that it wouldn't be long before extrication became essential.

'So,' she continued. 'What did you think?'

'About the kiss or the Church?'

'The Church, idiot.' The rebuke was friendly, cheeky.

'I think it's more important what *you* think,' Mordent said. He leant against the wall, both to avoid the river and the reminder of its depths and to focus on the entrance to the gallery. Lights were still on inside, and although the plasterboard blocked the view, its square haloed the light around the sides.

'I thought it was wonderful. Life-affirming.'

'Understood. But did any of it make sense?'

'Why, that's the magic. It doesn't have to make sense. But it does make you feel wonderful.'

'Like love?' Mordent felt like biting down on his tongue, but the words had escaped him. He realised Jessica would take it specifically, rather than generally, as intended.

'Yes,' she said, with a waver in her voice. 'Yes, like love.'

Over her shoulder Mordent saw Reflective Tony leave the gallery. He seemed to be alone. The flare of a match momentarily illuminated his face, replaced by a single-eyed burn and the ghostly exhalation of smoke.

He grabbed Jessica's shoulders, turned her around.

There was a gasp.

He kept his voice low. 'You recognise him?'

'Yes, yes I do.'

Mordent could tell from her intonation that her high was coming down fast. 'He broke your heart, didn't he?'

She nodded. His hands were still on her shoulders and he felt them tense. Looking down, he saw her fingers clench into fists.

'That's why I'm here,' Mordent said, voicing a partial truth. 'To make sure what he did to you he doesn't do to others.'

Jessica turned to him, her eyes bright. 'But it wasn't anything illegal,' she said. 'He was just a rat.'

Mordent shrugged. 'Do you want him to be caught like a rat? Or not.'

'I ... I don't know.'

'It still hurts, doesn't it?'

'Why yes, it does. Of course it does. But I'm away from him now. That deception, well, it led to nothing. And thankfully so. I would rather not be involved, Mr Mordent, to tell you the truth. Live and let live. Let things go. That sort of thing.'

Mordent pressed. 'But it led you here, didn't it? He was an advocate for the Church of Wire. Doesn't that strike you as strange?'

She hugged herself through her dress, her arms wrapped around. 'I would rather not think about it.'

Tony hadn't seen them. He flicked the stub of his cigarette skywards, where it arced like a substandard firework. Isabelle appeared silhouetted in the doorway. Tony took her arm and led her into the parking lot. Mordent followed them as far as his vision would allow. He saw them lean back against a vehicle, Isabelle's mouth on Tony's, more of a reaction than an action. Then they continued to walk out of sight.

He imagined their progress in his mind's eye. The weaving in and out of cars. The finding of keys. The turn of the ignition. At the back of the lot, twin headlights flared. The car followed a half-square pattern then came fully into view, turned onto the highway and headed into the depths of the city.

'Poor her,' Jessica whispered.

'Have you spoken to her?'

'Never. But she's been at all the meetings. I haven't seen her with *him* before. But she's pregnant, isn't she? Did you see that?'

'I had a hunch.'

They continued watching the lot, as though it might reveal more answers than it already had. Mordent's eyes flicked back to the gallery. Francisco was leaving. There was a girl on his arm who couldn't have been much more than twenty. She was leaning into him familiarly. Short bobbed black hair, pale white face, a smattering of make-up, and a red and gold dress that reached as far as her knees. Mordent guessed that, unlike most clergy, Francisco practiced what he preached. The girl was a dream in every sense of the word. Although he couldn't imagine that she thought the same of Carmide.

'The Church gives you what you need, doesn't it?' Mordent asked.

Jessica nodded.

Mordent felt for her then. To need so much that it could be satisfied by so little struck him as being painfully poignant. He moved his head toward hers, brushed her lips with his, then abandoned all uncertainty and dived in once more for a kiss.

Maybe it was just the moment, but it seemed the sweetest he had ever had.

25
A Body At Rest

Morning light fell on a tangle of flesh. As the sun rose, it created shadows and illuminations, revealed contours and indentations. A ruck of bedclothes concealed their feet in a knot. Mordent raised one eyelid, lowered it. Jessica's breathing was heavy, half into her pillow. He wondered if he might disengage without disturbance, decided against it. Through the window's magnification he could detect the progress of the sun's glare across his body. Within a few minutes, it was directly on his face.

One of Newton's Laws states that a body at rest will remain so unless an outside force acts upon it. The brilliant glare on his face acted as that force, and with some difficulty he edged his body away from Jessica's, drawing a sigh and mild movement but little else from her sleeping form. He stood with aching limbs, realised his naked body was viewable from the window of the apartment opposite, but felt good enough to leave the curtains open. As an afterthought, before he made his way to the bathroom, he drew a sheet over Jessica.

The floor was bare tile. His feet made a sucking noise as he walked. Shutting the bathroom door enclosed him in a space not much bigger than a toilet on a plane. He sat and discharged himself, rested his eyes. The hum of the refrigerator in the adjoining room added to the illusion of being thirty thousand feet above ground. Even so, he wasn't a member of the mile high club.

He ran through his feelings toward Jessica. Could be sure of nothing other than the Darwinian urge to fuck. Thankfully, the unfortunate intimation of *love* the previous evening seemed to have been forgotten within the heat of the sheets. Their coupling had proved more fruitful than the last time – maybe the moon had been up or the wind had been blowing in the right direction, but for whatever reason they had been syncopated. Not *fruitful* in the conception sense of the word – those precautions had been taken and were secure – but to the extent that they had slept blissfully afterwards, the traces of their lovemaking drying on their skin like glue residues or snail trails.

He stood. Splashed some water on his face. The bathroom mirror had a crack on one side that distorted his features. One direction lent him a scar, another a grin to rival that of the Joker, a further angle split his face and mirrored it back upon itself as though there were a fissure that revealed his future and his past in both directions to infinity.

It was then that he remembered the slightly distended stomach of Ms Isabelle Silk and wondered why it hadn't registered with him that day she had arrived at his office. Jessica was right: she was unquestionably pregnant. It was fairly clear that Tony was the father. And further evident why Ms Silk had engaged his services. Possibly she was also concerned by his links to the Church of Wire, but the reason she hadn't mentioned the organisation directly was that its relevance was tangential, due to her own personal crisis. The organisation had been a coat-hanger to hang the investigation on, but the pregnancy had been the impetus for his assignment.

It was then that he wondered if Isabelle Silk had ever been in jail.

There were a few phone calls he needed to make, a few appointments required.

He headed back into the bedroom. The sun's progress was now illuminating the back wall, as if it served as a cinema screen. Jessica was sitting up in bed, the sheet pulled up to her chin. A lazy smile played on her features. Mordent remembered back to Morgan's Bar, when he had assessed her age at late twenties. He had probably been right. And regardless that she wasn't the most attractive woman, a smile now featured on his lips. It hurt. He was using unfamiliar muscles, and while it felt genuine he remained fundamentally aware that everything would end in tears.

'Why, hello,' she said, with a coyness that betrayed the basic instincts fuelled during the night.

He nodded a response.

'I've been thinking,' she said. 'This business about Tony. Do you need me to help you?'

'You've changed your mind? Because of Ms Silk's pregnancy?'

Jessica nodded. Her eyes were shallow lagoons.

'Not at the moment,' Mordent said. 'Maybe in the future. Tony contacted you in jail, didn't he? No doubt made a lot of promises, subsequently broken. You're hanging onto the Church like a security blanket, either because you genuinely believe in it or because you don't want your memory of him to be entirely burnt. I can understand that. It makes sense. And it may well be that the Church is safe, whether Tony goes down or not. To what extent are you aware of his involvement?'

She blinked. Tear fragments clung like dew to her eyelashes. 'He canvasses. That much I'm aware. I don't really know more than that.'

'You're aware that he's contacted other women who have been in prison.'

She nodded. Wiped away those initial tears. 'I'm crying out of happiness, Mr Mordent. Sometimes happiness can be as unbearable as sadness.'

Mordent leant over the bed and kissed her forehead. Then began pulling on his clothes. 'I'm not even sure he's done anything criminal at all. Try not to worry.'

'It's not him I'm worrying about.'

'Even so. I'll call you later.'

Mordent finished dressing. He kissed Jessica again – a light brush on the mouth – then headed for the door. He was about to pull it closed when she called him back.

'One thing, Mr Mordent, if you don't mind? Your first name, please?'

'Stingray,' he winked, then left.

It was only later he realised that when Jessica had asked if he needed her to help him, she had been querying his intentions as to bedding her, rather than making him an offer. Insecurities obviously ran deep.

Newton had different laws for a body in motion than for one at rest. Every object in a state of motion tends to remain in that state unless an external force is applied to it. Now Mordent was fired up, he felt that he wasn't going to stop. There were people he needed to see, strings that required a tug: Kovacs, Silk, Tony. Probably Francisco Carmide himself. And who would be paying him to do this work? Probably no-one. Which was why he needed to contact Isabelle first and foremost. He made a call to her from his cell as he sat in his car, brusquely fixed an appointment within the hour. Then he headed out into traffic, his senses buzzing, with an overview now obvious within his head and the sure feeling that finally he was headed somewhere.

26
A Serpent Swallowing Its Tail

Mordent stood in his office with his back to the door. He was listening for the *click click* of high heels. Not those striding with determination and purpose to and from the agency further up the corridor, but those hesitant and nervous. Not that Ms Silk was a woman who appeared to have those attributes, but he had dented her veneer when he had previously told her his findings about Tony, and she must know that any further information couldn't be good news.

All it would need would be for her to admit it.

Meanwhile, outside, the rising sun had been obscured by low white clouds that scudded in from the east like grubby polar bears. Their undersides hung heavy with moisture. Mordent was prepared to bet on hail. The crisp cold morning had picked up a wind that battered at his office windows, which had seen better days. His shoulders shivered within his jacket; an involuntary sympathetic shrug for the winter that was on its way.

'So,' a voice said, 'what have you got for me?'

She had entered the room like a panther, like a dreamer. He glanced to her feet: sensible shoes. Her bare legs reached toward a skirt that met them at the knee. It was the antithesis of their previous meeting: black skirt white blouse replaced by white skirt black blouse. Her brunette hair curled on her shoulders like sleeping cats.

'Ms Silk.'

'Mordent.'

He gestured to the chair in front of his desk. 'Sit down.'

'Should I? Need I?'

He shrugged. 'We need to iron out a few issues, Ms Silk.' He glanced at her belly – the pregnancy mound was obvious when you looked for it, even if she was barely four months gone. Still, it was a risk to mention it. 'And perhaps you should rest. A woman in your condition.'

Her hands involuntarily touched her stomach. Any doubts dissolved. He sat first, as though to encourage her. After a moment, she followed.

'Is it so obvious? I thought I was concealing it well.'

'No need to conceal it, is there? Who are you hiding it from?'

'Some women prefer to wait for a scan before revealing their pregnancy, Mordent. Nothing sinister about it.'

'It's not Tony's then?'

Distaste flared across her face, her mouth took on a leaner, harder set. 'I think speculation as to the father of my child is none of your business. That's not what I'm paying you for.'

'No. You hired me to dig the dirt on Tony. I've just been wondering the reason why. If he were the father of your child, that would seem reason enough. And that knowledge would give me a better angle on the information I'm trying to retrieve. From what I saw last night, you two seemed pretty close. Unless I was dreaming.'

'I don't understand. Last night?'

'Following the meeting of your organisation. The Church of Wire. Down at the docks. You both seemed quite chummy in the car park.'

She stood. Her nostrils widened. 'I'm not paying you to spy on me, Mordent. I'm fully aware of my own whereabouts.'

'Calm down. If I'm following Tony and he leads me to you, there's not a lot I can do about it, is there? Now sit down and sit firm.'

Isabelle dithered, but Mordent knew she would relent. There

were questions she needed answering. Even if he didn't have those answers.

She smoothed out her skirt. Again he noticed her, in reflex, touch her stomach. Then she sat.

'So,' she said. 'Now you've satisfied yourself that you have the upper hand, perhaps you would like to share your information with me.'

He acknowledged her annoyance with a nod. Then leant back, the legs of his chair creaking. 'My concerns,' he said, 'relate to Tony Runcorn's involvement with the Church of Wire, which might well impact on his involvement with you. Perhaps you could share with me some information that – if you'd provided it right at the start – might have saved much messing about.'

She sighed. 'You seem to be a competent PI after all, Mordent. Despite my initial doubts.' She allowed a smile. 'I suppose all this is in confidence?' He nodded, but she was already continuing. 'Well, Mr Tony Runcorn approached me in my role as secretary at the Church. It is an … unusual organisation for a religious one. If I kept back a few details before, it was only because I didn't want you to prejudge us. But everything is above board, we're not some kind of cult. What we do require, though, are funds. And Mr Runcorn wished to invest in us. We took that investment and – I must say – are now stronger than ever.

'However, in my role as secretary, I became increasingly concerned as to where that money came from. I investigated a little, and inevitably that led me into closer contact with Tony –'

Mordent interrupted: 'And then he seduced you.'

She flushed, surprisingly. 'Then we became involved,' she said.

'As I said, then he seduced you in order to deflect you. It's not uncommon, Ms Silk. All of us – even you – can be foolish and susceptible to someone with charm. Quite where Tony gets it from I don't know, but he's obviously got something that makes the dames fall over him.'

Isabelle opened her mouth, then closed it again.

'And then you fell pregnant, and that was one fall too many. You hired me because you couldn't make the enquiries yourself, but you didn't give me all the information because you were hoping I wouldn't find anything. Basically, I was hired to *not* find something, and to satisfy your conscience that you had tried. Now I need to know what you want me to do.'

'Pardon?'

'I'm not some kind of public servant with a *do good* agenda nailed to my heart. You pay me, I work. You want this investigation to end, it will. What I'd say for certain, knowing Runcorn's predilection for wooing insecure females, is that that baby you're carrying wasn't created out of love, and you'd be a fool to yourself to believe it. I'd say that baby is tangible proof that he doesn't want you investigating that funding. And I'd say that means the funding is dodgy. Runcorn is known as a small-time crook – I don't know what business concerns he's suggested he might be involved in, but whatever he's told you, it won't have been the truth. Currently, if it does blow wide open, you'll be stood side by side with him. That child might grow up with a mother doing time. And if I crack this case quickly, the actual birth might take place in jail.'

Isabelle's hard veneer cracked. In slow motion Mordent watched the thin line of her mouth distort with the truth. Her face unbalanced, like that of a stroke victim. As he finished his last sentence, her hands fumbled for tissues and she buried her face in them, her body wracked with stifled yet heartfelt sobs.

'As I said,' Mordent continued, 'this can stop now. I don't need to do more than I have done. But then others might come after me. The IRS for example. So I have a suggestion to make, and that's continuing my investigation but keeping you out of it as much as I can. And to do that, I suggest you distance yourself from Tony. Have a lover's spat, split, whatever works for you. But keep your distance, and when he falls you might not fall with him.'

He leant back further, the chair creaked harder, suddenly there was a snap and he found himself on the floor amongst a kindling of timber.

Isabelle stood up, peered over at him from the other side of the desk. Her mascara had run and she was holding a tissue stained black. The grimace on her face had turned about, was approximating a smile. 'Until then,' she said, 'you had me for a moment.'

He struggled on the floor, managed to lift himself up. One of the broken struts had forced its way through his shirt, drawn a little blood. He held it like a stake freshly removed from a vampire and placed it on the desk.

'Excuse me,' he muttered.

Isabelle had regained her composure, dried her eyes. 'Do you think Tony is money-laundering through the Church of Wire?'

'I think it's a possibility. I've also other concerns about him that I'd rather not share at present. Either way, I think it's best for you to keep that distance.'

She nodded.

'There's something else I'd like to do,' he added, 'and that's talk to Francisco Carmide.'

She raised her eyebrows. 'You *have* been doing some digging.'

'I was there last night. In the audience. It was quite a show.'

'I'm glad you enjoyed it. I didn't see it myself.'

'Were you really asleep?'

'In a manner of speaking, yes.'

Mordent decided not to push it. But then said: 'The Church itself. It's a scam, right?'

Isabelle had managed to refix her hard persona. 'A scam? No, it's not a scam. And if you spoke to Francisco you would know it for sure. If it were a scam I wouldn't have approached you to start with, Mordent. I'm quite affronted.'

'Chill it. Can you set up a meeting between me and Carmide?'

'If you think it's necessary.'

'It would be useful.'

She shrugged. 'I trust you will be tactful?'

He nodded. He wanted her to go. The wound in his side had

begun hurting.

She stood. 'I'll phone you later today. And I understand about Tony. I guess it was over anyway. What I'll do about this – ' she gesticulated to her bump – 'is something for me to think about.'

'You're keeping it?'

'I'm not a complete bitch.' She turned on her flat soles and left.

Mordent moved around to the door and locked it. He sat on her still-warm chair and pulled up his shirt. The splinter had caused a four inch graze to open up from his right hip to under the armpit. The cut was mild, but it stung like crazy. He got up again, walked over to his side of the desk and kicked the remnants of his chair in retribution.

He leant by the windowsill, breathing heavily. Isabelle's suggestion of money-laundering was a good one. He hadn't yet gotten around to thinking about it. His main concern was the connection between Tony and the location of the last murder. That was something that he certainly wasn't going to run by Isabelle. Not in her condition.

He often found that the longer you leant on something the more circular it became. Until eventually you ended up back where you started. That didn't mean that starting in reverse would have got you the answer straightaway, just that you had to push to make those connections.

Detective work could – at a stretch – be equated to the symbol of the Ouroboros – a snake eating its own tail in the shape of a circle. This interlinking of cause and effect could set a man's head spinning. Invariably the answer was the most obvious, but you had to pass around the hoop to find the evidence to back it up. This repeated cyclical motion lent familiarity to different cases, made the job easier when it came to actual detection, but harder when it came to evidence.

Or maybe he was simply talking himself into a circle. Maybe he had banged his head when he hit the floor.

He made sure he had stopped bleeding, then put his jacket back on over his shirt. Unlocking the door, he wandered down the corridor to an office that he knew was empty. The chairs there had wheels. And they swivelled.

A few minutes later he was testing out his new piece of furniture. If he kicked his foot out quickly he could complete three revolutions. To an outsider, it might appear that he was chasing his own tail.

27
Social Visit (1)

Mid-morning saw him approaching the residence of Reflective Tony.

The air was as chill as a walk-in freezer. If the heater in his car had been working he would have pushed hot against cold, sidelined it; but it was a while since he'd had that luxury, and sometimes it was a struggle simply to keep the vehicle on the road. Leaves accumulated kerbside: the usual collection of mottled browns and greens, fulfilling a season cycle that had lasted for thousands of years. Whipped skywards by Mordent's tyres, they described an arc before settling down.

He parked in the same place as before, a few doors down, just for breathing space. Then he waited. Tony's car – the one he had driven Isabelle home in the night before – was parked in the driveway. The larger vehicle that the Frame used was not in sight. The probability was that the Frame wasn't there. Mordent hoped so.

It wasn't quite high noon, but it was time for a showdown.

Mordent had a plan, but it might not be a good one.

He got out of his vehicle and wandered a few doors up to Tony's house. Dogs could be heard barking from most back gardens, and he had to kick a couple of beer cans aside to smooth his path. Looking in Tony's neighbour's window, he couldn't see her star-jumping or couch-potatoing. Maybe she was out. A few more steps and he was on Tony's porch. He watched his hand cinematically as it rose and rapped three times on the wood.

A few moments more and he knocked again. There was a sound inside the house, like a sigh. But it was the house that had made the noise, not a human. Something creaking. Or perhaps wind soughing through a broken window.

The door suddenly opened. Tony's face looked haggard. Slept in. Stubble pushed through his skin like a pin picture. His shirt collar was unbuttoned halfway down his chest, and hair sprouted over the top like a garden gone to seed. This was all surface, however. His eyes clearly showed he was awake.

'What is it?'

Mordent had been banking on Tony not recognising him from the spat in the parking lot. He had been at a distance, after all.

Even so, he held only a handful of cards and had decided to reveal some of them up front.

He showed his PI badge. 'Name's Mordent. Can I come in for a chat?'

Tony shrugged. 'What is this about?'

'I'm making enquiries for a client of mine. I'm sure it's something we can smooth over.'

Tony raised an eyebrow, which also required grooming.

'For a lady,' Mordent added. 'As I said, nothing to worry about.'

Tony stood to one side, enough for Mordent to squeeze past. 'So long as it doesn't take long,' he said. 'I've got places to be.'

Mordent nodded. He waited in the narrow hallway for Tony to show him into the kitchen. Once he was there he looked around as if seeing it for the first time.

Tony pulled out a chair. Sat down. Beckoned for Mordent to do the same, then stood up again. 'Coffee?'

'Sure.'

Mordent watched Tony fill the kettle. Particles of water swirled like dust through a clear window.

The leaflets for the Church of Wire were no longer on the table.

'Black,' Mordent said, as the water got to bubbling and the spout ejected steam. 'No sugar.'

Maybe the silence had the effect of establishing order. Maybe they both wanted the other to speak first. Maybe it was simple courtesy. Maybe Tony was playing for time.

He put Mordent's cup in front of him. 'So, how can I help?'

Mordent watched the eddying blackness at the centre of the coffee cup. The kitchen was reflected atop it. A mirror in motion.

'I'm working for a client who wishes to remain nameless. She says you contacted her while she was in jail. Promised her the moon. But you were two- – maybe even three- – timing her. That's why I'm here.'

'Since when was that illegal?'

'Maybe it is, maybe it isn't. Maybe extortion is legal, maybe it isn't. What do you think?'

'Extortion?'

'While my client hasn't been particularly forthcoming, my instinct is that your involvement is likely to have been fuelled by money.'

'Your instinct, or your understanding?'

'One. The other. Or both. And both.'

Tony leant back. Mordent noticed the kitchen chairs were sturdier than his own office chairs. But then Tony was carrying less weight.

'Haven't I seen you before?'

'Your heavy played fisticuffs with me in a deserted car park.'

'Thought so.'

'Another reason why I suspect that what you're doing might not be legal.' Mordent blew on his coffee, creating a mini wave that crashed against the opposite side of the cup.

'Listen,' Tony leant forwards, 'we didn't have a clue who you were. And I don't like how you're throwing around this extortion thing. Truth be told, prison women are easy. When you get to a certain age, that appeals, you know what I mean? I'm not extorting money from anyone, just getting a little piece of the action for myself. Hell has no fury like a woman scorned. That's how the saying goes, don't it? There you have it. Dusted.'

'Maybe we see eye to eye on that score. Maybe there's something else. I've been tailing you for a few days. Seen you with another lady last night, leaving a religious art show.'

'It's a free country.'

'Seemed she was pregnant.'

'So she might be. Listen, what does this have to do with anything?'

'What would be your involvement with the Church of Wire?'

Tony stood. 'Look, you're not police, just a gumshoe snouting around trying to make something out of nothing. I don't have anything more to say to you.'

'I could always raise an assault charge on that incident in the car lot.'

Tony sat. Mordent knew what he was thinking. The assault was nothing, it was the location that was everything.

'Maybe I've been hasty. What do you want?'

'My client is financially insecure at the moment. She won't have much to pay me, never mind feed herself. What do you say that, as a matter of goodwill, you bankroll my fees so she don't owe me nothing?'

Tony ran a hand over his stubbled chin. 'And what does she get?'

Mordent shrugged. 'I say you're legit. That it was a matter of human error. That you didn't deliberately target her. That way she doesn't feel used, right?'

'How do I know she exists?'

'Pardon?'

'I said, how do I know she exists? Give me a name.'

'If she didn't exist, why would I be here?'

'That's what I've been thinking. Give me a name.'

'That's a matter of confidence between me and my client.'

'Look,' Tony raised his voice, 'I'm just after a goddamned name. Is that too much to ask? No name, no money.'

Mordent had only one name. 'Jessica Boothby,' he said.

'Right. *Jessica*. Now we're getting somewhere. You've got to understand, right, that I ain't exactly made of money myself. I can't be giving it up to every fleabit who comes in here claiming they know something I wanna pay for. What's your fee?'

Mordent made up a figure. 'One more thing,' he added. 'Nothing happens to Jessica, right?'

'Nothing other than what you're giving her, I imagine.' Tony's smile was wide and dirty. 'I remember Jessica all too well.' He downed the last of his coffee and got up from the table. 'Wait here.'

Mordent sat and drained his coffee as Reflective Tony headed upstairs. What had he achieved? He'd barely rattled Tony's cage. The only sure thing was that he wasn't hideously off track. Tony had accepted one charge to deflect another. Which meant that the second charge had to be worse than the first. Maybe it didn't take a PI to work that one out, but he also had a parting shot to fire.

The house gave another sigh as Tony returned. As though it gave him up.

'Here's your dough. Now scram.'

Tony threw a brown envelope onto the table. Mordent looked inside, counted the bills as though he really needed the money, then slipped it into his inside pocket, giving Tony a clear glimpse of his gun. He stood.

'Pleasure doing business with you.'

'Wish I could say the same,' Tony answered. He began hustling Mordent toward the door.

Mordent stopped in the frame. 'Just one thing,' he said. 'The parking lot. Heard there was a murder there the other day. Some coincidence. Don't you think?'

'I don't think nothing.' Tony's face contorted with an emotion Mordent couldn't quite define. 'Get going before I take more interest in you.'

Mordent nodded. 'Be seeing you.' He tapped the side of his jacket that held the envelope. Began to walk, then halted. 'Say, what's your pick-up line? *Does this smell like chloroform to you??*' He didn't wait for an answer, just turned his back and walked to his car.

27
Social Visit (2)

He was halfway back to the city when he had to pull over to answer his cell.

'Mordent.'

'It's Isabelle. I got that appointment with Francisco for you. Later this afternoon, three o'clock. How does that sound?'

'Sounds good.' He scribbled down the address – a hotel downtown.

'Listen,' she said. 'Don't go worrying him. How are you going to play it?'

'Tactfully,' he said, without any understanding of what that meant. He wondered if he should tell Isabelle he had seen Tony – decided against it. Instead he hung up, and headed to Morgan's Bar.

If there were a few hours to kill, then there was only one way to kill them. A barstool, a drink and his reflection.

He wasn't disappointed. Just after midday the bar was busy but the familiar stool that moulded to his backside was free.

He muttered a 'Usual' to Morgan and waited until the drink arrived. The bourbon scorched the back of his throat. If it was dry, he was dryer. There was a false taste in his mouth – a hung-over feeling born from lack of moisture and from pre-packaged food. His teeth were no longer the best. He wondered how a dead mouth might feel. Wondered if Martens down at the morgue knew.

As was his habit, he scanned the remainder of the clientele who were visible in the shadows. No-one there that he knew. There was a time when Morgan's was filled with cops and criminals alike, but either he was out of touch or they had moved on. The easy camaraderie between the two sides that had imbued his early days in the force was no longer evident. Some would say that was a loss, others – like Kovacs, who viewed it as corruption – saw it as a blessing. As for Mordent, while he had never had a drinking partner, he had always felt at home drinking in the same place as his contemporaries. He imagined it wouldn't be dissimilar to dressing as Chewbacca at a *Star Wars* convention. Anonymous yet universal simultaneously.

Half a glass down, he swirled the contents, wondered if his fortune might be read in the residue in the same way as a gypsy might read tea leaves. Not that he believed in that stuff. If the future could be told from the bottom of a cup then surely it could be told also from the crumbs of a pastrami sandwich, from the cracked surface of the clock that lost time in his parents' house, from the soil that surrounded dead bodies, from the smell of new born babies, from raindrops, cooking fat, the whorls of a bisected onion. If life was so much with us, then couldn't our paths be predicted from the swish of wet tyres on the road, the myriad reflections garnered when viewing oneself within a mirror within a mirror, the number of buttons on a shirt, the flashing cursor on a PC screen, the number of pixels making up a centrefold?

If he were a fortune teller he might be engaged by the direction of pointing fingers, the pattern of birthdays on a calendar, the sharpness of a drawing pin, the number of hairs on a camel. He could insist on the seriousness of the eyelets in a pair of thigh boots, the accumulation of *pops* to be had from bubble wrap, the number of moles that you couldn't see on your own back. He could charm women by predicting romance from looking at the backs of their knees, the pleats in their skirts, the patterns on their sweaters. And for himself:

from the floaters in his eyes, the colour of his shit, the number of microwaveable meals in his fridge, the amount of discarded packaging on the floor, the crumple in his bedclothes and the longing in his heart.

In short: the future must be just as predictable from all of those things as from studying palms, tea leaves, or a gullible victim's answers to loaded questions.

Most futures, to an extent, were predictable. Mordent knew almost for certain that within the next ten minutes he would be clutching a fresh glass, that at three o'clock he would be waiting in a downtown hotel, and that at some point during the night he would be sleeping. He could say for sure that during the next hour, cars would pass by the front of Morgan's Bar, Morgan himself would dry a certain number of glasses, and around the world people would be born, become ill, die, be impregnated, eat, sweat and shop.

In Mordent's experience, the real futures, the far-futures that might be full of uncertainty, were the futures that people really didn't want to know anyway. What could possibly be gained by a predicted date of death, illness, marriage break-up? Even a suggested likelihood of romance, a birth; good news might taint reality.

For him right then, life was best viewed as a burning cigarette. Starting with a spark, ending in ash.

As predicted, he ordered a second drink. With one elbow on the bar, the drink almost to his lips, he resembled Rodin's *The Thinker*. Maybe that was what fuelled all the nonsense that had flooded into his head. He checked his watch – there was still time to kill – downed the drink and left the bar. It was a short walk to Bukowski's, and there he grabbed the food his body was demanding. He ate in his car, then cleaned out his glove box. Before he knew it, that time was up.

Driving to the Gardner Hotel he realised he had no game plan when it came to Francisco. What business was it of his, anyway? His involvement in the case – if it even was a case – was tenuous at best. His knuckles shone white on the steering wheel.

The hotel was a fair one, mid-range, shy of shabby and a distant cousin to rich. It was the kind of hotel where the residents were often long-term: affordable rooms, decent food and proximity to services made it favourable. Mordent parked in the hotel car park – no valet service – and headed into the lobby. There was a long wooden desk fronted by a pretty girl in a blue uniform with a white hat meant to be set at a jaunty angle. Opposite the desk were several low tables beside dark mauve leather chairs. Newspapers lay open, from tabloids to broadsheets. Only one of the chairs was occupied: an elderly female with a handbag on her knees, dressed to go out and waiting for a taxi. At the back of the room was a bar with its shutters down. As far as Mordent was concerned, it was no bar.

He walked up to Miss Pretty and gave her a smile that hit like a bird against a window.

'Yes?'

Mordent wondered if she had gone on a customer service course. If so, the hotel needed their money back.

'I've an appointment with Mr Francisco Carmide at three o'clock. I believe he's resident here.'

'Unfortunately I cannot divulge whether guests are or are not staying at the hotel. Data protection.' She smiled.

Mordent sighed. 'It's quite straightforward. If you have a Mr Carmide here, then he's waiting for me.'

'Again, I cannot confirm whether or not a certain guest is staying at our establishment.' The smile remained fixed.

Mordent ran a hand through his hair. 'Then what would you suggest I do? Randomly wait for him to enter the lobby?'

'If you know he is here, sir, then I would suggest giving him a call. Presumably you've spoken to him if you've made an appointment?'

'You're making this unnecessarily complicated. All I need you to do is ask Mr Carmide to come and meet me in the lobby.'

'I would if I could, sir; but if I did so, that would confirm he is staying here. I'm not permitted to do that.'

'Why?'

She gave another sweet smile. Mordent felt like spoiling it. 'Because of data protection. Some of our guests prefer their details to remain private. Mr Carmide is one of those guests.' She hesitated, realised her mistake. 'That is, when he does stay here, occasionally. I'm not saying that he's here now.'

Mordent leant on the desk. His smile replaced hers.

'That's exactly what you've told me. Now, let's make this simple one more time. I know he's here, you know he's here. He's expecting me. I'll wander over to one of those leather chairs and look away while you call up to his room and let him know I'm here to see him. We'll keep it between ourselves. I assure you Mr Carmide is not going to kick up a stink. The only stink he'll kick up is if you keep both me and him waiting and don't do what I say.'

Mordent walked over to one of the chairs, not wishing to brook an argument. Without glancing back, he knew the only jaunty thing about the receptionist was her hat. He also knew she would be making that call.

What her rules did reveal to him, however, was the nature of the hotel. A residence where the security of the guests was at such a premium suggested a lot about those guests. Dodgy, shady, possibly infamous, even famous. If the good Mr Francisco Carmide was running a legitimate organisation then why were both the Church and he himself so difficult to find?

From where Mordent sat, the elevators were in full view. They covered ten floors. As he watched, the lights over one of the doors descended in a countdown. Each taken in a blink.

The ping that accompanied the elevator's arrival on the ground floor sounded like a spoon striking glass.

Carmide exited into the foyer. Looked around. His imposing height dominated his years, negated them. He wore casual trousers with a white shirt and had a cream cardigan draped over his shoulders. On his feet were sandals and socks. It was incongruous with the persona he had projected at the Church of Wire, yet somehow this get-up made him look all the more religious. Seeing Mordent sat, Carmide raised an eyebrow. Mordent reciprocated with a hand signal that inadvertently looked gay. Carmide headed over and Mordent stood. They shook hands, exchanged names, sat down.

'Well,' Carmide said. 'Isabelle speaks highly of you. To what do I owe the pleasure of this meeting?'

Mordent looked around. 'Are you okay speaking here in the lobby? Isn't there somewhere more private?'

Carmide shrugged, his shoulders like ferrets under the cardigan. 'The Church holds no secrets, Mr Mordent. It is as open as a palm.'

His accompanying gesture made the point in a way that irritated Mordent. He didn't need Carmide's religious principles rammed down his throat.

'Did Ms Silk say why I wanted to speak to you?'

'Only that it was Church business. I trust her judgement.'

Mordent leant back, the plush leather holding him like a mould. 'Truth is, Mr Carmide, before we begin I'd like some background on the Church. I'm a private investigator employed by a mutual client, and while my enquiries are only indirectly related to the Church, I feel an understanding of its principles would help with my case. I attended the meeting at the art gallery last night, but even so, I'm not quite sure what the Church is all about. Or – to be frank – of its legitimacy.'

Carmide smiled. 'You wouldn't be the first to ask those questions. As to its legitimacy, it is as legitimate as any organisation that expounds theological principles. While we try to work in the light, we do so from the dark. Any religion that explicitly states there is a God must be lying, Mr Mordent. There is no scientific proof of one, and I hold scientific principles dear. But science is not the only thing that guides us, and the theory that propels the Church is one that I believe will take us closer to His designs for this world. If, that is, He exists.'

'That's a very honest answer, Carmide.'

'Please call me Francisco. Honesty is the best policy, don't you think?'

'It's an honest answer, but it doesn't actually tell me much.

I find religious leaders to be a bit like politicians – all air, no substance. No offence.'

Francisco nodded. 'If you're asking if the Church is a money-making enterprise, fuelled by fleecing its congregational lambs, then the answer is no. If you were at yesterday's meeting, then you would have seen the collection box passed around at the end of the service. This simply funds our events. You will appreciate that last night was rather special. That camel didn't come cheap.'

'We all have to make a living,' Mordent agreed. 'Even if it isn't much of a living.' He glanced around the lobby of the hotel. 'Although, I can't imagine this comes cheap either.'

Francisco bristled, as though all the fibres in his cardigan had stood to attention. 'I used to be a successful businessman. My own living expenses are privately funded.'

Mordent held his palms open. 'My apologies. Tell me more about the principles under which the Church of Wire operates.'

Francisco sat back, crossed one leg over the other. Mordent could tell the socks were expensive. Unlike his, the only holes were the ones Carmide pushed his feet into.

'I've always been interested in the scriptures,' he said, 'and whether or not the creation of the world as described in Genesis is literal. If so, while it explains the creation of the Earth and its inhabitants, the details are sketchy at best. What about the way that humans interact with each other? Our hopes, fears, desires? Our innate nature to nurture? Where do our personalities come from? Our souls? So many unanswered questions, Mr Mordent. But then, when you question someone religious about their principles, how do they back them up? From their Holy Book, inevitably. So it led me to believe that the answers were in the Bible after all and I just hadn't seen them.

'So I looked again, with my mind open, and I saw those answers as clear as day. As you will have heard at the meeting, the Bible states that God created the world in six days, and on the seventh day he rested. We believe that while he rested he also created. Therefore all the idiosyncrasies of the world were created through *dream*. Wouldn't that be wonderful? As a concept, at the very least, you must admire it.'

'I admire facts, Francisco. I admire realities I can pick up and put down.'

'Maybe, Mr Mordent, your mind needs a little expansion. Let me give you some facts: animals, trees, the environment, humans. Our existence is irrefutable. But our desires, aspirations, the mystery of love: these are intangibles. But you don't deny that you have these feelings. So where do they come from? I believe that everything other than instinct – a force that is hammered into the psyche regardless of upbringing – came from God's dreaming. Once you accept that, everything falls into place. And we can embrace it.

'We often fear our emotions. That's because we don't understand them. We can understand them if we realise they come from God. Even from the subconscious of an unconscious God. What we can then do is harness them fully, ride them, exploit them – if need be. It's all about people taking charge of themselves and knowing their place in the world. That's what the message is with the Church of Wire.'

Mordent nodded. 'Your thesis hangs on the fact that if there is a God then he likes to get some kip.'

'It's all theory, isn't it? It has to be. Yet it is also about empowerment. When I worked in business I used to conduct lectures based on very similar principles. *Carpe diem*, etc. Even if my congregation doesn't fully believe the spiel, the likelihood is that they will benefit from it. If you don't see that as a charitable concern, Mr Mordent, then you are lacking in basic humanity.'

Mordent shifted. The seats weren't as comfortable as they appeared. 'What would interest me,' he said, 'is knowing exactly how much of this *you* believe. Whether it's just a theory or a belief system.'

'I believe it implicitly, as a principle. As a fact ... Well, it can be as hard to believe in facts as it can to believe in theories.

Nothing is fixed, everything is fluid: but then ...' Carmide leant forward, '... isn't that the exact substance of dreams?'

'I'm not here to argue with you,' Mordent said. 'I'm just trying to understand. The whole creationist argument seems built on flimsy ground. The book is the word, but who really wrote the book?'

'Yet everything is flimsy: from the miracle of birth to the negligee of a hooker. You raise an eyebrow at my metaphor? I don't claim to be *good*, Mr Mordent. We all have our vices, and I don't believe resisting those vices is the intention of our God. Rather, we should exalt in our aspirations and desires: because these come directly from God.'

'Anything goes?'

'Within reason.'

'The camel is starting to make sense.'

'Exactly, Mr Mordent. Exactly. Some people take things too literally because they need structure, but the lack of structure in life is a structure in itself. Let me expand. Some of the Christians who believe the world was created in six days find it hard to reconcile this with the overpowering scientific evidence that the Earth is billions of years old. So, to fit their beliefs, they have to redefine the word "day". Some believe the first day, when light was created, might have lasted a gazillion years in the way that we measure it. Some people believe that we are currently living within God's seventh day. That he is currently resting, and on the eighth day he might return.'

'What do *you* say?'

'That it's just a matter of semantics. Words – as you say – written in a book. Words are important, of course, but life is for living. Our Church hopes to open people up to the understanding that we can just celebrate life – because every aspect of life has come from God's imagination.'

Mordent found these ideas swirling in his head like cream stirred into coffee. A vortex of possibility. How much of the Church's doctrine he needed to digest was immaterial. Whether it was legit or not was a question that could be asked of every religious organisation in existence. Carmide could hold a good argument; that was important. But to what extent was he involved with Reflective Tony? Ultimately, that was the sole question he needed an answer to.

'I think I get it,' he said. 'What I'm now interested in is the relationship the Church has with Tony Runcorn.'

If Mordent expected a flicker of reaction on Carmide's face he was disappointed.

'Tony? He's one of the congregation, and he has supported the Church most generously. He's also involved with Isabelle, as you must surely know?'

Mordent ignored the question. 'To what extent do you trust Mr Runcorn?'

'Why, implicitly. Much of the funding for last night's escapade came from him. He pumps a lot of money into the Church.'

'You ever wondered why?'

'Because he believes in us.'

'If I were to tell you that Tony Runcorn is a small-time crook, who wouldn't have the money to buy himself a pizza most days, what would you say to that?'

'I'd say it belied the man that I knew.'

'If I also told you he caught fallen women so quickly that he's got an enviable collection of them, what would you say to that?'

'I guess that would be none of my business.'

'But if I also said that he has a connection with a site that has links to a murder investigation, *then* what would you say?'

'That I would leave it to the proper authorities?' Carmide's demeanour had transformed into the antithesis of a James Bond martini, stirred but not shaken. 'I can see you're trying to rattle me, Mr Mordent, but I've known Tony for some time. His relations with the Church have always been exemplary.'

Mordent leant forwards. 'I have a hunch he might be money-laundering through the Church. If he is, that would dent your reputation, wouldn't it? That would put a stop to your plans for world domination.'

Carmide laughed. 'I don't think world domination is my

goal, but if you insist.' Then he became serious. 'However, Isabelle did recommend I listen to you. I'm suspecting she is this "mutual client" you spoke of. So, she has her concerns as well, I imagine.'

'She might not be an angel, but she is one of the fallen. In my estimation, at least.'

Carmide looked spent. Suddenly, his face fell in and all the lines requisite of his age appeared as if they had been hiding under the bronzed surface. 'Oh dear,' he said. 'Oh dear.'

'None of this,' Mordent continued, 'is *fact* at the moment. Just suspicion. Just like the principles, I suppose, of the Church of Wire. But a different game, a dangerous game; perhaps.'

Carmide rolled up the sleeves of his cardigan, and Mordent realised the shirt underneath was short-sleeved. He distrusted short-sleeved shirts. He preferred sleeves you had to roll up to be ready for action. But those other shirts, they just weren't credible.

'I will need some time to think about this,' said Carmide. 'Are you passing details to the police?'

'Not yet. I'm just fishing, but when I start reeling I'll let you know.'

'Of course.' Carmide stood. Extended a hand. 'I would like to say it was a pleasure meeting you, Mr Mordent, but you've handed me a stick to a piñata disguising a beehive.'

Mordent nodded. 'Nice analogy. For what it's worth, I believe your intentions with the Church are sincere.'

Carmide muttered a thank you, but he was already turning away, absentmindedly wandering over to the elevators, his six foot plus size diminishing not only in perspective but in stature.

Mordent glanced across to the old woman still sat on one of the chairs, holding her purse. Then he wandered over to the receptionist.

'See, that didn't hurt. Say, that old lady, shouldn't you offer to chase up her taxi?'

The girl propped up her trained smile. 'Her? She sits there like that all day. Gives me the creeps. I think she's waiting for someone who'll never come.'

'Story of my life,' Mordent grinned. 'What time do you knock off?'

'Pardon?'

'When are you free? Would you like a drink?'

She sniffed. 'I don't think so.'

'Thought not. But don't blame me for asking. Hope I'm not the last offer you get. That you're not left waiting around like *her*.' He gesticulated over his shoulder to the old lady, then turned and tipped his hat to her. A smile, wrinkly and cracked, lit her face. 'Be seeing you,' he said, then left the building.

28
A Spot Of Violence

Mordent's cell rang as he reached his car. He fumbled inside his jacket pocket before managing to click the right buttons and press it to his ear.

'Mr Mordent?'

'That's me.'

'It's Jessica. How are you?'

'I'm doing fine. How are you?'

'I'm good. Good. Missing you, if that's okay.'

Mordent shrugged, realised what he'd done, and said, 'Sure.'

'Listen. I've been thinking. I've too much time by myself and I need something to do. Can I be your secretary? Would you allow that? I mean, it would be swell if you could. Plus, it would be a way of us getting to know each other, wouldn't it? Without getting all emotional, I mean. I mean, it's good to get emotional sometimes, but sometimes it isn't. It crossed my mind you might need someone to cross your i's and dot your t's for you.'

Mordent smiled. 'That wouldn't be a great start. Would it? Dotting the t's and crossing the i's?'

'Why I do believe I'm flustered, Stingray. Sincerely I am.'

Mordent couldn't help but smile wider. 'We can discuss it later,' he said. 'In principle, it might work. In practice, it could be something else entirely.'

'I wouldn't need payment of the regular kind.'

'I know, Jessica, I *do* know.'

There was a pause. 'So what have you been up to?'

'I've been paying a few social calls.'

'Anyone I know?'

Mordent sighed. 'I had a chat with Francisco Carmide.'

'Oh my. You do move in the most interesting circles.'

'You have a very glamorous view of the life of a PI.'

'What did you make of him?'

'I think he's serious about what he does, but in my mind there's a very thin line between deification and defecation.'

'Stingray!'

'I won't be apologising. But seriously, maybe he's one of the good guys.'

'Did you tell him about the bad guy?'

'I gave him some information on Tony to chew through. Now we stand back and watch.'

'Be careful, Stingray.'

'I will honey. Talk later.'

Mordent hung up.

Honey?

Where had *that* sprung from? If he wasn't careful he might start getting familiar.

He unlocked his car. The interior wasn't much warmer than outside. Already, dusk imbued the skyline with a cloudy reddish hue, like peering out from under bedclothes illuminated by torchlight. He considered what he had achieved that day. Guessed it didn't amount to much. Despite having rattled a few cages, he still wasn't sure what he was up against. Maybe Isabelle would pay him until Tony fell out like a weevil from a ship's biscuit? As for Bernard Maloney, he couldn't see how he could help him much further. That was best left in the hands of the police. Maybe it was coincidence that Tony had turned into that parking lot? Either way, he didn't see him as a killer. He could genuinely have been scouting for a location for the next service of the Church of Wire.

And the Church itself? Bonkers, obviously. Interesting, but no more than a placebo for a select clientele. Tony was running cash through it, that was for sure. Technically, he should report it to the police, but he wanted a sure-fire way to do so without necessarily bringing either Isabelle or the Church down. Giving Carmide a little time to sort his affairs was the best way to proceed.

He thrummed his fingers against his steering wheel, felt it reverberate beneath them. Switching on the engine he became cocooned by the satisfactory hum. There were times when he became awed by the capabilities of a vehicle. One moment he might be in a hotel car park downtown, and the next minute …

… he pulled into the parking lot by his office, took the stairs to the first floor. This time of night, the lights from the agency office across the hallway were usually on, but they must have packed up early, because it was deathly quiet. He fumbled for the keys in his pocket and approached the door to his office. Then he paused. Even in the half-light he could see that wood had splintered away from the frame.

He crouched, made his way across to the door in that position, his knees protesting. Once he was under the glass panel he ran a finger along the frame. The door had been jemmied open, then closed. Placing his eye right beside the lock he could see that it had been reset. He would need to use his key to open the door, which would either give a warning to anyone still inside or, if they had gone, have the intended effect of not announcing they had been there.

Gingerly he selected the correct key from the fob in his hand; inserted it as carefully into the lock, as though it might break. When it turned, the sound was magnified a thousand times in his head, as though he were simultaneously unlocking each and every lock in the city. Iron bolts drew back with a clunk.

He stood, one side to the door, then threw it open.

The office seemed empty. He kept his gun holstered. There was nothing worse than precipitating violence through expecting violence. Confidently he stepped into the room, then was immediately grabbed from behind. The words *vicelike grip* were a cliché in pulp novels, but Mordent accepted it as fact. His arms were pinned by his sides, and he decided not to waste any effort struggling. There wasn't a punch, wasn't a shot: therefore no immediate danger. If he were a gambling man like Hubie, he thought, then he would bet on the Frame. As if in answer, his desk light was switched on and Reflective Tony stood up from where he had been crouched out of sight.

'Fancy seeing you here,' Mordent said. In response, he felt the Frame's grip tighten.

A thin smile spread across Tony's face. 'You're not that difficult to track down. I have *connections*.'

'I'm sure you do.'

Tony walked around the desk, placed his hands on his hips. 'You're in over your head,' he said. 'You should stay out of my business.'

He drew a fist back, punched Mordent ineffectually in the stomach. Mordent gasped, made out it hurt more than it really did. There was no need to encourage a harder punch.

Tony skimmed his hands through Mordent's jacket pockets, removed the envelope containing the money he had given him earlier that day. He placed it in his own pocket without counting it. Reached out and gripped a hand around Mordent's neck, just underneath his chin.

'Lucky you haven't spent this already.'

The grip was tight enough that Mordent didn't answer. He was struggling to breathe.

Tony fired another punch into his stomach, caught a rib, and Mordent winced.

'This is more than Jessica Boothby, remember that. It's more than the Church of Wire. You stir me up, you stir others up. Others that don't want to be stirred, you get me? You stir up guys that are hibernating. You ever disturbed a hibernating bear? No, course you haven't. And you wouldn't want to.'

He released his grip. Mordent gasped. The Frame still held him tight; his breath on the back of Mordent's neck.

Tony was bouncing around the office, all revved up. He pulled open drawers, slugged out of Mordent's bottle of bourbon. There was little else available for him to do.

'You don't make much, do you?'

Mordent tried to shrug, couldn't.

'Just a jumped-up PI who thinks he knows it all.'

'That's your opinion.'

'I can see it.' Tony swept his arm to take in the room, the office.

Mordent could see Tony was struggling to make much of the situation. There was little to break, little statement to make. Either he'd get beaten up some more, which he could take, or Tony would have to decide he'd made his point and leave. It was all so ineffectual, and simply confirmed Tony as the small-time crook he knew him to be. The interesting part was who was backing him. And why.

'While you've got my full attention,' Mordent said, 'why don't you tell me how well *you're* doing?'

Tony grinned. 'I'm not some kind of cartoon villain who reveals his master plan before making an unsuccessful attempt to top you. All I'm saying is that this is a warning. Stay away from me. Stay away from Isabelle. Jessica you can keep. Stay away, as well, from the Church of Wire.'

'I'm my own boss,' said Mordent.

'So you might be. So am I.'

Tony wandered over to the window. Glanced out. As though he saw something there that made up his mind, he turned back and nodded to the Frame, who shuffled Mordent over to the chair on the visitor side of the desk.

'Tie him up,' Tony said.

Again, Mordent didn't struggle. There was no point. But he tensed his arms, hoping to create slack that might be of use later, once they had gone. The Frame pushed him down hard on the chair, sprung some twine around his wrists, then kicked his legs against the chair legs and bent and tied those too. It was almost comfortable, although Mordent would have preferred the other chair.

'We're going to give you an indication of what the Church of Wire is all about,' said Tony. He pulled a small bottle out of his pocket, together with a syringe.

It was then that Mordent had to resist the urge to struggle.

'You ever have nightmares, Mordent? The Church would preach that those are the work of God, but I would suggest the Devil. Wouldn't you?'

The Frame pulled Mordent's gun out of its holster and placed it on the desk in front of him. Then he yanked the sides of Mordent's jacket down over his arms, grabbed the right sleeve of his shirt where it was stitched at the shoulder, and ripped it down to his elbow. Meanwhile Tony had removed the stopper from the bottle, was filling the syringe. He tilted it, tapped it.

Then bent forward, so close that Mordent could smell his breath. 'Sweet dreams,' he said.

Mordent felt the tip of the needle push through his flesh. Tiny prick.

Tony stepped back. He looked at the syringe absentmindedly, was obviously considering what to do with it. Then he dropped it into his pocket.

'Remind me I've got this in here,' he said to the Frame.

Mordent sat facing the desk. Currently, there were no effects. The Frame moved into his eye-line.

'Right,' Tony said, 'we're off.' He was as casual as a relative leaving a party. Or a funeral.

'Hang on,' grunted the Frame. 'I've got a score to settle.'

He pulled his right arm back. To Mordent, his fist appeared like a piston, like a concrete slab, like Thor's hammer. Then it connected, and Mordent felt his face biffed like putty. His neck snapped back and he tasted blood. He ran his tongue around his teeth; none was loose. But then the second blow came and caught his tongue in that position. There was a sickening sound like the soft crack of meat on bone, and bile rose to the back of Mordent's throat.

Whether it was this or the effect of the drug, it was then that the lights began to dim, and Mordent's vision swung in and out of focus until all he could see was his gun as it lay on the table. It appeared pliable, as though it was made of rubber.

29
A Dream Within A Dream

Mordent regained consciousness. The gun remained on the table. Its barrel was pointing toward him and he projected himself into the hole. Darkness enfolded him, the smell of cordite invaded his senses, became all-empowering. Like crawling through a sewer pipe, he made his way along the barrel, the concave sides keeping him central.

Scratch marks representing the trajectories of bullets scored the black sides with silver streaks. The white sleeves of his shirt became streaked with dirt. The smell began to scorch the inside of his nose: powerful, pungent, acrid. His mouth closed, he pushed ahead.

There seemed no light at the end of the tunnel. He moved forward on his belly. The floor of the chamber was warm, and each time he inched ahead, that warmth ran deeper into his skin. Turning his head backwards he could no longer see the entry point. He forged ahead.

The blackness mimicked sleep. Sometimes he was unsure if his eyes were open or closed. Either way, he seemed to drift. Weird animals entered his reverie, appeared out of the darkness. Taxidermist jokes. He couldn't finger them.

Somewhere ahead, the sounds of gears turning resonated down the barrel. There was a soft clunk. Without seeing it, Mordent knew that a bullet had entered the chamber.

He pressed forward. After some time, the golden tip of the

bullet came into view, like the sun seen from space. It was beautiful in brass. There was a click, and he knew he had to make it to the bullet. The trigger had been cocked. As he moved, the elbows of his shirt and the knees of his trousers tore. Blood flowed from his body toward the bullet, confirming the angle of the weapon. The bullet fit snugly into the chamber, yet even so, he found he could squeeze atop it. He sat there, regaining breath that he hadn't realised he had lost. Within seconds, he was on the move again.

A blast exploded behind him, heat penetrated the depths of his organs, his fingers clung to the smooth sides of the bullet as it was propelled forward like a firework. Ahead of him, a pinprick of light expanded rapidly into a white circle, jagged at the edges. Suddenly he was free from the barrel, riding the bullet like General Buck Turgidson rode the atom bomb in *Dr Strangelove*. He felt for his hat, for a whoop, but it had been blown back in the barrel and his hand connected with thin hairs and skin.

The light was brief: a spasm of colour.

Splintering shards of wood flew past like arrows. He was burrowing into the desk, chewing his way forward. The top of the bullet heated up rapidly, burning hands that had to hold on. After what seemed like an eternity of pressure and noise, the bullet halted with a jerk, like the end of a fairground ride. He was embedded in the desk, surrounded in a wooden cocoon. The exertion left him breathless, and he slipped from the bullet and fell back into the chair.

His wrist and feet ties were taut. The twine ate into his skin like larvae. The word *serration* sprang into his mind. Across the expanse between his chair and the desk, the gun barrel was pointing toward him.

Fear searched and found each individual nerve-ending in his body. He became convinced the gun would fire. Concentrating, he tried to move the direction of the barrel with his mind. It became imperative. Wrinkles in his forehead bunched together with the effort. Imperceptibly, it seemed the angle of the gun was changing; yet simultaneously the trigger was being cocked.

As the fear widened inside him, so did the distance of the trigger from the plate. He couldn't voice his scream, but his nerves did it for him. With one final mental push he eased the barrel of the gun to one side just as the trigger came down and discharged the bullet from the gun.

There was a whoosh, a flash of impossible powder. He could see the barrel start to fill, as though the darkness within was expanding. As if waiting for a train at an underground station, he peered into that blackness: saw form and movement. Then, in a rush, the golden tip of the bullet became apparent, eased its way out and into the air.

The trajectory was skewed. The bullet discharged in slo-mo. He watched its progress as though syrup filled the air. Between them the distance was but a few feet, yet recalling Zeno's paradox of motion, he focused on derailment. For the bullet to move, it had to change the position it occupied. Yet in any one instant of time it was neither moving to where it was nor to where it was not. It couldn't move to where it was not, because no time elapsed for it to move there; it couldn't move to where it was, because it was already there. If at every instant of time there was no motion occurring, if everything was motionless at every instant – and time was composed entirely of instants – then motion was impossible.

Kovacs had once given him this paradox, even though at the time he had despoiled it. By him concentrating, the bullet slowed significantly until finally it halted completely – an inch or less from his chest.

He breathed out.

The bullet hit him.

He could feel it move through his body. Kinetic energy was imparted to the surrounding tissue, flinging it away from the bullet's path in a radial manner, producing a temporary cavity thirty times wider than its track. Shockwaves fanned out, damaging his tissue, organs and bones. While the cavity remained open for less than a second, the reverberation continued. One of his ribs splintered, causing further damage as the fragments travelled through the body as projectiles themselves.

He found himself hoping for an exit wound. If the bullet stayed within his body it would create the maximum tissue damage, transferring all of its kinetic energy to his internal organs. Yet his back was wedged against the chair. He was unsure of the type of bullet within the gun. A jacketed bullet was designed to fragment after impact, dividing its destructive power, while hollow-point and soft bullets flattened and spread, creating a wider area for their tracks and increasing the damage caused by shockwaves and cavitations.

The chair juddered as the bullet hit it, the back splintered and split like two swinging saloon doors, and somewhere within the wall behind him the bullet stopped like a brick in brick.

He exhaled. There was a wheezing sound. His head fell downward toward his chest but not into his lap.

When he opened his eyes, his bonds were loose. He pulled one hand free, regarded it. The twine had bit around in a circle. If he looked closely he could glimpse the white of bone. The flesh of his hand became a loose-fitting glove. He reached forward and his arm extended, the bone a smooth pole with his hand on the end – like the repeated extensions of a chimney sweep's brush. The horror of the sight was softened by the flexibility of his fingers: the comfort of touch.

His fingers reached the gun on the table; closed around the barrel. He contracted his arm and the gun came with it. There was a soft click as the bone fully retracted into his arm, and when he looked again he couldn't see a join. The gun was heavy in his hand. He turned it around, examined it from all angles. When his vision connected with the barrel, his gaze was transfixed.

It was like gazing through the top of a cone. Within the small hole, the blackness seemed to expand outwards. He fell into it and suddenly saw the universe for the very first time. Albeit without stars. He was engulfed and at one with it. Everything that mattered was matter, and it was a part of him and apart of him simultaneously. The enormity of his surrounding existence inflated his senses. He ballooned within the dark, swelled to fill it, the buttons on his shirt popping then disintegrating as they floated away from his self. His belt loosening, the twine around his ankles melting, he was freed from the chair and ejected into space.

He enjoyed this sensation for a moment, just as it awed him. And then he realised he was the progenitor of the experience. He could feel his hand still wrapped around the barrel of the gun.

The sense of the alternate confused. He flexed his hand at the same moment as his clothes relaxed from his body. Itchy trigger finger. Fired.

The blackness tore like a backdrop illuminated from behind by an arc light. Suddenly, all the dark fell away and it was light. Closing his eyes didn't halt the glare. He raised a hand, but the hand was no longer there. Nothing could be seen against the white. His was a phantom body made of pure light. Nothing else existed.

He seemed to hang for quite some time. The gun had dropped from his grasp. He no longer had a grasp.

Sometimes it was unclear whether his eyes were open or closed.

Sometimes it was unclear whether he had eyes or not.

Yet then, in the distance, as if emerging from a heat haze, a vertical line appeared.

Over time, the line grew, like a scorch mark burning through a white shirt; like a blade of grass revealed by melting snow. Moments later, a stick figure. Still later, form and substance. His head appeared fixed; it was impossible to look away.

He was reminded – somewhere in his mind's recesses – of out-of-body experiences and a beckoning to leave this world. He wasn't ready for this, but as the figure came closer and closer he realised that it was Jessica. Naked and completely smooth. She held out her arms to him. *Come here, Stingray*, he heard.

The light he was made of poured into her darkness.

He flooded into her crevices, illuminated her house.

30
And Relax

Someone was trying to clean his birdhouse with liquid.

His face stung.

He remembered one slap. Two.

A voice, echoing as though coming from a long and distant antechamber, called his name.

Like a tape it spooled on repeat.

Mordent. Mordent. Mordent.

A whisper. An incessant whisper.

Mordent.

He curled up in bed. He was a child. The covers were snug. It was time to get up for school. His mother's voice was low and warm. It infiltrated his ear like honey.

Mordent.

He gritted his teeth. Howled. Bit into something plastic. Water leaked into his throat.

Mordent. Wake up. Please.

The voice was insistent. Maybe he should do something about it. If only for the voice.

An eye.

Opened.

He blinked once. Twice.

There was a blur of colour, of light. A broken kaleidoscope. He felt faint and the room swung, as though his office was a box suspended from a crane by a rope.

His office.

He wasn't in bed.

There was his gun on the table in sharp focus. He blinked again. There were tears on his face that weren't his.

He leant forward and retched onto the floor.

Someone jumped backwards. Jitterbug steps.

Words poured out of him: a stream of bile more virulent than the insides of his stomach. Then he coughed. Once. Twice. Several times.

It wasn't even a hangover he could enjoy.

He lifted his head. Everything came into focus. Jessica sat on the corner of the desk watching him.

She looked like the perfect little secretary.

31
Playing Catch-Up

'What time is it?'

Jessica looked at her watch. 'It's after 2.00 pm. What time did you think it was?'

'I'm not sure what day I thought it was.'

'Who did this?'

Mordent deliberated whether or not to tell her. Decided he would. Decided not to tell her that he had given Tony her name.

'Our good friend Reflective Tony.'

'Reflective?'

'Just a nickname. What happened?'

She slid her legs off the desk. Walked over and began massaging his shoulders. 'Is this good?'

'You bet it is.'

'Well, I kept calling you yesterday evening. Thought it strange you didn't pick up. Thought it even stranger when you didn't answer in the morning. So I looked you up in the phone book and found you here, slobbering all over the stool, tied up.'

'Sexual experiment gone wrong.'

She laughed. 'Not with Tony, I hope.'

He forced a smile. 'Just kidding.' He realised she had dropped the Southern Belle accent. It made him trust her less, despite the situation.

'Anyway, I just kept slapping you until you showed the

whites of your eyes.'

'I was drugged.'

'So I gathered.'

Mordent grasped the arms of the chair, tried to stand, sank back down. He ran his tongue around the inside of his mouth. All his teeth seemed to be there, but when his tongue caught on them it hurt. He stuck it out: 'How does this look?' The motion was accompanied by a lisp.

'Not as bad as you think. You've got bruising though, left side of your face.'

He reached out to touch it. Saw the marks of the twine that had bit into his wrists. 'Ouch.'

'You're a big man, you'll get over it.'

He could tell she was putting on a brave face. He recalled her tears on his cheek. He owed her. Big time.

'Why did he do this to you?' Her voice was soft, low.

'Because I was poking my nose around.'

'You can't let him get away with it.'

'I won't.' Mordent closed his eyes. Stuff was still swimming. 'Say, Jessica?'

'Yes Stingray.'

'Give me a kiss, will you?'

She bent over him, her lips brushing his. Like two live wires touching, he felt a spark.

'You don't smell too good,' she said.

'Thankfully I can't say the same about you.'

She smiled. 'Are you going to be okay?'

'I guess so.'

'What did he use on you?'

'I'm not sure. I don't think I want to know.'

'You should get yourself checked out.' She perched back atop the desk.

'Maybe tomorrow.'

'Listen,' she said. 'Someone rang here while you were knocked out. I took the call now I'm your secretary. Guy called Marsham. Works for the police. You know him?'

'He's been kicking round some information for me.'

'Information is what he said he had.'

Mordent nodded. His neck felt loose, as though the massage had warmed the muscles like a softened squash ball. 'Maybe I should call him.'

'You feel up to it?'

'I don't know.'

'Maybe you should get some sleep?'

'I've been sleeping for the past 18 hours.' Mordent paused. 'Dreaming, for most of them.'

'Dreaming?'

'You don't want to know.' He tried to stand again, but his legs felt like springs that had been stretched to their limit and wouldn't recoil. 'Listen. Jessica.'

'Yes.'

'The Church of Wire. It's big on dreaming. From how I understand it, it's the basis of the religion. Have drugs been used during any of the services? Have you taken drugs?'

Jessica lowered her eyes. It reminded him that she wasn't as attractive as he sometimes thought she was. Age wasn't going to be kind to her. Live fast, age young.

'I may have dabbled in the past, Mr Mordent,' she said, slipping into her Southern Belle accent like a child talking soft to an admonishing mother, 'but I've never seen them used in Church. You don't need drugs to dream, do you?'

Mordent shrugged. He guessed not. But then Tony hadn't been trying to indoctrinate him. It was a warning. Bare-faced. There was no subterfuge. Tony knew Mordent could come after him. The drugs were just a symbol of how far he was prepared to go.

Mordent was prepared to go further.

He deliberated heading to the morgue and getting Martens to take a urine sample, but knew he wasn't going to make it official. Kovacs wouldn't back him if it came to the crunch; would be happy to argue that Mordent had self-injected. Besides, he wanted to pin more on Tony and whoever was behind him than a simple assault charge.

If Tony wanted to raise the stakes, that just meant Mordent

would give him more to lose.

He glanced at Jessica. She seemed to have assumed the secretary role. He guessed that under the circumstances he could hardly refuse.

'The job's yours,' he said, 'but I don't keep regular hours. This can't be just an excuse to spend time together. When I'm not here, that's when I really want *you* here. If we're both here it ain't gonna work. And I can't pay, either. I can barely feed myself. But you know this, right?'

She nodded. She hoisted her skirt over her thighs and shifted further onto the desk, leaning back in what Mordent assumed she believed was a seductive pose. He knew he was going to regret his decision.

'Listen,' he said. 'I'm going to get myself home. Your role starts now. Any messages, call me on my cell.'

'You sure you're going to be safe to drive, Stingray?'

'I'm sure.'

He tried to stand again, but it was useless.

'I'll call you a cab,' she said. And did.

32
A Coastal Kill

Mordent drank a bottle of bourbon, closed his eyes and went on the taxi rollercoaster.

Lights swirled behind his vision. His head swam like a fish fighting a whirlpool. Bile rose up and down his throat, never quite making his mouth – although he could clearly detect its acidic properties. He gripped hold of the door handle; an anchor to reality. His stomach lurched at every twist and turn, and when he was finally discharged, he ejected its contents onto the pavement, where steam rose in the cool sub-afternoon air.

He rubbed his eyes, paid the taxi driver and slowly made his way into his apartment.

Perhaps the hospital would have been a more sensible destination. But they would have asked questions for which he didn't have the answers.

His bed was made of marshmallow. He settled; sank. This time his dreams were normal, without the sensation of an uncontrollable reality. He woke twice, cleared his stomach from both ends, and return to the safety of sleep. The hallucinogens were being purged from his system. By the time he was ready to rise, it was already the morning of the following day.

Condensation clung to the inside of his windows, the trapped ghosts of his night-time breaths. He looked at his wrists. Thin red lines encircled them where the twine had bit, but they would heal. His legs ached from being tied in the same position for so long, and his gut ached from the retching, but Mordent had had worse mornings, and he simply thanked his lucky stars he was alive.

Now, he thought. *Game on.*

He lay for a while entertaining the fantasy of taking a baseball bat to Tony's face. Crunching the features to pulp.

It was quite within him to make that fantasy a reality.

With his internal workings getting back to normal, in the bathroom mirror he checked the damage the Frame had inflicted externally. His tongue was clearly bitten, but seemed to be healing. The human body was a miraculous system: from birth to death it shaped a life without the owner needing any awareness of its operation. Maybe the body was a cocoon – the transformation at death to a spirit making the butterfly analogy complete. But that smacked of religion, and he wasn't feeling particularly charitable. Instead, he showered, ate scrambled eggs and toast, settled back on the bed to make a call.

'Hello?'

'Marsham? It's Mordent. You left me this number.'

'Hey buddy. I was expecting your call sooner. You get the gen from someone else?'

'I don't *get* anything. I've been incommunicado for a day. What's up?'

'We've got another murder. Nasty, nasty, nasty. Listen, I'm off work today. You want this over the phone, or over a coffee?'

Mordent could hear the eagerness in Marsham's voice. It was an indication of how Mordent was still revered within the force. If Marsham wanted to tell him face to face, so be it. Even if his face currently belied that reputation.

'Coffee is fine. There's a joint called Bukowski's, down near Morgan's Bar. You know it?'

'Sure, I've driven past a few times.'

'I'll meet you there in an hour.'

Mordent hung up. Then he dialled Directory Enquiries and thenceforth the Gardner Hotel.

'I want to speak to Francisco Carmide.'

'May I ask who is calling?'

'Name's Mordent. I met Mr Carmide at the hotel yesterday – or maybe the day before. If you're the pretty girl on the desk you'll remember me, although I'm not quite as handsome as I was then.'

'I'm sorry, Mr Mordent, but my shift for this week started this morning. However, Mr Carmide is currently unavailable. He left the hotel about an hour ago. Can I leave him a message to call?'

Mordent gave his number. 'Tell him it's urgent. And you've been most helpful, much better than the other girl, who gave me the run-around.'

There was a pause, as if the receptionist was about to agree with him and then decided against it. 'No problem, Mr Mordent. I'll leave your message in his pigeonhole.'

Mordent dressed. His limbs ached as he put them through the various holes in his clothing. His gun hung like a dead weight against his chest. He remembered his car was still at his office, so ordered a cab. The ride to Bukowski's was uneventful – it wasn't the day for looking out of the window and speculating on the nature of existence. The driver wasn't chatty and the radio wasn't on. He passed slowly through the city with life's volume turned down, people and buildings barely registering on his eyes.

Once at Bukowski's he ordered coffee, thick and black. It slipped down his throat with the speed of a glacier, the texture of syrup. By the time Marsham entered – lowering his head as he ducked through the door – Mordent was on a second cup and starting to buzz.

Marsham raised a hand and a smile, pulled out the adjacent stool and sat, calling over the waitress for a cappuccino.

'How's it going? You've got a bit of a shiner going on.'

Mordent reflexively touched his face. 'As I said, I've been incommunicado.'

Marsham smiled. 'I'm guessing the other guy got off worse.'

Mordent grimaced. 'Not yet, but he will do. Tell me then. What have you got?'

Marsham looked around – disguising his intentions as effectively as a secret service officer pretending not to be one but looking like a secret service officer pretending not to be one.

'This didn't come from me, okay. The press don't have it yet and Kovacs is twitchy.'

'There's been another murder, you say?'

'Right. Does the name Donald Gaskins mean anything to you?'

Mordent shook his head. 'Vic or perp?'

'Perp. That was the name on the note left with the body. He was a serial killer executed in 1991 by electric chair at the Broad River Correctional Institution in South Carolina.'

'And I'm guessing the victim is a survivor of one of his attacks?'

Marsham shrugged. 'That's the assumption. No links other than the note and the manner of death so far, but it follows the same pattern. You can see why Kovacs is getting nervous.'

Mordent could. Kovacs liked it clean and tidy. This was far from clean and tidy.

'So, the victim …?'

'Little old lady, Mordent.' There was a break in Marsham's voice. 'Just a little old lady.'

Marsham's coffee came and he leant over it for a moment, drinking in the smell. When he lifted his head, Mordent wondered if the moisture on his eyelids was condensation or tears.

'You were called to the scene of the crime?'

'Yup. Both Barker and me. While she died two days ago, forensics reckon she'd been mutilated and tortured for at least a week. Her final release came through suffocation.'

Marsham sipped his coffee. 'You see,' he continued, 'while Gaskins was executed in 1991, his arrest came in 1975. Our victim, Judith Cantrell, would have been in her forties when Gaskins was in operation. Gaskins had two different periods of activity. There were his Serious Murders of people whom he knew and killed for personal reasons, generally with a shot to the head; but before that were his Coastal Kills – these are his classifications, not ours. The Coastal Kills were ones he committed for pure personal pleasure. The victims were generally hitchhikers on the coastal highways. They could be male or female. One every six weeks, to relieve what he called his "bothersomeness". Those victims were all tortured and mutilated, while he attempted to keep them alive for as long as possible.'

Marsham wiped sweat from his brow. The heat was cranked up in Bukowski's and they could have written their names on the condensation covering the window.

He continued: 'Gaskins confessed to eighty or ninety of these crimes, although it's always been assumed the figures were exaggerated. Kovacs is obtaining data on people who later claimed they had narrow escapes. I'm certain our victim will appear on that list. Whether she really got away or just made it up – as people do – who knows? Whichever way, it all caught up with her. There has to be someone on the inside trailing these cases to find these guys. And while it's inter-state, it falls on Kovacs, as the crimes are committed here. At least, till the FBI get hold of it.'

'Surprised they haven't already.'

'Kovacs is trying to contain it, but he's sitting on a pressure cooker.'

'Anything else I need to know?'

'Only if you want details of the mutilations. But, to be honest, they're not relevant.'

'On my stomach it probably wouldn't be a good idea.'

'Truth be told, Barker and I scored some compassionate leave. It was a sight I don't want to relive.'

Mordent nodded. He felt it would take a lot to unnerve Marsham. He was grateful for him taking some time out to fill him in.

He swung the conversation around to guys that he knew at the precinct, took the sting out of Marsham's distress. After a good three quarter hour – during which they also ordered and ate some sandwiches – he patted Marsham on the back and got up to leave.

'I appreciate it,' he said. 'Will put in a good word for you whenever I can.'

'Thanks buddy,' replied Marsham. 'Although I get the feeling that your days of influence are over.' He grinned.

Mordent slipped on a rueful smile. 'You mightn't be wrong, but maybe there'll be a vacancy should Kovacs fall.'

'Maybe,' Marsham said.

They left it at that.

Mordent exited the warmth of Bukowski's and wandered the few blocks to his office. His breath preceded him like cigar smoke. Pedestrians wrapped in long heavy coats, scarves and gloves burrowed their way past him. Suddenly the seasons had changed – just a few days had tipped the scales. At times like these, Mordent couldn't imagine that it might ever be summer – a time for shirtsleeves and short skirts. The cold weather negated the past just as easily as the warm season would roll into the future. When he died, he thought, he would prefer it to be at this time of year. He wanted someone to have to work hard to break the earth to dig his grave.

His mind wandered over the crimes of the Coastal Killer. Of how many lives he might have taken and how many persons were left unaccountable. Of how many graves might be unmarked, of how many relatives wouldn't find solace. Life was a tragedy for some: usually the underprivileged, but it also had a habit of ripping its claws into each and every strata of society. Ultimately, no-one was safe from death. And no-one knew when it might come.

He pieced together what he had, but it wasn't much. Everything hung on whether or not Tony had scouted a location for a serial killer to leave a body. If he hadn't, then this trail of thought came to an end. Whatever Isabelle Silk decided to do with the information about Tony's activities was up to her. The same went for Francisco Carmide. If he could take one fish out of the water then the past few days would have been worth it. The serial killings – although of interest – were best left to the police.

It was then that a trickle of an idea entered his head, and instead of heading straight to his office he got in his car and headed over to Bernard Maloney's place.

33
Start At The Beginning

Maloney lived outside of the city in a tidy three-storey townhouse. The avenue was lined with trees. Mordent was no aboriculturist, but he suspected they were oak. The grass verges were blanketed in leaves: the usual gamut of browns, reds, greens and an artist's palette of colours in-between. There was a colonial feel to the area, but in reality it had spread out from the city and was a new development for those financially mobile and with an urge to believe they lived in a place other than where they did.

Mordent had called Maloney in advance. He had been at home, hadn't returned to work, although tentatively might do so within the next few weeks. His wife's death had hit him hard. If he had expected closure after weeks of stress while she had been missing, then it hadn't happened. Mordent knew the feeling. When his wife, Maria, had first left him, he had spent weeks blaming himself. After a while, drink had replaced her. After a further while, other women had.

He had an idea it might be a while before Maloney gained his level of acceptance.

He parked and walked the steps to the front door, rang the bell. As the wind picked up and blew leaves over the porch, he felt like a trick-or-treater. The door opened before he could decide what he would do for the trick.

Maloney stared out through glasses that seemed too large for his face. He was wearing a grey tank top over a white shirt, brown corduroy trousers, and granddad slippers. He looked to have aged since Mordent had last seen him: but then again, he would, and had.

'Come in, Mordent. The place is a bit untidy, but I know you understand.'

Mordent entered the house. There was a funereal air to the place. Curtains were drawn and dust motes caught the pale rays that gathered at the edges. Being in unfamiliar properties always unnerved him; reminded him of his time on the force, when breaking into a potential perp's house held all kinds of possibilities. But he didn't need to follow Maloney with a gun raised. Instead he dug his hands deep into his pockets and tried to shake off the spectre of death.

They ascended to the first floor. Maloney stepped ahead and opened the curtains in what would have been their dining-room. Polished wooden floors had seen their best days, bearing scuff marks from shoes that should have been kept downstairs. The table was covered in crumbs, as though left for birds. Maloney saw Mordent's glance and shrugged. *This is how men live without women*, he seemed to be saying. Mordent could find no argument in that.

They pulled out chairs, echoing scrapes.

'Do you have any news?' Maloney's voice was low, tired.

'I've got a lead that the police haven't. For the moment, I'm keeping it to myself. You're aware of these other murders, I imagine? The papers are starting to fill up with them.'

Maloney shrugged. 'I've tried to keep away from the news.'

'Then I'll make it brief. I previously told you on the phone that there had been another murder linked to that of your wife. Since then, there have been two others. It appears that we have a serial killer on our hands who is killing the survivors of previous serial killers. Some sick individual. What's puzzling me is, how does he know who to target?'

Maloney raised his eyebrows. 'Beats me. Tessa barely mentioned her previous attack. I guess there would be a police record of it somewhere.'

'Exactly. It has to be someone on the force. But why now?'

'Hmmm?'

'Why now and not years ago? You see, something needs to have started this. There has to have been an impetus. I was hoping you might be able to shed some light on it. Before she went missing, did anything happen?'

Maloney leant back. 'When everything is normal, how do you remember details? Something completely unimportant at the time, that gains importance only following another act – how do you pin that down? Don't think I haven't been trying.'

'You sure there's nothing happened in the past year that was out of the ordinary? No contact made that could have been someone sounding out your situation. See: these crimes have been planned well in advance. Not only that, but they're going to be finite. I'd be surprised if another one happens in our area. The chances of any more serial killer survivors having moved into our city and become known to the new killer are minimal. Someone's got an overview, but it can't last. For all these to be happening within a short time-span, it has needed to have been meticulously prepared. I'm betting that your wife had contact with this guy before her disappearance. Or if not with her, then with an accomplice.'

'An accomplice?'

'I'm fairly sure this guy isn't acting alone. You heard of Tony Runcorn?'

Maloney shook his head. 'Means nothing to me.'

Mordent shrugged. 'Was a long shot.'

'In any event, Mordent, I've been through all this with the police. There's nothing additional I can think of.'

'I understand, but tell me this: would you have told the police about an incident where the police had *already* been involved?'

Maloney leant forwards on his chair. 'Well …' He stopped. Thought. Scratched stubble with dirty fingernails. 'Well. You may have something there. We had an attempted break in. Would have been about ten months ago. An officer came round before we rang them. We laughed about it at the time. Tessa said how efficient they were, but he said he'd been investigating another break-in in the area. Our downstairs window was forced, but as far as it could be determined no access was gained.'

'Did you see that officer yourself?'

'No, Tessa mentioned it when I returned from work.'

'You wouldn't have the guy's name lying around?'

'I doubt it. As far as I remember she said he just took some details and would let us know if anything came of their investigation at the other house. I fixed up the window and that was it. You think there's something in this?'

'I dunno. My gut says maybe, my head wonders if we have enough to follow it up. I'll make enquiries.'

Mordent stood to leave. Maloney reached out for him, but the distance between them over the table was too great.

'Keep me informed,' he simply said.

Mordent nodded. 'I'll let myself out.'

He made his way back through the dark house. Once outside, he examined the windows, noted the one that had been fixed. The fresh brass clasp was clear. What would it have taken for someone to force the window and then return in uniform to check out the house? Maybe it was nothing. Maybe it would lead to nothing. But with the little that he had, at least this was a little more.

He sat in his car. Wondered what would be best. Marsham wouldn't be at work, and this was no job for Martens. There was only one thing to do and that was to call Kovacs.

He drove a short distance from Maloney's house and parked up. Was this the time to exchange the information he had about Tony? He decided to play it by ear.

The phone was answered within the time specified by the police charter. Mordent was impressed. He asked for Kovacs and ended up in the right office. Thurlow picked up.

'Thurlow. Is Kovacs there? I need to speak to him.'

'He's pretty tied up, Mordent. How's the drink problem?'

'No longer a problem. Look, I need to speak to him. Tell him it's urgent. It's about the recent murders.'

There was a pause. 'The Residue Killer?'

'If that's what you're calling him, then yes.'

'Could be a *her*, Mordent. Suspect everyone.'

'Listen, Thurlow, just get me Kovacs. Is he there?'

Again, a pause. Mordent imagined Thurlow looking around the office space, scanning for Kovacs. 'Can't say as I can see him. Why don't you give me the information and I'll pass it on?'

'I'd rather speak to him direct. I need to trade this info. No offence, Thurlow.'

'None taken.'

'When will he be back?'

'I dunno. Give me your number. I'll get him to call you.'

'Thanks.'

Mordent hung up. He headed toward the city, leaving all the pretty trees and buildings behind. Even without their leaves, the trees were impressive – like multi-fingered hands pushing through the earth and reaching toward the sky.

Traffic was thinner out here, but like a magnet pushing through iron filings he accumulated cars all around him by the time the outskirts of the city came into view. Or to use a different analogy, it was like the meeting of tributaries as they headed toward the sea.

Sometimes, all you needed to do was work backwards and head toward the source. One thing Kovacs should have done was to query who might have accessed those serial killer files in the past year. He must have realised the killer's information came from that source. Surely it was simple? Follow the trail in reverse, rather than predict the future. But sometimes the obvious things are those you least think of. If he could prod Kovacs in that direction maybe he wouldn't need to trade his suspicions about Tony checking out the location.

So, maybe it was withholding information. But after the incident with the syringe, Tony was going to be his.

About a mile out from his office his cell rang. He weaved a way through the traffic and pulled up at the sidewalk. His phone indicated *Number withheld*.

'Mordent? It's Francisco Carmide. You were trying to get hold of me.'

'That's right. Listen, have you spoken to Tony Runcorn yet, about what we discussed the other day?'

'I've been exceptionally busy, Mr Mordent. This is a delicate matter that requires some thought. I don't want to rush into anything.'

'I suggest you hold fire for a moment. I've some new information that suggests there's more to Tony than I first thought. Currently, I don't want you poking a stick into that particular snake's hole. He'll either hide, or come out all guns blazing. Can you do that for me?'

'Why, of course. If you think it's for the best.'

'I think it's best for the Church, Carmide. And your reputation. Tell me something, though. Whenabouts did you start having dealings with Tony?'

'I'd say about five months ago. I set up the Church two years ago, but funds were slow to trickle in. It's since Tony's involvement that we've expanded. Without the knowledge you've given me, Mordent, I would say I'd have a lot to thank him for.'

'The congregation before he attended – would you say it was small?'

'Double figures at some meetings. But we all have to start somewhere.'

'I find starting at the beginning bears the best results. Has Tony any close friends within the organisation, other than you and Isabelle?'

'I wouldn't say I was a close friend, but obviously I've had dealings with him. He's usually with Isabelle. But to be honest, I tend not to fraternise with the congregation. If Tony has any connections with them I wouldn't know.'

'Well, thanks for calling me back, Mr Carmide. I appreciate you can only tell me what you know.'

'Indeed.'

Carmide hung up. Mordent chewed his lip. More things needed to add up. He was never good at math, but the sums weren't sitting right. Maybe it was because the sums were greater than their total parts.

He pulled back into traffic, being absorbed like water into a sponge. If you were far enough away you would see only a continuous movement, rather than individual cars. Mordent was thinking he was too far away from what was going on. He needed to get that bit closer, too close if necessary. But before he could do so he needed to be tooled up.

Taped to the underside of his desk drawer in his office was a key to a left luggage locker.

It wasn't often that he used it.

But today would be one of those occasions.

34

If It Looks Sweet, And It Smells Sweet, And It Tastes Sweet, Then It Is Sweet

There was a girl in his elevator. One of the agency types. All legs and tan tights with a straight skirt and make-up. She avoided looking his way, her eyes searching the corners as if inspecting for dust. Unwittingly this gave Mordent's eyes free range to rove over her body, appraise her beauty and her curves. He willed the elevator to break, but fate wasn't on his side and an electronic *ping* ended his reverie.

He motioned for her to exit the elevator first. Not because he was gentlemanly, but all the better to watch her from the rear as she tottered down the corridor.

Outside his office he glanced at the damaged door. He vaguely remembered giving Jessica his spare key. Trying the handle, it was indeed locked. He entered with caution, but everything was as it should be. Jessica had tidied. The twine was gone from the floor. There had been nothing else to take care of. He wondered if she had spent some time in the office, filing her nails and waiting for the phone to ring.

It had crossed his mind that she might be there. Part of him wanted her to be there. And then part of him didn't.

Dames were always fine so long as they weren't in the way.

Since he had met Jessica she had proved useful in a variety of situations, but there would come a point when the case would be over, and from then onwards she would be surplus to requirements. He no more needed a secretary than he needed a wife. And you only needed a secretary when you had a wife. Eye candy for the office. Nothing more, nothing less.

If Jessica hadn't turned up, would he still be strapped to the chair? He doubted it. Once he had awoken he could have shouted. One of the agency girls would have heard him. He entertained a brief fantasy of the one in the elevator coming in and finding him helpless. Then strapping on bubble wrap gloves and playing nurse. He became distracted, almost forgot why he was there; then shook his head and knelt behind his desk. Opened the drawer and removed the key taped to the underside.

He whistled to himself as he locked up the office, then headed over to the train station and the left luggage locker.

The station was wide open: wide and open. Wind scoured it. In the days of steam, engines would have puffed like bulls. Sausages of metal muscle. Nowadays the trains were much more efficient, yet there were no such improvements to the passengers, most of whom appeared to be travelling for the first time if you took vagueness and uncertainty as indicators.

Mordent cut through them, walking with determination and purpose. He located the locker, opened it and pulled out a canvas bag knotted at the top. It was heavy, but he avoided the temptation to swing it over his shoulder. Instead he grasped it by the neck, twisted the slack around his fist and headed back to his vehicle.

There was a piece of wasteland Mordent was aware of at the back of the station. He pulled up alongside it, then slipped through some wire netting that had been pulled away at the base. It had been a while since he was last there; was thankful it remained undeveloped. There was still a chance that the body might be found, and with the latest forensics a slim possibility that the murder might be linked back to him. Most days he never thought anything of it: but some days it rested on his back as though the corpse were pressing down on him, trying to reach his eyes with its fingers.

Castillo had had to die. Both of them had known it. Plain and simple. He recalled that summer night, over 12 years earlier, when he had assembled the weapon that was now contained in the bag. Unconventional but effective. Crossbow bolts were harder to trace than bullets, didn't bear marks that identified them as having been fired from a specific weapon. Maybe it was reckless to have kept it, but the key hadn't always rested under that desk drawer. When he had killed Castillo he had still been on the force. The key had inhabited at least four different hiding places. But he preferred to keep the weapon rather than discard it. As far as he was concerned, that minimised the likelihood of it being found.

Castillo had met him with a view to blackmail. He had had information regarding some of Mordent's informants and their connection to the force. Mordent would have been the fall guy, the nature of his involvement inarguable, and an easy target to avoid the stain spreading to other senior officers who were involved. He hadn't been willing to take that rap. He had agreed to meet with Castillo, and once he had seen the evidence and been as convinced as he possibly could be that he had everything required, he had socked the guy in the face, tied his hands behind his back and sent the crossbow bolt through the base of his skull.

It had been a dirty job, but one that had to be done. Pay a blackmailer once and you'd always be paying. But not only that, other guys' lives had been at stake. His ring of informants had fanned out like ripples from a stone thrown in a pond. He had had to protect them, and to protect himself.

This was his justification. Castillo wasn't the only person he'd killed outside of his official capacities. Maybe he wouldn't be the last.

He scanned the waste ground. A sign indicating that guard dogs were on the premises was attached to the wire fence, but it was faded and he was certain the area hadn't been patrolled for years. Nevertheless, it wasn't easy to find cover. Eventually he hunkered down behind some trees, opened the canvas bag and removed the four separate sections of the crossbow individually wrapped in muslin cloth.

It was a cinch putting it together. Memories drifted in and out like the tide obliterating yet uncovering footprints.

Castillo had blubbed before he had died. Tears streaming down his face. Mordent knew what it was to fear death – or rather, the absence of life. Death was about the loss of existence. It was a crime to take it, but on this occasion he held no guilt. Castillo had never approached the fringes of his memory with an accusing finger.

What that taught him was that there were echelons when it came to good and bad; that the boundaries between them might blur, but that the inherently good – the mostly good – would be justified.

With the crossbow completed, he popped it back into the canvas bag. It was bulky now, difficult to handle with the material wrapped around it. But better to assemble it there than on Reflective Tony's front porch.

Low clouds scudded over the waste ground. Pinpricks of light appeared in the sky and fell as rain. Mordent pulled his collar up around him and walked quickly back to his car. Inside, the rain battered the windscreen in a sudden shower, rendering the view a pointillist painting, which, as the rain just as suddenly halted, melted down the glass.

He turned the key in the ignition and set off for Tony's.

The downpour's journey to the drains was obstructed by leaves. As he headed uphill, the water cascaded like a group of children running to a playground, tumbling and falling over each other. The crossbow sat on the passenger seat like a kidnap victim: quiet and expectant. There were a couple of other items in the bag: a crowbar and a third of a roll of masking tape. Mordent had wrapped the tape around Castillo's hands after slugging him, but had not gagged his mouth. Train noises had been a sufficient dampener. The squeal of metal on metal merging with Castillo's pleas had negated them. And the crossbow was a quiet weapon. A soft thud, like a backwards suck, and the job was done.

Tony being in a residential area – albeit one where the neighbours probably weren't unused to a bit of violence and no doubt were frequently drugged up themselves – Mordent would have to be more cautious. Even if the intention was to scare Tony, not kill him. If he accidentally *did* kill him, forensics were much in advance of when he had last used the crossbow. Mordent didn't want both his chickens and eggs to be in the same basket.

This time he parked a block away from Tony's. He didn't want his vehicle associated with the street, even if the precaution ruled out a quick getaway. He sat in the car awhile. Thought better of his plan and drove a square taking in Tony's house. The Frame's vehicle wasn't parked outside, and he hoped that meant that either Tony was alone or that the property was empty, in which case he would gain the element of surprise. After rounding the fourth corner he parked again where he had done the night before, loaded up the crossbow and picked up the bag, with his hand inside clutching the shaft.

It wasn't quite high noon, but as Mordent walked up Tony's street, weapon in hand, he could feel tension building. The anticipation of revenge.

Where his palm held the crossbow there was the intimation of sweat.

As before, he glanced through the window of the property next to Tony's. The woman who had unknowingly played a bit part in his fantasy was stretched out asleep on her sofa. There was a movie playing on her plasma screen, but in a blink he was beyond it, and while the scene was familiar he couldn't place it.

Just for a moment he was distracted, and he found himself outside Tony's door without preamble.

He knocked.

It seemed quiet inside. Not so much an absence of noise, more a case of noise being withheld.

He hadn't spent all that time in the force without becoming attuned to danger.

Something was up.

Tony was a small-time crook and it didn't take much for Mordent to read his mind. If he was wary of a visitor he would be stood quietly just the other side of the door. It was a blind spot from the windows at the front of the property. Tony's expectation would be for a visitor to knock again and then – if they were inquisitive – to wander around the back. Mordent had to break that expectation. And he did.

He knocked once again – harder – just hard enough to give Tony the impression he meant business. Then waited. As Tony no doubt listened out for footsteps heading around the back, Mordent leant back, put his shoulder against the door, and in one movement split it away from the frame and caromed into the interior.

It was dark inside. He felt the door hit something solid, and almost tripped as that something fell to the ground. Mordent kicked out: once, twice. Connected with a soft body that emitted a low groan. He reached out for a light switch, flicked it. The narrow corridor revealed itself. Tony lay on the floor clutching his stomach. Mordent unsheathed the crossbow and pointed it low. Then pushed the door closed behind him, the latch slipping back in as if nothing had happened. Mordent thanked his lucky stars Tony hadn't upgraded his property. The door was as flimsy as balsa.

It seemed Tony had been caught unawares. He was dressed in his underpants.

'Jeez.' He wheezed out the word. Struggled to lift himself up with one hand.

'I suggest you stay put,' Mordent growled. 'We've got some unfinished business to settle.'

All the bravado from Mordent's office had fled from Tony's face. 'What are you doing with that?'

Mordent moved the crossbow up and down, scanning Tony's body. 'I haven't decided yet. Either way, it'll cause some pain.'

'Just keep in mind who you're dealing with.'

The threat was unconvincing.

'You're low-life, Tony. You know it and I know it. We all

know it. Laundering money through the Church is one thing, fleecing dames is another. But being in cahoots with a serial killer, that's gonna count a lot of years.'

'What?'

'I know you haven't forgotten I saw you in that disused parking lot. That's why you tried to scare me off – maybe kill me – with that hallucinogen the other day. So, either the killer is you – which I very much doubt – or your hood – which I doubt even more, he hasn't the brains for this type of thing – or it's a third party. That's the name I've come for this morning. And I won't be leaving till I get it.'

Tony shrugged. 'You've got nothing on me. You can't pin me for those crimes.'

'Maybe I can't. But I can turn my knowledge in to the police, and I'm sure you don't want them investigating. Besides, I *have* got something on you. Something tangible. This.'

Mordent fired the crossbow, and the shot hit Tony soft yet hard in the thigh.

'Fuck!' Tony's face contorted with pain. 'What was that for?'

'Payback for the drug.' Mordent smiled. 'Revenge is sweet.'

Tony clutched his thigh, blood running through his fingers, as Mordent calmly reached into the bag, pulled out another bolt and loaded it into the bow.

'Not just a surface wound, but no real damage done,' Mordent said. 'So now we're quits. But I kill you if you don't give me the info.'

'You wouldn't kill me.'

'Maybe I would, maybe I wouldn't. Maybe you thought I'd never use this thing. Maybe I did. The odds are fifty-fifty: either I will or I won't. Same with the odds of you telling me: either you will or you won't. The odds are not lengthened or shortened by me having fired this already. They remain fifty-fifty. Good to keep things simple, don't you think?'

Maybe it was the look in Mordent's eyes, but the look in Tony's changed. Mordent assumed he was thinking through the options, balancing helping the police with their enquiries against withholding information. Adding up the other misdemeanours that might be added or subtracted during a subsequent investigation.

'You haven't thought this through,' Tony said. 'You drop me in and I get you for using that thing.'

'I think your crimes outweigh mine. Quit stalling and spill the beans.'

'And if I do?'

'Then *I* think through your options. I've spoken to Carmide about your money-laundering. I'm sure he'll want to drop that connection without much fuss. What you do with the dames is your business – what goes around comes around. What you did with me, well, payback came and went. So that leaves your connection to the serial killer. I know there's also a connection there to the force. Maybe the money-laundering is tied into it, maybe it isn't. You tell me.'

Tony glanced at the wound in his leg. The bleeding had staunched. It had been a clean shot.

'I don't know a great deal about the murders,' he said. 'Someone at the Church asked me to scout for an abandoned location. Somewhere central, but hidden. It was the only involvement I had, and I thought it was connected to a Church meeting. Once the act had taken place, I realised what was going on. I went back to my source and made a financial arrangement. There was nothing else I needed to know.'

Mordent hefted the weight of the crossbow in his grip. Mulled things over. It could be the truth, but something bugged him.

'How come this guy got you involved at all? Why risk it?'

Tony shrugged. 'He's heavily into the Church, that's all I know. I get the feeling he feels he's protected.'

'By God?'

'By God.'

Mordent snorted. But there was no second-guessing the mind of a nutter. He'd heard worse.

'That's your info,' said Tony. 'Are we quits?'

'You know I need more than that. I need a name.'

'And this is just between you and me? How can I trust you?'

'I think we've gone beyond trust. Just give me the name.'

Tony thought it over. 'Thurlow,' he said.

'Thurlow?'

'Yeh, Thurlow. He's on the force.' Tony smiled.

'Thurlow can't be the killer.'

'Didn't say he was. What I said was that Thurlow asked me to scout the location. He turned to the Church after a period of drink. He's clued up on it. Would do anything for it. Ask him.'

'I know him. I will.'

Mordent paused. The urge of the day had passed. It was similar to the moment after climax when the anticipation and adrenalin dissipated in an instant and he wondered how it ever became heightened in the first place. He guessed he was going to have to let Tony go. Then watch his own back for a while. It didn't pay to make enemies, but it wouldn't do him any favours to shut Tony up permanently. His job for Isabelle was done: he'd flushed out the rat. And he'd gained a lead that could further the Residue Killer case and bring in more money from Maloney. Sorted.

'We're done here,' he said. 'I don't want to see you again anytime soon.'

Tony nodded. 'Likewise.'

Mordent turned to go, then heard a loud thump upstairs. Like something falling off a bed.

'You got a woman up there?' He gestured toward the ceiling.

Tony's smile was thin.

It was enough.

The masking tape was thick. Mordent flipped Tony over and, with his knee in his back, wrapped tape around his wrists.

'Wait here,' he said, deliberately superfluously. Then headed upstairs.

Maybe it was his imagination, but the house seemed darker than it had been when he had broken in the other night. The stairwell enclosed him, his vision reduced to black and white. He felt that shadows of the walls were falling inwards, as if he were ascending into a cone.

Once in the main bedroom he switched on the light. Jessica

was stripped to her underwear, lying in a foetal position on the floor. Her hands were tied behind her back with twine, and on the dresser next to the bed a syringe pointed skyward like a rocket.

He knelt down beside her, turned her face to his. Her eyes were like two black-spotted billiard balls, her jaw was slack and she was drooling. Mordent loosened the twine and massaged her wrists, lifted her onto the bed and stretched out her body. She sprang back into the foetal position like a coiled spring.

He pulled a cover over her. Picked up the syringe from the table and filled it with the remainder of the drug that sat in a small bottle beside it. For a moment he considered not tapping it to let out the air bubbles, then did.

His descent of the stairs carried a premonition of the hell he was about to put Tony through. A hell that he deserved.

35
Another Spot of Violence

Again, shadows encroached on his vision. As he descended the stairs, it seemed that a door was closed at the bottom. Then the door moved and he realised it was the Frame.

He had left the crossbow in the bedroom. Turning swiftly, he began to head up, but with a speed belying his weight, the Frame thundered up behind him, struck out with something hard and caught Mordent on the back of his left heel. Pain shot through his leg as though it were racing upstairs ahead of him. His knee gave way and he slipped belly forwards. The Frame pulled on his leg and began dragging him downstairs. Mordent tried to kick him with his right leg, but if it connected then it was ineffective. As he reached the bottom step, he felt the scruff of his jacket constrict as the Frame wrapped a meaty hand around it. Hauled to his feet, he was then thrown toward the kitchen. He hit a chair hard, the back digging into his solar plexus. Trying to pick it up, he turned to face the Frame, but the chair was easily knocked out of his grip and he dropped to the floor, mimicking Jessica's pose as he waited for the kicks to rain down.

Instead the Frame spoke: 'Didn't think we'd see you again. At least, not till we went back to your office and found you'd worked your way free. Picked up a sweet replacement though.' He grinned, grabbed at his crotch. The gesture was so incongruous that Mordent stopped thinking of him purely as a caricatured heavy and realised he was a human being.

Mordent glanced over to Tony, who was still lying on the floor. His mouth had now been taped over, and his eyes were wide.

The Frame followed his look. 'He talks too much,' he said.

'Sounds like you've got something to hide.' Mordent shifted into a seated position, his back against the chair, his legs stretched out on the floor. The back of his left ankle hurt like hell. He noticed his crowbar by the foot of the stairs, realised what the Frame had used.

'We've all got something to hide,' said the Frame. 'Some of us hide behind others. Tony, he hides behind me. Me, I hide behind myself.'

'You're not as stupid as you look.'

'That's the point.'

Mordent felt his stomach where the chair had hit. There would be bruising come morning. Should he see morning.

'So,' he said. 'You're the Residue Killer.'

The Frame's brow furrowed. 'Is that what they're calling him? Nope, I'm not the Residue Killer. Hasn't Tony explained that?'

'Tony gave me the name of Thurlow.'

The Frame laughed; it didn't sound funny. 'Thurlow ain't the killer either.'

'You know who is?'

'What's it to you?'

'Let's just say I have an interest.'

The Frame became distracted. His eyes roved over the room, as if searching for something to play with. There was an edge of uninterest that puzzled Mordent, then he noticed something the Frame hadn't seen: the syringe hanging loosely at the back of the big man's leg.

Maybe it had only penetrated his trouser, maybe it had nicked the flesh. Mordent couldn't recall releasing it, but it had gotten there somehow. If he were lucky, it might slowly drip-feed into the bloodstream. If he were unlucky, the Frame would spot it and discharge it into Mordent's own body. He'd taken that trip before, didn't fancy a return ticket.

The Frame turned and saw the crowbar, picked it up; then walked into the kitchen, his movements stiff as though battling wind. Picking up another of the chairs, he turned it so the reverse faced him, sat down and rested his arms on the back.

'So,' he said. 'What do I do now?'

'If I were you, I'd contact the guys that are behind Tony's church money-laundering venture. Tell them Tony screwed up and you want a new employer. Do away with him, if you have to, to prove your worth. I'm sure they'd be ready to pay a hood with some intelligence.'

The Frame sighed. That sigh seemed to come from deeper inside him than it had a right to. He toyed with the crowbar, hefting its weight in both hands, seesawing it between them. 'Could be a plan,' he said.

'You let me go with the girl and we call it quits. I've got the information I came for.'

The Frame sighed again. 'It's that simple, right?' He crossed his legs under the chair and the syringe fell to the floor. He didn't notice.

'Right.'

'Yet you've got me and Tony figured for the Residue Killer. That's nothing to do with us. And the money-laundering is nothing to do with me.'

'As an employee you're getting the proceeds.' Mordent bit back his tongue. Perhaps he shouldn't remind the Frame of the depth of his involvement.

But the Frame was drifting again. His eyes wandered around the room and he moved one hand from the crowbar to rub the top of his head. It was a dreamlike motion in a sleepy state, but Mordent knew the drug wasn't designed to render the subject comatose – it contained an unpredictable twist.

He glanced at Tony on the floor. He was quietly trying to unpick the tape, but it was stuck hard and fast and his fingers merely wavered ineffectually like sea anemone antennae.

'Seems I've got some tidying up to do,' said the Frame. He stood, placed the crowbar on the seat of the chair and lumbered across the room like Frankenstein's monster in leaded boots. There was an opened packet of lentils near the draining board and he picked it up, folded down the lip and sealed it with the sticky flap that came with the packaging. Opening the cupboard door, he placed it carefully alongside the other pulses.

Mordent watched as, that done, he collected a beer can by the drainer, squeezed it between his two palms and placed it within a carrier bag hung on the back door handle, with the remains of other cans that were ready for recycling.

Following that, he wandered around the rest of the kitchen, opening both cupboards and the fridge, moving a few items around, sniffing a couple that Mordent presumed were close to their use-by dates. An opened pre-packed salami went in the food bin.

Muttering accompanied the Frame's actions, but it was too low to be heard. He wandered past Mordent, who remained still, the pain in his leg an unknown factor when it came to defence. The Frame picked up the crowbar and placed it on the windowsill, then returned the chair to the table, making sure that it was square, with the back pressed tight against the wooden top.

There was that sigh again. Almost preternatural. Then the Frame picked up the crowbar again and wandered over to Tony. Kneeling down beside him, he raised the bar and stove his head in.

There was a sickening crunch as he repeated the action, as innocently as a child attacking a piñata. Bile rose in Mordent's throat and he struggled to his feet, ignoring the pain in his left leg. Tony's face had been a picture of fear as the bar had been raised: then in an instant it had crumpled, and in several instants had been less than a bloody pulp. His gagged scream, stifled by the suddenness of the action, died along with him. It was over far too quickly, viewed far too slowly. The Frame's shoulders sagged and he placed the bar on the floor, breathed heavily, wiped his eyes.

Mordent clutched the side of the table to steady himself. The pain in his leg was seriously debilitating. He glanced at the back door, wondered if it was locked. Then realised with a jolt that he was carrying his gun – the crossbow incident had confused him.

He drew the gun and held it cocked by his side. Waited to see what the Frame would do.

Minutes passed. The Frame remained in the same position, one knee on the floor, the other at an angle. Then with one hand he started to poke at the remains of Tony's face, as if checking whether or not a package of meat had defrosted. Tentative movements that sank into the remnants of flesh. Mordent was suddenly reminded of King Kong holding Fay Wray in the palm of its hand; the idle curiosity that bridged the gap between beauty and the beast.

He wondered what the Frame was seeing.

It made sense to do nothing. He had all the time in the world and a gun in his hand.

Then he heard footsteps upstairs and remembered Jessica.

36
Crime Scene

He held his breath. Counted the steps from the bedroom to the door, from the door to the foot of the stairs, and then the descending footfalls as she made her way down.

He glanced over at the Frame, who had picked up the crowbar and was using it to root around within Tony's smashed face like a shaman poking chicken entrails with a stick to predict the future. Mordent had a pretty good idea of what that future might contain.

He saw Jessica's toes, feet, ankles, calves, knees, thighs, panties, waist, stomach, bra, neck, chin, mouth, nose, eyes, forehead and hair arrive into view in that order. She looked beautiful. For the first time since he had met her he found himself really wanting her. Yet this was neither the time nor the place. Jessica glanced over to the Frame bent over Tony, but whether or not she could see the details, no scream came from her mouth. Mordent realised she was still drugged up. In one hand she carried the crossbow that he had left on the bedroom floor.

She remained stood at the bottom of the stairs. She had a clear view to Mordent, but it seemed she hadn't seen him. He gestured with his gun for her to come over, but it didn't register. It was difficult to see her eyes from that distance, but they seemed not quite there. He realised he was trapped in a house with two armed and drugged crazies, and he wanted to shoot only one of them.

Again, the scene froze as if in a tableaux. Time crept by inexorably. Mordent became aware of pedestrian noises outside, the TV from next door. A wasp in its death throes curled and buzzed ineffectually against a window pane. His own breathing seemed laboured, as if he had run a hundred yards. He realised that the pain in his leg was even worse than he had thought – his breathlessness was directly connected to it. The gun was warm in his hand.

Then, as if a light had been switched on in Jessica's head, she let the crossbow drop to the floor. The bolt fell out of it, but it didn't discharge. The Frame lifted his head, turned to see her. His expression was unreadable, but Jessica's was as clear as day. She advanced toward Mordent, a smile on her face.

'Hey, Stingray, how about you and me getting some action.'

Mordent's tongue swelled in his mouth. He couldn't get any words out.

'I didn't hear you arrive,' she continued, in her fake Southern Belle accent. 'Why honey, you might have told me you were coming.'

She continued walking and entered the kitchen. Behind her, the Frame stood like a presumed dead killer in a horror movie. One that rises again when the victim's back is turned.

Jessica slipped one finger where her bra bit into her left shoulder, unhooked it. 'Why,' she said, 'you've got me all hot and bothered.'

Mordent found his tongue unloosen. 'Just get over here,' he said, as calmly as possible.

'I love it when you order me around.'

She continued to walk closer. The Frame had entered the doorway to the kitchen, filling it.

'I've been so lonely,' she said. 'I need a man to take care of me, Stingray. I can't look after myself. I'm just a poor, defenceless female.'

'Get over here,' yelled Mordent. He couldn't risk shooting the Frame with Jessica stood in front of him. And he had a feeling he couldn't reason with either of them.

'Oh my.'

Behind her, the Frame continued to advance. He raised the hand holding the crowbar. Despite Jessica's size in comparison, her closer proximity to Mordent made her equal in perspective. Mordent might have a chance to shoot the crowbar-carrying arm, but it would be tricky. There would come a point, however, when the only alternative would be to risk it.

Jessica suddenly halted. 'Hey,' she said, 'what are you doing with that gun?'

She started to back away.

Mordent fired into the ceiling. Plaster fell like clumpy snow.

'Get over here!' he shouted.

But he had scared her out of the reverie, and she knew something was wrong. What she didn't realise was wrong was the wrong that was stood behind her.

The crowbar rose. Mordent sighted his gun for a shot.

And then suddenly it was over. The Frame slumped forward and fell onto Jessica, pushing her to the floor, where she cracked her head. Mordent now had a clear view to the doorway. Isabelle Silk stood there, with the crossbow in her hand.

'I would blow into it,' she said, the crossbow raised, one hand on her hip, 'but that would be a bit tacky, wouldn't it?'

Then she fell away in a dead faint.

Mordent turned a chair around, sat on it, surveyed the scene.

Over by the front door, Tony lay in a pool of blood, his head wrecked against the canvas of the floor like some surrealist sculpture. Beside him, his pregnant girlfriend had collapsed with half her body resting on the foot of the stairs, her knees pushed together so that it looked like she was simply relaxing, her white business shirt bulging with baby. The soles of Isabelle's shoes were wet.

Directly in front of Mordent, Jessica lay squashed by the Frame. A cut oozed red from her forehead and one of her teeth lay two inches from her mouth. An outstretched hand almost touched Mordent's right shoe. It could have been an accusing finger, but she was still breathing and therefore wasn't dead. Her eyes were closed and Mordent knew she still ruminated with the residue of the drug.

Atop her, the Frame lay stretched like a collapsed wall. A tiny hole in the back of his jacket was the only indication of a wound. Isabelle had either got lucky or was a hot shot – Mordent suspected the latter. He was dead; there was no question of it. The bolt was embedded in his heart, but Isabelle was no Cupid.

Mordent felt tired. He rubbed his hand over his face. Knew he would have to ease the Frame off Jessica before she suffocated. Knew that with the lost tooth he'd find it hard to make love to her again. Knew that he should never have done it in the first place.

So this is how it ends, he thought. He would have to call the cops. Explain the situation in an interview room where in his distant past he had been on the other side of the desk. Where he had sometimes used violence to make a point. Here, violence was all around him. Just as it was in the world at large. Violence was a force – every action had an equal and opposite reaction. What went around came around.

He bent down, pulled up his trouser leg and examined the blue-black bruise spotted with red that was his ankle. He touched his hands to his face, traced the faint indentations the Frame's fist had made a few days beforehand, stuck out his tongue and realised it was healing.

All this would heal in time. The good guys had won.

He hefted himself to his feet and then to the floor. Knelt beside the Frame and attempted to lift him, couldn't do it. Instead he grabbed Jessica by the arm and pulled. Her face slid against the floor as she was squeezed out from underneath the Frame, giving the appearance of a leer.

Once she was out, he rolled her onto her back. She looked old.

She opened her eyes. 'Hey Stingray,' she said. Then she slept.

37
Godzilla v Mechagodzilla

'Let's get this straight.' Kovacs leant across the desk, his arms folded flat on the wood.

Mordent sighed. They had gotten it straight for the past hour, but Kovacs was a stickler for procedure. Though if he was hoping to lay a trap he would be sadly disappointed.

'You're investigating Tony Runcorn on behalf of his girlfriend, Isabelle Silk. She's due to have his child and has concerns over his dodgy business connections. Right?'

Mordent nodded.

'So this has been going on for some time, and you're aware – like us – that Tony's a small-time crook. Tell me again why you visited him today.'

Mordent leant back in the chair, posed relaxation. 'Tony found out that I was investigating him. He abducted my secretary, Jessica Boothby. At least, I had a suspicion that had happened. So I went on over to find out.'

Kovacs continued leaning forwards. He interlinked his fingers. 'So, you get there and Tony is dead. Shot in his thigh with the crossbow by Cyril Beckworth, known in the trade as the Frame, and once immobilised had his face smashed in. Beckworth appears drugged up, as does Boothby. There's an altercation and Beckworth smashes something into your leg. You're incapacitated. Beckworth comes after you again and

Boothby gets in the way. Silk arrives, picks up the crossbow, kills him. You'd testify it was self-defence?'

'Absolutely, Kovacs. Silk saved my life.'

Kovacs smiled. It was a smile Mordent wasn't happy with.

'Doesn't quite explain your prints on the crossbow. Does it?'

Mordent shrugged. 'I picked it up afterwards. I know I shouldn't have. But we've been through this. It was traumatic.'

'Boothby's prints are on the bow too.'

'So she also picked it up. Listen Kovacs, you know as well as I do that a jury can't convict any of us with all our prints over that bow. Silk's story will tie with mine – I've no doubt of it. Boothby's may or may not – but she was drugged up. She'll concur with the kidnap though. And that's all the info you need. The bad guys are dead. Period.'

Kovacs looked as if he was about to whisper how much he'd love to pin something on Mordent. But he restrained himself. Mordent knew that admission would hurt. Besides, there was nothing to pin. Mordent genuinely hadn't killed either of them. All he was leaving out was the Church of Wire and Tony's possible connection to the serial killer. Although he was ready to use that now, to get out of there.

Kovacs sighed. 'The women's stories tie with yours,' he said. 'Although I get the feeling you're holding something back.'

Mordent leant forward, edging into the space on the desk. He saw Kovacs wanted to move back, yet didn't. Throughout the interview the desk territory had gone back and forth like a tug of war. Like the battle between Godzilla and Mechagodzilla in those old Japanese movies.

'No charges, right?' said Mordent.

Kovacs shrugged. 'There's nothing to charge you with.'

'Same with Silk and Boothby?'

'Again, all the evidence puts Tony's murder on Beckworth and Beckworth's murder in self-defence on Silk. Maybe if Beckworth was going to brain you and I was Silk I wouldn't have fired the bow, but a jury won't convict on that, so there's no point taking it to court. As you say, the bad guys are dead. So what's the trade off?'

'When I was tailing Runcorn he headed to the location of one of those murders you've been investigating. Prior to the murder. Seems a bit too much of a coincidence to me.'

Kovacs sat up. 'You're saying Runcorn is the Residue Killer?'

Mordent smiled. 'I *doubt* Runcorn is the Residue Killer. I think he was scouting a location for the Residue Killer. I'm saying I think he knew who he was.'

'Beckworth?'

'What do you think?'

'I don't think Beckworth had the intelligence.'

'He played a dumb game, I agree, but I think he was smarter than he looked.'

'Smart enough to take a shot in the back?'

'Just a feeling I had. But no, I don't think Beckworth was the killer. I think Runcorn was being used, but I don't know why.'

'Which location?'

'The disused parking lot. Runcorn went inside while Beckworth beat me up outside. Couple of days before the murder. Just thought you might like to know.'

Kovacs nodded, in thought. 'You didn't ask Runcorn about it?'

Mordent leant back. 'Dude, he was dead.'

Kovacs shook his head. 'Previously.'

'Nope.'

'And you didn't think to tell me this before.'

'Wasn't sure it was relevant. Could have been just a coincidence. Might have been something I could use against Tony. I would have brought it up today, if his head hadn't been stoved in when I arrived.'

Kovacs nodded, again, fell into thought. Mordent saw behind the veil. The tiredness etched into Kovacs' face. The accumulation of years of police work hanging heavy on his jowls. This was a different Kovacs from the one he'd once known. He suddenly felt sorry for him. Even someone as meticulous as Kovacs couldn't fight time.

And whichever way you looked at it, time was always against you.

'This Residue Killer,' Mordent ventured, 'I'm guessing he's a tough nut to crack.'

'You could say that.'

'Tessa Maloney's husband tells me they had a break-in a few months before her abduction. That's something else I need to pass on.'

'Oh?'

'Just a hunch I had about the killer casing the joint. Maybe you could check if it was reported. We all know there has to be a link to the force to account for the killer having the information about the survivors of the previous attacks. I'm guessing you won't have a record of it.'

'I'll contact Maloney to check.' Kovacs stood. 'And thanks.'

'Thanks?'

'Yeah, thanks. Now get out of here.'

Mordent got.

38
Bad Egg

Mordent stopped at the front desk before he left the building. Bartholomew was on duty.

'Mordent. How the devil are you?'

'I'm good, Bartholomew. How's the wife and kids?'

Bartholomew smiled. 'They're good, thanks.'

'Glad to hear it.' Mordent leant on the counter. 'Say, do you know if Thurlow is in today? There's something I need to talk to him about.'

'I'll take a look.' Bartholomew tapped away at the PC next to him. 'What you doing here anyway?'

'Helping Kovacs with an enquiry.'

'Go okay?'

'Just dandy. What you got?'

Bartholomew ran his finger down the screen. 'Thurlow is off the roster for a couple of days. Had worked 12 straight.'

Mordent rubbed his chin. 'Need to see him before then, if possible.'

Bartholomew shrugged. 'He won't be in.'

'You got a home address?'

'I can't give you that info, Mordent. You know that.'

'Could be important.'

'So could my job.'

'New Commissioner a stickler for the rules, like Kovacs?'

'You could say that.'

'Tell you what,' Mordent pulled a pen out from his inside jacket pocket and placed it on the counter. 'Just write it down with my pen and no-one will know.'

Bartholomew laughed. 'Doesn't work like that.'

Mordent smiled. 'I know.' He reached for the pen and knocked it off the counter, on Bartholomew's side. 'Oops.'

Bartholomew bent down to retrieve it. 'It's gone under the desk.'

'Sorry. Can you get it? Was a present from my mother.'

'Didn't know you had a mother.'

Bartholomew rooted around for the pen while Mordent leant over the desk and double-clicked Thurlow's name on the roster. His contact details were displayed and Mordent memorised the first line of the address and the zip code. The screen was back to normal by the time Bartholomew returned with the pen.

'Thanks.'

'No worries.'

Mordent whistled as he left the building, hobbling on his crippled leg. He wasn't sure if Bartholomew had known what he was doing, but if so, good on him for playing along. If there was anything he hated, it was a stickler for the rules. And also a rat. He hated rats. And Thurlow was a rat who needed flushing.

Not that he would have given Kovacs that info. There were some things he needed to check out for himself.

It was fast approaching evening. The once clear sky discoloured with the sun's descent. Reds streaked against the blue like hot wax directed by a hairdryer. Darkness hunched Mordent's shoulders, the space within his car diminished until it was all that existed. Outside no longer mattered. The focus was the vehicle, and the vehicle was moving in a sea of lights.

Thurlow lived on the opposite side of the city. It would take some traversing during rush hour, but this gave Mordent time to think. The buck didn't stop with Thurlow, that was for sure. He was simply another cog in a buckled wheel. If the Church were implicated, the killings might have been conceived as warped sacrificial offerings to God, but Carmide and Silk were far too upper-class to entertain such ideas. The killer's need was basic, the methods precise. Religion was a sprawling city compared with the enclosed, small-town mind of a serial killer. Although, in some respects, the motives of both could be equally unfathomable.

Traffic hemmed Mordent in. Cars stopped, started, juddered, stalled. Some days he wished he could turn on the sirens and cut through like a joy rider. There was a thrill to be had from the chase, yet he was moving inexorably toward Thurlow; glacial progress. If this were a movie, the director would speed up the film: give the appearance of motion in an otherwise motionless shot.

Mordent decided to make some calls, nudged his phone out of his trouser pocket. He hadn't had the chance to talk to either Isabelle or Jessica once the police had arrived at Tony's apartment. He wasn't sure if he'd get the chance now. But before he dialled, he remembered Martens down at the morgue. Martens who hadn't phoned through the final murder, the one attributed to Donald Gaskins, the mutilation of the old lady. If he was lucky, he might catch him at the start of his shift.

The noise of the phone ringing segued with that of car horns either side as traffic squeezed him back like an orange pip between finger and thumb. After a handful of rings, Martens picked up.

'Morgue.'

'Martens. It's Mordent.'

'So it is.'

'Forgotten about me?'

There was a pause. 'Not at all. I was expecting you to call.'

'That's funny, because I was expecting *you* to call. Wasn't there a slip of paper with the name of Donald Gaskins on it a while back? I thought I gave you instructions to pass that kind of stuff onto me.'

'Yeh, well. I had other instructions.'

'Listen Martens, I know Kovacs wanted it kept quiet, but you've got something you want kept quiet as well. Fornicating with a stiff one takes on a new meaning for you, doesn't it?'

The silence that followed was uncomfortable.

'So what do you want to know?'

'Just confirmation of information I got elsewhere. This old lady, I hear she was cut up pretty bad. I know Donald Gaskins had a stab at her before and failed, and I know the Residue Killer tidied up. What I want to know is if there's anything else I *need* to know. If you're aware of any leads Kovacs might have.'

'You've got what I know, Mordent. I'm kept in the dark down here.'

'I imagine you feel at home.'

'Look, Mordent. The heat is on. It's not as easy to pass information as it was in the good old days. This new commissioner: I wouldn't be surprised if he's monitoring calls in and out of the building. We can't be alluding to my indiscretion, if you know what I mean.'

'Then you know my cell phone number. You should contact me instead of me contacting you.'

Martens sighed. It was a wispy sound that Mordent barely heard over the running of his engine. 'It's not like the old days. I had Thurlow down here earlier, nosing around a couple of stiffs I believe you had a hand in. I had to send him packing too.'

'Thurlow?'

'Yeh, he wanted to check out the Runcorn and Beckworth bodies.'

'Did he tell you why?'

'Not exactly. I said I needed authorisation from Kovacs, and he just shrugged and left.'

'Okay Martens. That's all the info I need. Thanks.'

'Thanks? You feeling okay. Sure there's not another jibe you want to get in about me and a corpse.'

'Nah, you're okay, Martens. I'll save my jokes for another day.'

Mordent hung up and wondered what Thurlow had been doing down at the morgue on his day off.

Then he rang Ms Isabelle Silk, but her line went to answer machine. The recorded message was surprisingly chirpy. He imagined she would be less so. He hung up before the message finished.

He tried Jessica next. The fact that she was third on his list was a good indication of his feelings.

'Hello?'

'Jessica, it's Mordent.'

'Oh. Stingray.'

'Yeh, Stingray.'

'I'm not feeling too good, Stingray. I just got home from the hospital. They were going to do some procedure to flush the drug out of my body, but decided against it. It's gone anyway. Transitory. But you know what it's like.'

'Yeah, I know what it's like. Hey sweetie, I'm sorry I got you into this.'

'You? I thought I got *you* into this.'

'Sometimes that's the way that it looks.'

'Listen, Stingray. I have to go. I need to sleep, to dream something normal. You know what I mean?'

'I know what you mean.'

'I might end up re-evaluating my life. Events like this put a fresh perspective on things, a new spin. I haven't always been good, Stingray. I guess I need to be.'

'I'll call you.'

'I know you will. Night, Stingray.'

'Night, Jessica.'

Mordent threw his phone onto the passenger seat, where it bounced once and then disappeared into the foot well. He swore. Up ahead, the traffic began to disperse like chewing gum pulled away from tarmac, strands spreading in various directions. He began to breathe again. His car was a cocoon, protecting him against the outside world until he was ready to rejoin it, revitalised and transformed. Sometimes Mordent thought he could live in his car. And if he didn't get more paying cases, he might have to.

He reached over and switched on the radio, listened to some jazz, which soothed his savage breast until he found himself rolling into the suburban district where Thurlow lived. He parked opposite the house, stilled the engine, muted the radio, and sat.

Silence muffled the night.

He ran over what he knew of Thurlow. Precious little. Thurlow had started on the force a few months before Mordent had finished. He'd never made it much further than a beat cop and seemed content treading pavements. Thurlow himself had said he had a sister-in-law with a drink problem, that night he'd found Mordent in the gutter. But Reflective Tony had intimated that Thurlow had turned to the Church of Wire following his own battle with drink. Who knew which was correct? Truth be told, Mordent had no more on Thurlow than the word of a dead crook. Still, it was enough to be making a house call.

He pulled out his gun, checked it, reholstered.

Monochrome had fallen. He exited his car, the closing door sounding like a gunshot from a silencer. Mordent pulled the collar of his coat around his neck, the brim of his hat downwards. The soles of his feet tapped out Morse code on the asphalt, but it was a signal he was unable to interpret. A light was on in Thurlow's home. The building itself was a one-storey wooden affair, a poor cousin to Tony's, but compact and no doubt sufficient for Thurlow's needs. Mordent was pleased to see it. It intimated there wasn't a Mrs Thurlow and baby Thurlows that would need to be dealt with. It was going to be just how he liked it: one on one.

The porch creaked. Inside the apartment a flickering television picture threw silhouettes against the curtains, like a malfunctioning zoetrope. Mordent raised a fist and knocked. He questioned his wisdom in the seconds before the door opened – his body, mind and soul weren't in a state ready for action. But then they were, and he saw his hand reach for the collar of Thurlow's shirt as he came into view, and then charge him backwards into the apartment up against the nearest wall, his left leg kicking the door shut behind him in one swift movement so streamlined that he might have been practising it for months.

'What the fuck!'

In contrast, Thurlow's reaction was unprepared, inelegant and ineffective.

'You've got some questions to answer, Thurlow.'

'Mordent?'

'Who else?'

Mordent tightened his grip on Thurlow's collar. His fingers were aching. One pull and Thurlow could get free, but he suspected there'd be little resistance.

'I don't understand.'

Mordent pushed his other hand up against Thurlow's chest. 'Maybe you don't, but I'm sure that you will. I hear you were down at the morgue today. Just what was your interest in Reflective Tony Runcorn and his associate, Cyril Beckworth, otherwise known as the Frame?'

Mordent's face was so close to Thurlow's that he almost had to duck as Thurlow's expression dropped.

Then he lost his grip as Thurlow's body sagged and slipped to the floor, his legs folding like a deckchair.

Thurlow leant back against the wall, his legs now stretched in front of him. Mordent looked around and pulled out a chair, straddled Thurlow's legs with it and sat down, removing his gun from his holster and holding it nonchalantly in front of him.

'I get the feeling, Thurlow, that your chickens just came home to roost.'

Thurlow seemed slack-jawed. As though he'd had a stroke. Eventually consciousness returned, although he maintained a wide-eyed stare that Mordent attributed to shock.

'The Church is all I have,' he said.

'I didn't say nothing about any church. What do you know about Runcorn?'

'I knew Tony was money-laundering through the Church, but I wanted it to grow, so I did nothing about it. Even so, I thought I could use that knowledge to get him to give me a hand.'

'What church are you talking about?'

'The Church of Wire. It's my spiritual home. Ever since I ditched the drink, that place has opened up a whole new world to me.'

'So you've got an allegiance to this place?'

'You could say that.'

'And Runcorn was running money through it?'

Thurlow shifted his back, gained some comfort. 'Any cop could tell that. Fortunately for him, I was the only cop there.'

'And you wouldn't shop him?'

'I told you, I need the Church. More than I ever needed the drink.'

'And then you decided to blackmail him over it?'

Thurlow shook his head. 'It wasn't like that.'

'You're right, it wasn't. You needed Tony to scout a location for a murder, am I right? You knew he wouldn't say no, because of his connection to the Church. And I'm guessing you didn't want to do it yourself, because it would dirty your hands more than you intended.'

'I'm not sure I follow.'

Thurlow's words belied their intonation. Mordent had a feeling he might collapse again, even from the floor.

Mordent leant forwards. 'Just what is the connection between you, Tony, the Church of Wire and the Residue Killer?'

Thurlow looked up. The wide-eyedness left. Instead, his face calmed like a billowing cloth that had descended to cover a table, became tightly smoothed at the edges.

'God,' he said.

'Oh Lord,' sighed Mordent.

39
The Trouble With A Mask Is It Never Changes

It was usually through the distortion at the bottom of a glass that Mordent wondered if it mattered whether religious beliefs held truth or not.

He'd decided the answer depended less on the big picture and more on the small. What mattered most was if the individual *believed* they were true. Because if they did, any action in that name was justifiable to them. Religion absolved culpability.

Thurlow had been content for those murders to take place because he had been told they were part of God's higher plan. If he had held no belief in God, or in the surrealistic values that the Church of Wire contained, then he would have discarded the notion as unacceptable. But his unquestioning belief that had taken him by the hand had led him to go along with them. There were some days when Mordent couldn't stop shaking his head.

Yet if he extrapolated the idea of belief and stripped it away from religion, rather uneasily he found that similar justifications were fuelled by the ritual following of society's assumed commands. The entirety of life, in fact, was circumscribed by pre-ordained rituals: school, work, marriage, children, retirement, death. And those who didn't adhere to the path were outcasts or misfits. Were these much different from the guidelines that religion demanded were followed? If anything, the rules of society dictated how your life should be on Earth, and the rules of religion dictated how your life would be post-Earth. Look at them closely, and the differences were marginal.

Not that Thurlow viewed it with such clarity.

'The Residue Killer is tidying up,' he said. 'Those unfortunates should have died the first time around. It was the will of God. Somehow they sidestepped fate. When such things happen, God's plan becomes unbalanced. We had to go back in to restore the equilibrium.'

'And the victims?'

'They were already victims. They had gained an extended life, but you can only cheat fate for so long. I feel sorry for them, but they'd *had* those extra years. They were winners, in the end, not losers.'

Mordent drew back his fist. 'Was the mutilation of an old lady necessary to fulfil this plan?'

Thurlow shrugged. 'In theory she should have been mutilated twenty years earlier. She had gained that extra time. She was lucky, but the balance still had to be restored.'

Mordent let his fist fall to his side. 'But you aren't the Residue Killer. You're distanced from all this. It's like me having a button right here that lets me kill a rabbit in another room. If I can't see the rabbit then it's easier to push the button. You're absolving yourself from the criminal act by dressing it up as something different, but it's still a criminal act. *Thou shalt not kill.* I thought that was in the Bible? Or is that inconvenient to acknowledge, because it doesn't fit with the master plan?'

'These people were already dead,' Thurlow mumbled. 'And who said anything about the Bible? The Church I belong to is the Church of Wire. Their values are different, even if the ends are the same.'

'You saying Carmide put you up to this? To investigate the records of those killers and find the victims that had escaped, the loose ends that needed tidying up?'

'Not Carmide. Carmide has nothing to do with this. The

killer had a visitation during an hallucinogenic experience. Believe me, he takes no delight in the physicality of the killings, but it's essential to maintain the equilibrium.'

Mordent sat back in the chair, his gun barrel still directed at Thurlow; the casual intimation of violence.

'So you say,' he said. 'And the killer's name is …?'

Thurlow shook his head. 'I can't tell you. And it doesn't matter now. The last of the victims was Judith Cantrell, the old lady who emerged unscathed from Donald Gaskins. I was unable to trace any other serial killer escapees. The job is at an end. My work is done.'

'You sure it's not because the killer is now dead? Tony Runcorn or Cyril Beckworth?'

Thurlow smiled a faint smile, a weary smile. 'I only used Runcorn to keep some distance between myself and the murders. That was a bad idea, because he wasn't as stupid as he looked, and the blackmail angle I had over the money-laundering didn't stop him from turning the tables on me. But scouting out a venue was the total sum of his involvement. As for Beckworth, I never spoke to him. Never work with adults or children, they say. I'd add small-time crooks to that list.'

'I'd add bent cops.'

Thurlow laughed. 'That included yourself, when you were on the force, no doubt.'

Mordent stood, kicked Thurlow's legs apart, and toe-poked him in the balls.

Thurlow gasped, bent double and clutched between his legs. 'Jesus.'

'I don't think you should take the Lord's name in vain,' Mordent said. 'That might upset the fucking equilibrium.'

Thurlow looked up, just about managed a wheeze, then returned his gaze to the floor.

'You've had it, Thurlow. Your life is over as of now. Kovacs is looking for a fall guy and you'll be the one. Who is the Residue Killer?'

Thurlow just shook his head, rolled sideways and curled up like a foetus in the womb. Except there was no womb and

Mordent wasn't a good mother. He kicked Thurlow twice more: once in the back, once in the knees.

Then he returned to the chair and watched Thurlow tighten.

Maybe he would tell, eventually. Maybe he wouldn't. Maybe he was right and the Residue Killer's work was done.

Four people had died. Six if you included Reflective Tony and the Frame. Did it really matter?

Mordent felt it did.

He pulled out his phone. Speed-dialled a number.

'Kovacs?'

If Mordent had started the case with an A then he'd finally reached the Z.

Zee or *Zed*. It didn't matter how you pronounced it, the end result was the same. If Mordent could be bothered, there was an analogy to be had with religion, but the shutters were closing and he was far too tired.

Sometimes, making no sense simply made sense.

40
A Killer In Their Midst

A chill wind blew downtown. It picked up fast-food wrappers and dirty-danced them. Flyers for nightclubs became ripped from staples that were pinned to chipboard over boarded-up windows. Coats were pulled tight around human frames. The only thing the wind couldn't budge was the graffiti that adorned the brick buildings – tag curlicues rendered through spray cans – although it gave a damn good try. Mordent huddled amongst the masses, queuing to enter a disused pizza joint. Ironically, this meeting of the Church of Wire was being held just a stone's throw from Hubie's place. He was intending to go there afterwards, to catch up and wind down. Meantime Jessica was pressed against him, her face in a fur. He could feel her body warmth through both of their coats.

It was her last meeting. No doubt Mordent's too. She had persuaded him to attend by way of a goodbye. Their relationship had faltered since the kidnap. A few desultory fucks and a smattering of kisses. He didn't blame her. She might have been raped in Tony's apartment, either by Tony alone or together with the Frame. Jessica hadn't wanted the details. Thankfully, she had no memory of it. The drug had temporarily obliterated her synaptic responses, but the medical evidence was fact. There was no resolution to be had: the deaths of Runcorn and Beckworth had not given her the closure she needed. Mordent knew too that he wouldn't be her salvation.

And neither, in this instance, would the Church.

'Stingray.'

The voice was pure honey in his ear.

'Yes?'

'Just checking you're still there. You stepped out for a moment.'

Mordent nodded. His thoughts often strayed. And just as they weren't faithful, neither was he. A few days earlier, as he had been considering whether or not to stand by Jessica despite her best intentions to leave, he had paid a visit to Astrid in her brownstone.

He remembered looking up at Astrid from his position on the floor. She was wearing bubble-wrap gloves, and baby oil ran in and around the bubbles like a rat in a laboratory maze, making them shine.

'I got these made for you,' Astrid said, with a wicked smile. 'They fit my grip perfectly.'

She descended her hand over his erection and his mouth opened in an 'O'.

Later, they drank cappuccinos over Astrid's kitchen table. She gripped the cup with both hands for warmth, although it was only cold outside; inside, her homely apartment matched her homely persona. Her natural blonde hair wisped each side of her face. Not for the first time, Mordent wondered what life would be like living with her permanently, although he expected he would somehow taint her; that the permanence of such a relationship would blend into mediocrity, and it was only the short time they had together that gave their interaction a charge.

And of course, despite Astrid's professionalism, he knew that her seemingly avid interest in him was a façade, and he was no more her favourite customer than the next man who knocked on her door.

'How did it go,' she said, 'with those cases you had? You've got more bruising.'

Mordent nodded. 'It's over,' he said. 'And I don't really know if it went well or not. But I got paid, so I suspect that it did.'

'Perhaps you would be better off in another line of work.'

'Perhaps.'

Mordent sank the remainder of the cappuccino. At the bottom of the glass, undissolved dregs resembled mud. 'There was something I wanted to ask you. There's a girl – well, a woman – I'm not sure about. She's damaged and she's clingy and it probably wouldn't work out, but I'm just wondering if I should try.'

Astrid smiled. 'If you have to wonder, then it wouldn't. But then we're all damaged, Mordent. It just manifests itself in different ways.'

She had kissed him on the cheek when he left. If he thought hard enough, he could feel the presence of it now – an almost visible marker in the cold air and the wind. Jessica turned to him, kissed him in almost the same spot, but not quite – like a child pushing coloured shapes through a plastic box, she didn't quite attain perfection.

'The line's moving,' she said.

She was right. They were beginning to shuffle into the building.

Inside, there was no pomp or camel. There weren't even any chairs. People were directed to stand in rows according to their height. Mordent found himself placed in front of Jessica, who snaked a hand to find his within the pocket of his jacket. Her fingers were cold.

An area before the audience had been raised – an apparently hastily-constructed chipboard platform. Mordent didn't expect to see Isabelle that evening. She was convalescing somewhere in Virginia, paid for by her parents. He had held a brief conversation with her over the telephone, an awkward exchange in which she had promised a cheque in full payment of his services – something she had since delivered. Despite the shock of her seeing Tony's head reduced to pulp and then killing his killer, her pregnancy was on course and the baby would be okay. She had thanked him at the end of the call, but Mordent wasn't sure if she had meant it. Her usual direct and stringent manner had been reduced to a series of monosyllabic answers. He felt responsible for her, but knew she would bounce back. Everyone did, eventually.

After a short wait and no fanfare, Carmide appeared from the back of the room and walked toward the stage. Maybe it was perspective, but he appeared shorter, his shoulders hunched together, defeated.

'Friends, newcomers and subversives. Welcome to the Church of Wire.' He clasped his hands together, less in prayer than in comfort. 'Please forgive the less salubrious nature of our surroundings,' he continued. 'However, one of our major benefactors has regrettably left our organisation, and the style and frequency of our events have been severely curtailed. Indeed, this may be the final meeting of our Church, unless further funding is established. I'm sure each and every one of you here would like to support us to the best of your ability, and in that regard, when we pass our collection box around later, we hope that your generosity will reflect your enthusiasm.

'Some of you may also have become aware that the reputation of the Church has been tainted in the press. While any articles so far have been low-key, it is luck rather than a lack of prurient interest that we have to thank for this. In response to those articles, please be assured that any illegal activities are not supported by us, and any drug-use to facilitate your dreaming is not recommended. Remember, each of us holds the key to our own existence, and this can be found inside without the necessity to resort to outside stimulation. If there are any misguided souls who would like to discuss this with me directly on a one-to-one basis afterwards, please do so.

'And now the unpleasantries are out of the way, here is today's service.'

The Beach Boys' 'Good Vibrations' began to play from a boom box situated at the side of the stage. The congregation sang and danced, and Mordent was unsure whether their enthusiasm had been dampened or heightened by Carmide's speech. There was the usual mix of rich and poor, old and young, male and female. Mordent realised the Church would live on, somehow, if this body of people wanted it to. It took a lot to kill religion, because for some people the death of religion meant the death of hope.

And someone within the audience was no doubt more fervent than most. Someone who had been willing to kill to satisfy the demands of a dream delivered by their God. Someone misguided, sick and without excuse. Mordent was positive the Residue Killer must be within the abandoned building. But simply turning his head from side to side wasn't going to be sufficient to reveal them. Outside, he knew, Kovacs and his team were massing to await the conclusion of the event. Mordent had liaised with Carmide to arrange this service with his full cooperation. The Church's gatherings being arranged purely by flyers and word of mouth, Carmide had no information as to its members' identities. Neither did Isabelle Silk. Mordent might suppose that the man who sang and applauded the loudest was more likely to be the killer, but that kind of evidence didn't sit well with the courts.

Gentle interrogation, DNA sampling and the existence or non-existence of alibis usually did the trick. Kovacs had promised that this would be done tactfully, and Carmide had seen no reason not to acquiesce. Mordent had given him all the gory details, and colour had drained from Carmide's face as he had done so. His enthusiasm for a swansong, however, had remained strong.

As the music died and Carmide began to drone on about the significance of connecting with dreams in order to connect with God, Mordent felt Jessica's hand in his. He ran his thumb over her fingers, tucked it into her palm. She reciprocated. They played a blind game of thumb war. Finally he released her grip like a bird sanctuary releasing a pigeon back into the wild after having nursed a broken leg. A mute understanding passed between them. Carmide signalled the playing of the last song, which Mordent recognised as 'Dreaming' by Blondie. Carmide left the stage before it finished, and Mordent dropped a singular coin into the collection as it passed: it didn't sound as though there were many brothers in the tin. Red and blue lights illuminated the interior of the old pizza parlour like a '70s discothèque.

As the crowd began to disperse, Mordent followed Carmide out back.

'Not a bad turn-out.'

Carmide shrugged. It was almost a duck. 'Do you think they'll find the killer?'

'We can only hope.'

Carmide sat on an upturned crate. 'I fear the Church is finished.'

'You've got a lot of support out there.'

'Maybe I have. The public can be fickle, though. They're always looking for something new.'

'You need another benefactor.'

Carmide sighed. 'Money is dirty, Mordent. It taints all who come into contact with it.'

'So does religion.'

A smile cracked through the weariness. 'In your worldview. I tend to be more upbeat.'

Carmide glanced over Mordent's shoulder. 'I have a visitor.'

Mordent turned and saw Jessica in the doorway, leaning against the frame.

'Hi,' she said.

Mordent was about to introduce her, but Carmide beckoned her in. 'No introductions required,' Carmide said. 'I know you're well acquainted. I'm trying to get Jessica to take over Isabelle Silk's role, but she's rather reluctant. I was hoping you might be able to persuade her.'

Mordent glanced querulously at Jessica, but she shook her head. 'I've decided against it,' she said. 'In fact, I'm going away for a while. Revisiting my Southern roots, if you will.' She moved toward Mordent and reached out her hand, let him shake it. 'You've been very kind. Perhaps under other circumstances ...'

Mordent nodded. Something welled in the pit of his stomach. He wished he could put it down to poor food choices or drink.

'As have you,' Jessica said to Carmide. 'When I found the Church, it was just what I needed, but I feel my needs have been supplanted for now.'

Carmide nodded. 'You know where we are,' he said. 'Meantime, if there's anything I can do ...' He opened his hands in an expansive gesture.

'I would be content if you could just give me a lift back into a more habitable part of the city,' Jessica said. 'That is,' she nodded to Mordent, 'if that's okay with you.'

'Of course,' Mordent growled. 'We're done here, anyway.'

She leant over and kissed his cheek again. 'Be seeing you.'

'Be seeing you,' Mordent replied, knowing full well that would never be the case.

The three headed out back. Kovacs gave Mordent a nod and watched as Carmide led Jessica to his car. Then Kovacs raised an eyebrow. Mordent reciprocated with a finger.

41
Say Hello To Oblivion

Mordent walked in the opposite direction to the police vehicles and was inside the dank interior of Hubie's apartment block before Carmide had started his engine.

Never to look back.

He ascended the stairwell with heavy legs. Someone was slouched in one corner, and he stepped over him, his hand hovering near his holstered gun. But all that emitted from the prone figure were snores.

At Hubie's door he raised his hand to knock, but it was opened before his knuckles hit glass.

'Jesus,' said Hubie. 'I didn't think you'd arrive. Have you seen the cops outside?'

Mordent smiled, wryly. 'They're with me,' he said. 'Kind of.'

Hubie hustled him inside. Locked the door. 'You got the stuff?'

'Don't be so excited, Hubie. This is a one off. Between you and me. As I said on the phone, I just need someone by me while I use it. Then it's your turn.'

'I know what you said.'

Hubie gestured toward his bedroom. 'Best we do it in here. But the cops, what's that all about?'

'With any luck you'll read about it in the papers in the morning. If luck is on Kovacs' side, that is.'

Hubie nodded. 'You sure this is safe?'

Mordent pulled out two glass bottles from his pocket. He'd appropriated them from the cabinet in Reflective Tony's bedroom when he'd scouted the place before the cops had arrived. 'I don't even know what it is,' he said. 'But if you need a place to go that's more subsuming than Morgan's Bar, I think you're gonna find it here.'

Mordent slung off his jacket, rolled up his sleeve and lay on Hubie's bed, trying not to think of the activities that no doubt had been performed there.

Hubie filled one of the syringes Mordent had brought with him. 'You sure about this?'

Mordent sat up. 'Listen. It's been a devil of a few weeks. Sometimes you need a good wash before you go back on the street. Think of it as colonic irrigation for the mind. That's what I need right now. I need to be flushed out. For you, it'll be just a weird trip.'

Hubie nodded; prepared Mordent's arm.

Mordent lay back, his head sinking into the pillow. He needed to be taken out of himself, needed a dream. Needed a replacement for Jessica and the stimulus she had been igniting in his brain. Then – and only then – would this be finally over.

The needle sank deep and he became numbed, floated away like a beach ball; embraced a light adventure as he was carried in the wind.

42
The Honey Ward

I knew who was ringing at two in the morning even before I picked up the phone.

And I still picked up the phone.

'Mordent,' he said, 'how're things?'

'Pretty grim.'

'I might have a job for you.'

'You know I don't do that shit anymore.'

'Clean, eh?'

'Damn right.'

'So.' And then there was the pause that I'd known would be coming. 'All that stuff I got on you has washed away, has it?'

I rubbed my eyes with my right hand and wished the telephone away from my left.

'Mordent?'

'Yep.'

'At the track on Wednesday. Just in time for the three o'clock.'

'In broad daylight?'

'Make something up.'

The phone died and I returned to bed. Two hours later I was still awake. It didn't do to argue with Seymour, but my growing reputation as a bent cop was something I loathed to exaggerate. Still, the reed that bends survives longer than the oak. I found myself getting up and making coffee as the dawn started to push its way into the room. God knows I needed something to occupy my mind.

It was easy to find Seymour at the track. The people who weren't congregating around the horses were milling around him. *Despite the strong autumnal heat, which made eating ice cream still a distinct pleasure, he was wearing a thick camel hair coat that hung down to his knees. Young women, those with an eye for money, vied to press themselves against him, and older women who should have known better fluttered long black eyelashes under ridiculous hats. He looked for all the world like the king of his particular castle, although I'd been in the business long enough to see crime moguls come and go, and the ground he was stood on was just as apt to crumble as it was for the best of them.*

I stood to one side, gum in my mouth, and waited for the race to begin. All eyes would be on the track, and then, if Seymour wanted and the need was that desperate, he could come over and try to sell me whatever business he had. Not that I wanted it. Life had been quiet of late, and I preferred to keep it that way. But even inertia has a price. Stability comes no cheaper than war.

There was a tangible anticipation running through the crowd like a Mexican wave. The horses were backed into the stalls, and the thumping of the jockeys' hearts might well have matched the music that was pumping through the sound system and then stopped. I'd placed a bet before I came down to the stand. Hotel Maid. It was something I felt like handling right now instead of the case.

Then an arm went up. I breathed out. And they were off.

I just had time to wonder if jockeys ever sat on horses while flat racing; then I knew that Seymour was stood behind me, because I could taste his Cuban cigar when I licked my lips.

'So, what's the deal?' I asked.

'I got a job for you.'

'So I gathered. I didn't come here to watch midgets ride for the hell of it. You ever watch flat racing, Seymour? I mean, really watch it? Take a look at it now. Look at those jockeys' asses bobbing in the air like beckoning tarts. Feel the rush of those animals. They might as well be creatures from another planet when we step outside of the horsebox and really understand them for what they are. The whole thing's patently ridiculous.'

'You finished?'

I spat my gum into the ground and rubbed the toe of my brogue over the dirt, covering it up.

'This is the last time,' I said. 'Understand. Otherwise, I won't be in a position to help you out no more. Sometime, someone will trace me back to you, or vice versa, and I'll be off the force. I'm not sticking everything I got against that.'

'You've got nothing, Mordent. You ain't even got a dime or a dame.'

'I've got what I want. A nice clean house and a girl whenever I want one. I eat out. What more does a man need?'

'You eat out in late-night diners, and I've seen some of the girls you've hung around with. Believe me, Mordent, you'll never have nothing to lose.'

I bit back on the double negative and said nothing. Okay, so he was right. I couldn't even keep my apartment tidy, never mind the rest of my life.

'This is the deal, and this doesn't go any further than ourselves. Understand?'

I nodded. Hotel Maid was out in front, but few people seemed to be cheering for her. I had a hunch that she wasn't the favourite and would soon be eating turf.

Seymour continued, his voice dropping to such a low whisper that if it wasn't for the underlying growl I would never have been able to hear.

'Someone's been after my girls. The honeys I keep up at the shack. Each night when they go to bed, I lock the door behind them, and each morning when I return, I find their shoes are wet and soiled. They won't say anything. They don't even look scared, and that worries me more. With my reputation, they should be terrified if they had even a hint of something to hide. But they aren't, so I'm reckoning that whatever they're doing must be fucking failsafe.'

'Maybe they're doing each other.'

'I'm close enough to crack your skull, Mordent.'

'It was only a suggestion.'

'Well suggest something else. I've put three men in the room with them so far, and all of those men reckon nothing has happened. The fuck it hasn't! Three bullets are now embedded in their heads, and they're bolt upright in the foundations of the Seymour Apartments being built overlooking the docks. Unless you want to be inside the

fourth pillar, then you better come up with something.'

'And if I don't do it?'

'Then your chief and the media both get that file we know I got.'

I knew that file intimately. One slip seven years earlier when the bullet from my gun had shot that kid instead of the gangster I'd been aiming at ... The ramifications of that had gone far deeper than I'd expected. I hadn't been young at the time, but I'd been on the road to promotion and getting greedy. The street had been deserted anyway, but before I'd had time to work things through, Seymour had been there, cleaning up and whispering suggestions in my ear. As it happens, I never did get the promotion anyway. But I'd been beholden to Seymour ever since.

'Okay, I'll do it, but on one condition.'

'I don't do conditions.'

'You'll do this one. If I'm successful then I get to keep the file. No more cover-ups.'

'And if I don't agree?'

'Then the entire underworld and police force knows you're stupid enough to let someone diddle your girls.'

'And if you don't find out who's doing it?'

'Then I'm the fourth support at the docks, remember?'

I could hear Seymour clenching his teeth behind me. If there was anything he hated it was a compromise, and it would take several seconds for him to convince himself that he held all the cards.

'Okay,' *he said; and I felt the smoke from his cigar on my neck.*

Then he said: 'Fuck!'; *and I looked up to see Hotel Maid romping home.*

What Seymour had described as a **shack** *was a veritable palace to the likes of the lowlifes and coppers I was used to hanging around with. The large white ornate façade reflected the sun to such an extent that it was like driving into pure light as one approached the entrance. You could imagine God living in a place like that. That is, if he were still at home. Inside, the opulence continued, built on shady business deals and crack cocaine. But no-one had ever been able to pin anything on Seymour. His lawyers would have made good grease monkeys, because nothing ever stuck. Some of that was down to me, and I wondered how many other cops were caught in his craw; yet it was only me that I was* concerned about, and making this deal for the last time that I'd have to.

It felt peculiar entering by the front entrance, even though I'd done so many times before. Usually with a posse in tow and knowing that I'd already tipped off the house. I glanced at the butler who admitted me, and wondered how easy it might be to buy him. Maybe even now a call could be going back to my superior at the station. But if I had a choice then it was Hobson's – perhaps they should rename that Seymour's – and I'd only get an ulcer worrying much further than I already did.

I was shown into the library, and clichéville didn't end there. Spread out over a table was a scale model of Seymour's Apartments overlooking the docks. I wondered which of his three henchmen was in which of the three pillars, and whether or not I'd face seaward come the time that I might happen to join them.

It was late already, ten o'clock, and Seymour was dressed in a silk dressing gown and wearing slippers, sucking on the tip of a mahogany pipe. I'd never seen him without a cigar, but the homely image figured somehow. Surely that's all any of us want at the end of the day – somewhere to put our feet up and call our own?

'Mordent.' The way he said it sounded more like a dismissal than a welcome.

'Enough of the formalities,' I said, 'tell me more about these girls.'

He put the pipe down on a mantelpiece that was completely free of dust. Then he motioned me toward a black leather sofa and sat down in the armchair opposite. I immediately sank into the material and knew it was a power thing. There was a real log fire burning in the grate. I looked up at him like a small boy caught up in circumstance.

'I've been collecting girls,' he said. 'Volunteers, of course. A harem of sorts, if you will. We all need our indulgences, don't you think?'

I made as if to nod, but then thought better of it. I wanted no more complicity than I was already up to my neck in.

'They get all they want here. They're not whores or second-class stock. Most of them are very well bred. You might find that they're on your missing files should you investigate their names, which obviously I'm not going to give you, but they all came here of their free will when they started out.'

'But not free to go …?' I knew the answer before I asked the question.

'That would be ... as the dramatists say, inconvenient.'

He smiled, and his teeth were yellow in the firelight. Not for the first time, I wished I'd never pulled the trigger when I could see the kid cycling into the corner of my vision. Split-second decisions, who needs them when we have all the time in the world?

'So they're going somewhere or someone is coming in? That's the gist of it, right?'

He nodded. As if voicing it would magnify the weakness.

'But then they come back?'

He nodded again.

I found myself scratching my head. 'I still don't get the deal here. I don't understand it.'

'You don't have to understand it. You just have to see where they go.'

'CCTV?'

'They're not fucking stupid. Any cunt can dismantle that!'

'Technology's pretty damn good these days ...'

'I wouldn't have brought you here if it wasn't a last resort.'

Thin lines were beginning to bulge on his forehead, like tributaries unsure of their route toward the sea. It might have been the glow from the fire but I was sure his face was turning red. It struck me then: he really had tried everything in his power. What we were dealing with here was something out of the other.

'Come on then,' I said wearily. 'Take me to them.'

We moved out of the library and he led me upstairs. The carpets must have been an inch thick under my brogues, and the wooden banisters were so highly polished that my hands glided along them like the puck glides across the table in a game of air hockey. Crime does pay, I thought. But could Seymour sleep at night? With a voluntary harem of honeys I guess he didn't need to.

On the third floor, he paused outside a pair of magnificently-carved doors. Whorls of contorted shapes intertwined in a nonsense picture. I could see something was ticking over in his head, but I wasn't sure what. It unnerved me for a moment. I can read most situations. It was only when he turned to look at me that I knew what he intended to say.

'These girls are mine, you understand?' His voice was quiet, the menace understated. 'Under no circumstances – none at all – do you touch them.'

I nodded. My mouth hung open. Then he knocked three times, and a key was turned in reply.

The doors swung wide onto a massive room that must have taken up an entire wing of the house. Twelve beds were lined up beside each other, with a pink-lacquered dressing table facing the wall at the foot of each of them. It was like a beautified hospital ward. The carpet was pink too, as were the walls and even the ceiling. Pink also dripped from the girls as they stood combing each other's hair in a bizarre pre-sleep ritual that was as perfect as a daisy chain. Apart from the girl who had opened the door to us, each of them had her eyes fixed on the task in hand. Then Seymour clapped three times in quick succession and they stopped what they were doing and formed a line.

My eyes ran over them quickly. It was true they were extraordinarily beautiful. A flawlessness that, perhaps, people like me didn't deserve to see. There was an intentional mix that was obvious, from the white-skinned to the dark, from the blonde through to the redhead, and from the differing colours and shapes of their eyes. Seymour must have hunted high and low for such excellence, and my fists clenched at the thought that they had enslaved themselves to him. I wondered how many of them had shared his bed.

Seymour knew I was staring, and I realised that he was giving me the time to do so. Like a reclusive art collector, he was proud of his accumulated masterpieces. But I felt no gratification that he could appreciate beauty, only anger that he needed to possess it.

When he spoke, his voice was devoid of its usual gruffness. There was an underlying fatherly nuance that increased my detest.

'Mordent will be your bodyguard for this evening. Treat him well and with respect.'

Before I knew it, the door was closed. Bolts were slammed across it from the outside. I was locked in with 12 beautiful women, and my pulse should have been racing round the track of my body. But all I felt was increasing panic and impending dread.

The room was silent.

The honeys resumed combing their hair. The girl who had let us into the room fetched a chair and placed it against the door. She motioned for me to sit down, and in an instant I fell to desire. Her hair was a soft dark brown, and curled tantalisingly at the corners of her mouth. Her eyes were speckled turquoise like a chipping sparrow's *eggs, polished until they shone. Her mouth, her lips ... It was all I could do not to press myself against her and force my flesh against hers. Was this why the other bodyguards had died? Not because the girls were escaping into some other, hidden world, but because it was they themselves who had been pulled into divine debauchery by the lustre that was before them?*

I almost fell into the chair, my legs were so weak. And when she brought over black coffee and a slice of angel-food cake my hands were shaking as I took them. I mouthed my thanks, but no sound came out, and in reply she mouthed something that I couldn't hear. It was then that I realised the room was silent because of something that I hadn't had the wherewithal to consider up to that point. The girls were mute. Or rather, their tongues had been cut out.

I awoke in total darkness. My face and neck were swollen and it was difficult to breathe. Gradually my eyes accustomed to the dark, and I made out the massed outline of the girls, crowded into one corner of the room. I knew I'd been drugged – the coffee, probably, or the cake – and wondered how long I'd been out. If I hadn't anticipated it then I would have woken at morning, only to find a gun at my head and the fourth pillar my likely destination. But the litre of milk that lined my stomach on top of the hamburgers I'd eaten at Lou's Diner had had the desired effect. Sopped up anything else in my system and nullified the sedative.

From my position I couldn't quite see what was happening, but I figured on staying put until it became obvious. Seymour hadn't told me the whole story, that was evident, but I hadn't yet determined why. It was plain that the girls couldn't speak, and he must have known I'd work that one out. He'd also have known that was some heavy shit to keep from the authorities, so either he'd expected to waste me or he'd had some other reason for bringing me there. There was an itch at the back of my mind. I suddenly had an overwhelming urge to open the door and run, to get the hell out of there. The realisation that I didn't need to be there, that I had come to Seymour's place by choice, grated on my nerves.

It was then that a square foot of floor opened around the girls, as a simultaneous reflected square of rippled light hit the ceiling. Their surprisingly naked bodies were illuminated by the glow. I watched as they each slipped into the water and disappeared.

I made my way across the room, holding onto the bedsteads for guidance. A piece of chalk lay next to a pile of clothes and shoes, and while I struggled with the knowledge that some kind of portal had obviously been opened, I couldn't doubt the evidence of my eyes and refused to believe I'd been duped by dreams. Even as I watched, the water held in the square fanned out a little, touched my brogues as the surrounding floor turned to dirt. Tiny flowers pushed their way through the soil: brilliant reds and yellows. Water lilies bobbed to the surface, as though helium balloons floating to the uppermost reaches of the sky. The scene transformed itself before me, and as I squinted into the distance, I saw the fall and rise of fishtails, heard the high-pitched mermaid calls. Slowly I removed my shoes, and then I stopped.

The door unbolted behind me and Seymour entered the room.

He stood quietly and I could smell the pipe tobacco coil into my nostrils. It seemed so incongruous against the gentle wind that blew across the lagoon.

'I had to show someone,' he said. 'Someone I could trust.'

I imagined how difficult it must have been for him to admit that the only person in that category was me.

'You knew then?'

'Of course I knew. I had to have a ruse to get you here. I was going crazy keeping this to myself.'

'The other bodyguards ...?'

'Never came in here. Can you imagine showing those idiots this?'

'I don't understand ...'

'You don't have to understand, but you value perfection. You appreciate the finer things in life even if you've never had the cash to explore them. Show this to any of my cronies and they wouldn't know what to do with it. But you, you can see the beauty in all of this. Can't you? Mordent?'

I faced the open water that looked so inviting, and my eyes took in the view. Far out, in deeper water perhaps, the 12 mermaids had found their mermen. They were coupling with an intensity that went beyond the grimy instincts that I succumbed to in motel rooms or dark back alleys. More rapturously, I knew for certain, than Seymour ever did. Immediately I was jealous, then just as quickly the feeling abated.

Human emotion just didn't cut with this scenario.

When I turned to face Seymour, I saw he had my file in his hands. There were photographs in there, together with the marked bullet that I had shot from my gun and that had ripped into the flesh of the boy. I took it from him and we never spoke again.

When it came down to it, all you needed was the nerve to disbelieve.

OTHER TELOS TITLES

CRIME

PRISCILLA MASTERS
WINDING UP THE SERPENT
CATCH THE FALLEN SPARROW
A WREATH FOR MY SISTER
AND NONE SHALL SLEEP
SCARING CROWS
EMBROIDERING SHROUDS

MIKE RIPLEY
JUST ANOTHER ANGEL
ANGEL TOUCH
ANGEL HUNT
ANGEL ON THE INSIDE
ANGEL CONFIDENTIAL
ANGEL CITY
ANGELS IN ARMS
FAMILY OF ANGELS
BOOTLEGGED ANGEL
THAT ANGEL LOOK
LIGHTS, CAMERA, ANGEL
ANGEL UNDERGROUND

ANDREW PUCKETT
BLOODHOUND
DESOLATION POINT
SHADOWS BEHIND A SCREEN

ANDREW HOOK
THE IMMORTALISTS
CHURCH OF WIRE

TONY RICHARDS
THE DESERT KEEPS ITS DEAD

44997285R00167

Made in the USA
Charleston, SC
09 August 2015